Luck of the Draw

CARRIE JACOBS

for Grandma
who may or may not have inspired Agnes and Millie
(she totally inspired Agnes and Millie)

Chapter One

"Not this year, Agnes." Or any other year. Sarah Winchester would rather smack a piñata full of bees than get wrangled into the stupid Love Drawing. She'd come to Sonny's Diner for pie, not to be accosted by the president of the Ladies' Society.

"Oh, but Sarah, you must! You'll have a wonderful time." The older woman waved a slip of paper in one hand and held out a pen with the other, beckoning Sarah to join her in her booth.

"No." She softened her firm word with a warm smile and stayed on her stool at the counter. Being matched with a random partner at the Ladies' Society Valentine's Day event felt more desperate than swiping through a dating app, which Sarah also had zero interest in doing. Even if she had time for a man, which she didn't, she didn't have the interest.

The older woman clucked her tongue in disapproval and wrote Sarah's name on the entry form with a flourish.

Sarah's smile vanished. "Agnes, don't you dare." Her legs tensed to jump off the stool and snatch the paper, but she knew she'd never make it in time.

Agnes folded the form and slid it through the slot on top of the ancient wooden – and padlocked – box with the words Hickory Hollow Ladies' Society engraved on the lid. "Oops." Agnes tapped her ear – an ear that had never needed a hearing aid – and said, "I didn't hear you, dear."

"It's not nice to lie." Sara tsked, wagging her finger.

Agnes gave her a mock-horrified expression. "Oh, I would never." With a triumphant grin, she added, "See you at the ball, dear."

"They should kick you out of here," Sarah said with affection, her dark curls swinging as she shook her head.

Agnes and her old lady club were a permanent fixture at Sonny's Diner. They set up shop in a corner booth. Not that booth, that one, and unsuspecting visitors who unknowingly sat there were subjected to scathing looks of disapproval if the ladies should happen to come in. Nearly a decade ago, the talk of the town was when Sonny, the diner's owner, boldly refused to let them put a permanent 'reserved' sign on the booth.

A steaming cup of coffee magically appeared on the counter, courtesy of Corinne, the best waitress – and best friend – ever. "I got married just to avoid their matchmaking schemes," she joked.

Agnes piped up. "It's not a scheme. The Hickory Hollow Ladies' Society has been holding the Love Drawing every year since 1846 and we've had at least one marriage every single year. Even during the Civil War," she added proudly as she stood and pulled on her coat.

Corinne leaned her hip against the counter. "Tell us about the first drawing, Agnes. Was it your idea or Millie's?"

Agnes pretended to be affronted. "You should respect your elders." She wiggled her fingers and winked at them as she left the diner.

Corinne moved the Ladies' Society box off the table and put it under the counter. Yeah, that was their spot, too. She wiped down the table, then came back to the counter. "Tough day?"

Sarah let out a deep breath and lifted the cup to blow on the coffee. She promptly sloshed hot coffee down the front of her scrubs. "Crap. Yeah, rough day. But I can't talk about it." Not to mention she'd just been unwillingly entered into the stupid Love Drawing. One more item for the "lousy day" list.

Without missing a beat, Corinne produced napkins from her spot behind the counter. "Not even in hypotheticals, huh?"

She wiped at her shirt. "Nope."

"Must be about Tanner. Poor kid."

Tanner Atkins, the high school basketball star, had taken a bad fall on a jump shot and messed up his leg in front of pretty much the whole town last evening. Sarah was the technician who'd done his MRI, and had witnessed Tanner's parents' wrath when the doctor explained the extent of the injury. Sarah was no fortune teller, but she'd bet the farm Tanner's college scholarship offers would be drying up. And heaven knew an academic ride wasn't happening.

"I can't tell you anything, even if you guess."

Corinne had heard enough of Sarah's HIPAA lectures to know when to quit. "I'll stop fishing. Sorry you had a rough day, but the apple crumb pie's fresh. Want a piece?"

"Absolutely."

Corinne turned around and opened the glass door of the cooler. She unwrapped a slice of pie and set it in front of Sarah with a fork she snagged from under the counter. "Hey, the day's not a total waste. Agnes got you all fixed up for the Love Drawing. Maybe you'll end up with the love of your life."

Sarah poked her finger toward her throat and made a gagging noise. "Harvey is the love of my life. Besides, you've seen what this town has to offer."

"Maybe we'll get some newcomers before then."

"Newcomers? Yeah, right. People don't move in. Or out. You're born here, you grow up here, you get old here, then you die here." She speared the pie.

"Such a cynic."

Around a bite of sugary goodness, she said, "Realist."

"Call it what you want, but I don't think I've ever seen you so pessimistic about Hickory Hollow."

Sarah reached back and rubbed her neck. "I don't think I've ever felt so pessimistic. I'm just tired. I need something new. Exciting. And not a man, either. The last thing I need is one of those."

Corinne refilled her coffee cup. "Maybe the drawing will be a good thing. I heard it's the biggest event the ladies have ever put together, so at least it'll be fun."

"Depending entirely on who I get stuck with."

"I'll be right back." Corinne walked away to check on the only table of customers left in the diner while Sarah finished her pie and coffee.

Rain mixed with snow shone in the circles of brightness from the pole lights in the parking lot. Sarah hated this time of year. The days were supposedly getting longer, but it was so dark and dreary it was impossible to tell.

Corinne returned with the coffee decanter and gestured to Sarah's cup.

"No, thanks." Sarah pushed her empty mug and pie plate toward Corinne. "I'm gonna head out. Genius me, I was in such a hurry to leave work I left my coat."

"Good thing you're pretty," Corinne teased.

"Ha." Sarah put money on the counter and blew a kiss.

Driving home, her mood soured further when a sudden downpour burst from the black sky. Huge, fat drops of rain mixed with wet ice splattered against her windshield, reminding her she needed new wiper blades. It was after six, already full dark, and the driving rain made seeing nearly impossible. Sarah flipped her lights to high beams and slowed to a crawl.

Empty cornfields on either side of the road gave her no landmarks to focus on, and made it impossible to gauge how far away from home she was. A mile? Five miles? Her shoulders ached from hunching toward the steering wheel. Hot air blasted from the vents but it still wasn't enough to completely get rid of the chill in the air.

Ahead, faint light from a handful of houses situated on the right-hand side of the road helped orient her. The sleet calmed just enough for her to see the small red taillights of a vehicle about a hundred yards ahead of her.

A second later, those red lights swam wildly back and forth as the car fishtailed, then swirled out of view until the head-lights faced Sarah, then the taillights were in view again, whirling back around in a surreal arc. The lights came to an abrupt dead stop, punctuated by a bang so loud Sarah felt it in her chest. "Be okay, be okay, be okay," she whispered over and over.

Sarah took her foot off the gas. Even so, her own tires spun and caught again. She eased forward, heart pounding, trying to hurry, but mindful of her own safety. She eased to the side of the road and threw her hazard lights on. Grabbing her cell phone, she dialed 9-1-1 and jumped out of the car. The icy rain soaked through her thin scrubs almost immediately.

"Hello?" She hurried to the minivan, which now had a tele-phone pole for a hood ornament. Her slip-resistant work shoes offered little help against the ice on the road. Steam rose from under the crumpled hood.

"9-1-1, what's your emergency?" a man's voice came across the line.

Rapping on the driver's window, she hunched over to

shield her phone from the rain. The driver was reclined against his seat, unmoving, the deflated airbag hanging limp from the steering wheel. Sarah smacked her palm against the window to get his attention, her fingers already numb.

"One vehicle accident on Route 37, near the old mill. Driver appears to be unconscious."

"Ma'am, what is your name?" His voice was clipped but calm.

"Sarah. Winchester."

"What is your phone number?"

She hurriedly gave the dispatcher her number and rapped on the window again. "He lost control and hit a pole. I can't get the door open." She babbled whatever information she thought they'd need. Her teeth chattered almost as loud as her voice. For a second, she thought she heard a cry, but it was impossible to isolate it from the noise of the phone, the hissing from the van's front end, and her own violent shaking.

"Is the driver moving?"

Her fingers felt like they'd frozen into a claw as she held the phone. "No, he appears to be unconscious. I keep knocking on the window, but he's not moving." She couldn't remember if she'd already told the dispatcher that information.

"Are there any other passengers?"

"The back windows are tinted. I can't see.' She cupped her hand against the rear door window and tried to peer inside, but she couldn't see anything. Once again, the noise that sounded like a cry rose up, louder this time, and longer. "I think there's a child in the back seat." She tried the door handle again. Nothing. She tried the back door, then ran around to the passenger side and slid against the slick muddy ground, falling hard onto her side. The phone flew out of her hand and skittered across the slick ground.

Slipping, she eased to her feet and gingerly limped to her

phone, then back to the car to try the passenger doors. The front passenger door was crumpled, the front end of the car now partially in the seat. Hot tears scratched the backs of her eyes. What if there had been a passenger in the front... She pushed the thought away. It wouldn't do any good to think about anything beyond the here and now.

Sarah grabbed the door and pulled, but other than a sickening fingers-on-a-chalkboard screech, nothing happened.

"Hello?" she yelled.

There was no response. She looked back to her own vehicle. It would probably be better to go sit in her car and wait since there was nothing more she could do.

She'd taken one step when a cry from a tiny voice inside the minivan sounded a lot like, "Help!"

Shoving her freezing wet hair off her face, she tried the door again, knowing it was futile.

Crying. Unmistakable this time.

Her phone had gone dead at some point, probably when it hit the frozen ground. A shiver rocked her, but she tried not to think about how cold she was. Or how much her ankle and elbow hurt from where she'd fallen. Forcing her voice to be calm, she said, "Hi, sweetheart, everything's going to be okay." Why did people say that? She looked at the driver. Maybe everything was going to be very not okay.

"My name's Sarah. Can you tell me your name?"

The child cried harder. She tried to guess the age. Not an infant, maybe a bit older than a toddler? Definitely in a car seat, but she couldn't make anything out. The glow from the dash barely reached the driver and it was as dark outside as midnight.

She hunched over to protect her face from the stinging rain that now contained little shards of ice.

"Help!" the child cried, wrenching Sarah's heart and rooting her to the spot.

The man groaned and lifted a hand.

"Sir? You shouldn't move." She tapped the glass.

He groaned again and the child resumed its terrified cries for help.

Sarah's entire jaw chattered. She shook so badly she had to brace her hands against the side of the car. "Honey? It's going to be okay. Your daddy bumped his head. Sir, don't move."

Sirens screamed in the distance. Sarah nearly wilted with relief.

"The helpers are coming to get you and your daddy and make everything better."

"Daddy?" the child sobbed.

"It's okay, sweetheart, just… still and it'll… okay." It was getting harder to think of comforting things to say to the child in the back seat and the groaning man.

Bright lights sliced through the darkness. Sarah squinted, watching them approach. "Almost here."

The ambulance pulled beside the wrecked car, joined a few moments later by a fire truck and police car. People in the houses finally noticed the commotion and peered out their windows.

Sarah moved toward her own car, her teeth no longer chattering. She put one foot in front of the other to get out of the way, watching the ground carefully because her numb legs fought to cooperate. The numbness wasn't all bad, though. At least she wasn't cold anymore.

"You okay?"

The voice came at her through a tunnel.

Her head felt fuzzy, like she'd been drugged. Her car was so far away, but she needed to go home. Taking another step forward, the ground shifted and she stumbled.

Strong arms grabbed her and held her steady. Voices and lights and noise and the driving rain all fell away and Sarah was suddenly so very, very tired. She needed to lie down.

"Whoa, stand up." The voice wasn't particularly friendly, but the arms were comforting, and they were taking her somewhere. Her feet tangled together and she lost her balance.

The huff of annoyance was clear in her mind, even if she couldn't quite place its owner. A second later, she was lifted into the air and it occurred to her that she needed to swim. Because the rain was so heavy.

"Stay still!" the annoyed voice barked.

She obeyed the sharp voice. Apparently she was swimming wrong. She stopped waving her arms and kicking her feet and decided to just float. The flashing lights were gone, replaced with a steady glow as they moved inside.

"Millie, we need to get her warm."

The voices floated around her like a dream.

"Put her here and get the blankets," Annoyed Voice said.

Suddenly, she was freezing again, her body shivering uncontrollably, her teeth chattering so hard she bit her cheek and tasted blood.

Annoyed Voice said, "We have to get these wet clothes off her."

Sarah felt them wrestle her shoes, socks, pants, and shirt off until she was in her wet bra and panties.

He said, "I'll wait in the kitchen while you… finish."

Millie's voice was close and soothing. "Should we let the ambulance people check her?"

His voice moved away as he spoke and Millie took off her undergarments. "They're already gone with the two patients from the van. She'll be fine here. We just have to get her warm."

Sarah couldn't stop whatever was happening to her. She

couldn't make sense of it. She couldn't even open her eyes as a blanket was wrapped around her.

A while later, maybe minutes, maybe hours, Annoyed Voice was back. "Here's a towel. I'll put more wood on the fire."

Sarah felt the towel being wrapped around her head, soaking up the freezing water from her hair.

The violent shaking subsided, and Sarah's mind felt a little clearer. She forced her eyes open and studied her captors. Millie Van Houten stood beside the sofa, holding Sarah's shirt. Her tight silver curls glowed like a halo in the firelight. Why had Millie kidnapped her? She squinted, her vision blurry. She was wrapped in several blankets and couldn't free her arms. She felt like a burrito.

A giggle bubbled up her throat and escaped her lips.

Millie's head turned. "Sarah, dear, are you okay?"

Her gaze slid to the fireplace, where Annoyed Voice stoked the flames higher. Were they going to cook her? Maybe she really was a burrito. If she was, she probably wouldn't fit in the microwave. It made sense.

"Sarah? Honey? I called your parents to let them know you're here." Millie perched on the edge of the sofa and squeezed the towel covering Sarah's hair.

Annoyed Voice stood up and glared down at her. She couldn't make out his features, but he was tall and well-built. He wore jeans and a flannel shirt. A wolf was curled up by the fireplace. Maybe they were going to feed her to the wolf.

Millie said, "Do you think she'll be okay?"

"She'll be fine." He then spoke to Sarah. "That was really stupid. Another five minutes and you'd have ended up with permanent brain damage from hypothermia."

She wanted to ask why he was yelling at her. All she'd done was call 9-1-1 and try to help a frightened child. Trying to avoid his gaze, she pulled her neck deeper into the blanket but couldn't get away.

The fog in her brain lifted, bit by bit, and the feeling slowly returned to her fingers, even though she couldn't quite feel her toes. Her eyeballs felt like lead weights.

"The car…"

Millie's warm hands scrunched her wet hair with a towel. "Your car's fine, dear."

"No." Sarah was getting frustrated that her words weren't coming out right. "Other car."

"They're going to be just fine. The little girl was perfectly fine, and rode along to the hospital with her daddy."

"Congrats, you saved them, hero."

"Rowan!" Millie fixed a stern gaze on him. "Enough."

He stormed away and a door slammed. Millie shook her head, her silver curls never moving, and sighed. "He's a good boy. But if he takes that tone again, I'll box his ears."

Chapter Two

Rowan crossed the lawn carefully to Sarah's car, a gray Hyundai Elantra, and was surprised to find it still idling. Probably no one had heard the quiet engine over the commotion. Getting in the driver's seat, he turned off the hazard lights and pulled the car into Millie's driveway. He sat there as tiny balls of ice bounced off the windshield. In the rear view mirror, he watched the last burning flare on the road extinguish. The tow truck would pick up the wrecked car after the ice storm let up a bit.

People were so stupid. How that woman thought standing in the freezing rain in those thin clothes was going to do anything *except* give her a nice case of hypothermia, he'd never know. Sure, she'd been the one to call 9-1-1, but she should have waited in her car.

He sucked in an irritated breath. If she'd have fallen on Millie's lawn, Millie would have gone out to try to help her and there would be two frozen corpses on Millie's lawn right now. It was one thing when people wanted to be stupid on their own, but... He swallowed hard. Millie was all he had aside from Blue. If anything happened to her... especially because of someone's stupidity... He shoved the thoughts away. Millie was fine. The worst hadn't happened, despite this woman's best efforts.

He looked around the interior of her car, probably only a year old. Maybe two. Spotless. He turned the car off and on a hunch, went back to open the trunk. Snorting in disgust, it was just as he'd suspected. She didn't even have a blanket or emergency kit. Nothing except a spare tire – flat, from the looks of it – and a jack he was certain she couldn't operate. Not even a set of jumper cables. He slammed the trunk shut.

Who lived out in the country and drove around in January *this* unprepared? Stupid people, that's who. People who couldn't conceive of their precious cell phones not having signal. People who had other people waiting at home who'd notice if they were late.

Rowan pulled his coat tighter and grabbed the bucket of rock salt from Millie's porch. He threw liberal handfuls over the sidewalk and driveway. When he was done, he put the bucket back in its spot. He snatched Sarah's purse from her car and took it inside Millie's cozy ranch home, setting it and her keys on the table by the door. She'd probably need her freaking lipstick or nail file or something just as useless from the bulky quilted bag.

He rolled his eyes, betting she paid three hundred dollars for this ugly purse to carry around stuff she probably never even used.

Like he'd said. People were stupid.

"Are you sure she'll be all right?" Millie came up behind him, her voice hushed.

"Yeah. Just keep her warm. I'm going to head home."

"Oh no, you're not. It's dangerous out there. Don't believe

me? Check the front yard." She planted her fists on her hips, her tone brooking no discussion.

"Blue—"

"Blue is just fine where he's at."

The old German Shepherd snoozed beside the fireplace, his big paws twitching as he chased something in his dreams.

"Fine." Rowan relented. He hadn't really wanted to take Blue back out in this weather anyway. And he didn't want to leave Millie alone in case Sarah took a turn for the worse. Unlikely, to be sure, but not impossible.

"Ease up. She was trying to do the right thing."

"Yeah, well, she could have…" he trailed off. Millie's face was a stern mask. Little old lady or not, Rowan knew she had the upper hand. "Fine. If you need anything, I'll be in the basement."

Millie pursed her lips, but said nothing, so Rowan escaped to the downstairs, where he could watch TV in peace. Which he did. Until the power went out.

"Are you freaking kidding me?" he muttered. The air chilled quickly without the furnace running. Reluctantly, he went upstairs to the living room, glad he'd cleaned the fireplace and gotten a nice blaze going.

Millie was nowhere to be seen, and the couch was empty. Blue was still asleep.

"Auntie? Where are you?"

She called out, "In the bedroom. I was trying to find some clothes for Sarah, but now we can't see."

He had to laugh a little. Millie was several inches shorter than Sarah, who was short herself, and a fair amount wider. "I'll get the flashlight."

Feeling his way through the kitchen, he located the junk drawer and found the flashlight in the exact same spot it had occupied since the sixties. Not the same flashlight, of course, although the original was probably in a box in the attic.

Rowan flicked it on and went to Millie's bedroom. Ignoring Sarah, he shined the flashlight into the closet. Millie pushed clothes back and forth on the hangers. "I don't think I have anything that will work. Rowan, go get your sweatpants and one of those flannel shirts for Sarah. They'll be big, but at least they'll do the job."

He bristled a little bit at being ordered to give Sarah his own clothes, but he did as his aunt requested. Demanded. Whatever. Without a word, he went down the hall to the guest bedroom where he had some old clothes for when he worked at Millie's house, and picked the rattiest pair of sweatpants and stiffest flannel shirt. For good measure, he grabbed a pair of thick, scratchy socks he'd never worn. To be fair, they'd be warm. The flashlight cast eerie shadows along the walls and around the corners. It made him uneasy.

Back in Millie's room, he ignored Sarah's outstretched hand, her bare arm poking out from the blankets, and set the pile of clothes on the bed. He handed Millie the flashlight before he turned and walked to the living room. He put another log on the fire and reached over to scratch Blue, who woke up and gave a huge yawn, then stood, licked Rowan's neck, turned in a circle, and lay back down with a huff.

"Who's a good boy?" Rowan asked quietly, scratching Blue's head.

Blue's tail thumped against the floor. He knew the answer to that.

Sitting in the recliner closest to the dog, Rowan kept his attention on the fire as Sarah came into the living room and sat on the far end of the couch. His clothes swallowed her up, but her eyes still managed to spit defiance and fire. Millie took her place in the twin recliner next to Sarah.

"I didn't catch your name," Sarah said.

Without looking in her direction, he scowled. "I didn't give it."

Millie cleared her throat. "My incorrigible nephew is Rowan Graham. Rowan, stop being so rude."

"Sorry, Auntie." He forced himself to look at Sarah. "I'm Rowan Graham. So very pleased to meet you."

She rolled her eyes. "Sarah Winchester. Likewise."

"You need to have some emergency supplies in your trunk. You don't even have a set of jumper cables. You probably won't be so lucky next time."

"I'll take it under advisement, Captain Safety." Her tone dripped sarcasm. "You sound like my dad."

"Sounds like *he* has some sense." He turned back to the fireplace. She was the one who made this whole evening crazy, and *she* was eye rolling and getting snippy? Nice. Maybe he should have left her car idling along the road until it ran out of gas.

Millie and Sarah talked and laughed until almost midnight, while Rowan did his best to ignore them and keep the fire blazing to stave off the chill. When the power flicked back on, Rowan went downstairs to reset the furnace and make sure it kicked on.

Back upstairs, he found Millie pulling out every extra blanket and pillow she owned and dividing them up among the three of them. "Oh, dear, I only have one guest room."

He grabbed a stack of blankets. "I have to keep an eye on the fire anyway, so I'll take the couch."

"I can take the couch," Sarah said. She stood, his clothes swallowing up her petite frame.

Rowan stopped and looked at her. "Guess you didn't hear me. I'm taking the couch. Good night." He slapped the pillow at the end of the couch and flung the blanket out, then sat on the couch and toed his boots off.

Sarah looked like she was going to argue, and for a moment he hoped she did. He was itching for a good argument. Especially one he'd win. In the end, she followed Millie down the hall and went into the guest bedroom without another word.

Hopefully, it was the last he'd see of her.

Chapter Three

In the morning, Sarah looked around the unfamiliar room. Her mouth felt like she had a hangover, dry and foul. The loud floral bedspread reminded her she was in Millie's house. The ancient floral wallpaper confirmed it.

Most of the house had a floral scent from Millie's liberally applied signature perfume, but this room smelled different. The pillow smelled faintly like Old Spice, clean and masculine. She hadn't been close enough to Rowan to smell him, but it made sense.

Stretching, she pulled the covers back and slipped out of bed, eternally grateful the bedroom had its own bathroom attached. She felt like a little kid as she rolled the pantlegs of Rowan's sweatpants up so she wouldn't trip. When she finished, she gathered up her still-damp underwear, bra, and rolled them into her scrubs. The blankets were neatly folded on the couch, the fireplace cold. She peeked into the kitchen, where Millie was making coffee. There was no sign of Rowan or his dog.

"Good morning. Thanks for letting me stay last night." Sarah didn't want to think what might have happened if the accident had occurred just a hundred yards farther in either direction, with no houses, and no one paying attention.

Turning, Millie smiled widely. "You're welcome, dear. I'll make you some breakfast."

"Thank you so much, but I have to get home and check on Harvey, then get to work."

"Are you sure? I have waffles."

"I'm sure." She hugged the older woman. "I really appreciate it, though. And I'll get these clothes back to you."

"No hurry."

Sarah grabbed her keys and slipped her shoes on. She shoved her wadded up clothes into her massive purse and gave Millie one last wave before heading outside. It was wet outside, but the temperature had risen, so the ice was gone. Remnants of rock salt crunched with each step. She was still kicking herself for leaving her coat at work. The heavy flannel shirt was a big improvement over her thin scrubs, but it was by no means warm. She supposed it served her right for being so dumb. Lesson learned. It wasn't a mistake she'd ever make again.

Grateful there was no frost on her windows, Sarah started the car and let it warm up for a minute before carefully backing out of Millie's driveway. The pole was splintered and bent where the van had impacted it. Pieces of the headlight littered the ground.

She was halfway home before she realized Rowan must have moved her car for her.

Rowan. He was gruff and annoying, but he seemed to have an affectionate relationship with Millie. And he obviously loved his dog, so he couldn't be all bad. She couldn't figure out why he'd been so annoyed with her. Okay, if she was completely objective, he wasn't wrong that she'd been stupid to stand out in the freezing rain that long. But in her defense, she hadn't realized how long it had been, or how cold she was, until she was being carried into the house. Who could expect her to walk away from a child crying for help?

Her own little brick ranch house was a welcome sight. She pulled into her garage, hit the button to close the overhead door, and went into the house. The garage opened to the laundry room. She dropped her clothes in front of the washer, then went through the kitchen into the living room to look in on Harvey.

"Hey, buddy."

The turtle, a red-eared slider to be specific, stood on his rock, his head outstretched. He clearly did not approve of her being gone all night.

She breathed a sigh of relief to see him safe and sound. "Yes, I know, you're starving, right?" She reached into the tank and rubbed his head. "You're always starving, you little pig."

Harvey was offended, but he hid it well.

Satisfied that the filter and heat lamp were working properly, some of the tension left her shoulders. It wasn't a big deal to leave Harvey alone overnight, but she was always paranoid that something would go wrong with his terrarium, especially with the power outage.

She went to the kitchen, plugged her phone into the charger, reset the time on the microwave, got a carrot top from the fridge, dropped it in his tank, then showered and dressed for work. Checking her watch, she figured she either had time to inhale a bowl of cereal or run through the drive-through for coffee.

The drive-through also sold muffins. Decision made.

Twisting her hair up into a tight bun, she decided to skip putting on makeup, even though she felt pale as death.

Checking on Harvey one more time, she smiled as he wrestled the carrot into submission. Her cell phone was still dead.

Luckily today was her short shift, so she could stop at the wireless store after work.

Dropping Rowan's clothes on the pile with her damp scrubs, she contemplated throwing the load into the washer, then checked her watch again. Nope. It would wait until later. She tugged on her backup coat, an ugly old thing, but warmth trumped cute. She'd definitely learned a lesson on that score.

Back in her car, she felt like she'd just left work. What a long, eventful, sleepless night. Stopping at the drive-through, she ordered her muffin and coffee and headed to the hospital.

Her department wasn't exactly part of the hospital, even though they were housed in a wing of the main building. They were lucky enough to have an office that ran 9-5 through the week and 9-12 on Saturdays, instead of the 24/7 operation of the main hospital. Sarah was one of three MRI technicians, the others being Julie and Becky, and they rotated Saturdays. Whoever worked Saturday got a half-day on Wednesday to make up the time. She knew it was just a corporate ploy to keep them from getting into overtime, but it suited her just fine. Especially since today was her half-day Wednesday.

She parked in her designated space in the employee lot and hurried up the sidewalk. While the heavy glass doors slid open, she brushed the muffin crumbs off her shirt.

The office door was already unlocked. "Hey, Julie."

"Heard you had an eventful night." Julie slid a handful of file folders into the slot for scheduled patients.

"How'd you hear?" She shrugged out of her coat and hung it over her other one.

"Max told me you called in the wreck over on Bricker Drive." Julie's husband was a 9-1-1 dispatcher.

"I didn't even recognize his voice."

"I'm sure you had more important things to worry about. You okay?"

They worked side by side, running through the routine of opening the office. "I'm fine. I was a good bit behind this mini-van, I saw it spin around, so I stopped and called 9-1-1. It was right in front of Millie Van Houten's place." She left out the part about her encounter with hypothermia.

"Oh, geez. The whole town will know the story before noon."

"You'll probably also hear that I stayed in her guest room. It was so icy I couldn't go home." She took her stack of files. "Her nephew was there, too."

"Rowan? I heard he was back."

"You know him?" Sarah's hand froze in midair.

"Not well. He went to school with Max. I've met him two or three times. Nice guy."

Sarah begged to differ, but the first patient came in, so the conversation died there. Max had grown up in a neighboring town, so it made more sense that she'd never met Rowan if he hadn't lived in Hickory Hollow until recently. The morning schedule was packed, so time to clock out came as a happy surprise.

Becky, the third tech, was taking another patient to the back. "Enjoy your afternoon."

Sarah waved on her way out, glad she was leaving. The ice storm had caused a significant amount of slip and fall accidents, giving them their busiest day in weeks.

The parking lot of Sonny's Diner was empty when she pulled in. There were no customers inside, so when Corinne brought her club sandwich and French fries, she slid into the booth across from her with a cup of coffee. She watched the door as she sipped.

"Has it been this slow all day?" Sarah dragged a french fry through gravy and popped it in her mouth.

"No." Corinne leaned forward and rubbed her lower back.

"This morning was insane. Standing room only. I'm hoping everyone is full from breakfast and won't be in again today. How come you're here?"

"I work Saturday, so today's my half day."

Corinne blinked at her. "You work Saturday. *This* Saturday." She poked a finger onto the table for emphasis.

"Yeah, wh… oh, no." Sarah squeezed her eyes shut and pressed the heel of her hand to her forehead. "I completely forgot you're moving this weekend."

After a long pause, Corinne said, "It's fine."

It wasn't fine, and she felt terrible. "My parents are still coming over with the truck. I just won't be there until after twelve."

"I thought they were coming with you."

Sarah shook her head, her curls bouncing just above her shoulders. "No, I remember now. I told Dad I had to work because it's Becky's kid's birthday. They'll be there by six. I'll text and – Ah, crap."

"What?"

"My phone's dead. I'm going to see if I can get it fixed after I'm done here. It's been a crazy twenty-four hours." As much as she missed her phone, it was kind of nice to not have it attached to her hand.

"Do tell."

Sarah launched into her tale, focusing on Rowan's crappy attitude and deliberately minimizing the severity of her own actions to avoid a safety lecture. "He didn't have to act so pissy. It was like I'd personally offended him by being out in the cold too long."

"Wow, yeah, no need to be so rude, even if he wasn't totally wrong."

"Exactly. You can be right without being smug and jerky about it."

"It's kind of romantic, though, him carrying you into the house."

Sarah snorted. "There was *nothing* romantic about it, trust me." She pushed her empty plate away. "He was like some reclusive lumberjack with zero social skills that should be living out in the woods somewhere instead of being around people."

Corinne snickered. "Lumberjacks can be hot. And an isolated cabin away from people? Sounds pretty good to me."

"You need to get out of the diner. Take a vacation."

"Whatever that is." She looked up as the bells on the door jingled. "I guess I should go wait on those people who just came in."

"Probably." Sarah put some bills on the table and pulled her coat on. "Off to waste the afternoon messing with my stupid phone."

"Have fun."

She waved on her way out of the diner. By the middle of the afternoon, she had a shiny new phone that cost more than her first car, a flower delivery scheduled for Millie, and a small box of crickets for Harvey from the pet store.

As soon as she got home, she gave Harvey a fresh cricket and changed into yoga pants and a sweatshirt. While her new phone synced with her most recent backup, she crossed her fingers that her contacts would transfer without a hitch, and she grudgingly decided to take some of Rowan's advice and at least put a blanket in her car. With even more reluctance, she went to the hall closet and dug out the set of jumper cables her dad had given her several years ago and insisted she keep in her car. Oops.

She supposed a neat, clean trunk was slightly less important than having a few basic items on hand in case of emergency. Her destroyed phone was a stark reminder that she might not always be able to call for help. As much as it pained her to admit, Rowan's point was valid, if his approach was not.

Knowing it would annoy her if she heard things rattling around in the trunk, she went to the closet in her spare bedroom and found a pretty canvas utility tote she'd felt pressured to order at a home party a coworker had hosted several years ago. She dug through the stash of quilts she'd made, picking one with a pattern she never really loved. She folded it, put it in the tote bag, and set the jumper cables on top.

After some more thought, she added a pair of sweatpants, a sweatshirt, and pair of heavy socks. There. Now she was prepared.

The phone was still updating, so she took the tote to the car and found herself annoyed at the sense of accomplishment she felt. She didn't want Rowan to have been so right. A little right, fine, but this was ridiculous.

At least she didn't have to admit it to his grumpy, smug face. Which she planned to never lay eyes on again.

Chapter Four

"Settle down." Rowan scratched Blue's ears.

He'd been barking out the side window for the better part of ten minutes.

"What's the problem, anyway?"

Bark! Bark! Bark! Blue's tail whipped back and forth so fast it was a blur.

Rowan moved the curtain and chuckled. The neighbor's cat sat in the window across the street, mocking Blue by steadfastly ignoring him and casually licking his paws. "That cat's kind of a jerk, huh?"

Blue barked in agreement.

"If I let you go over there, you'd get your butt kicked." He scratched Blue's head and said the magic words. "Let's go for a walk."

The barking stopped abruptly as Blue turned and sprinted for the door.

"Hey, you forgetting something?" Rowan picked up the leash from the hall table and held it up.

Blue sprinted back to where Rowan stood and waited for

the leash to clip to his collar, his front paws dancing back and forth, then darted back toward the door.

Rowan snapped his fingers, and Blue immediately went to heel. As excited as he was to go outside, he stayed by Rowan's side as they walked down the sidewalk, past the houses in their neighborhood. Even though he was retired, he still obeyed the commands he'd been taught.

At the end of the street, they headed into the park, which was normally empty this time of year. Thanks to the crazy Pennsylvania weather – two solid weeks of temperatures in the teens, ice storm yesterday, and now temps in the mid-forties – it was full of kids and families shaking off their cabin fever.

Blue did his business and Rowan bagged the results and tossed them in the closest trash can. They strolled around the trail at the perimeter of the park, then circled back to the street. The mild day was a nice change from the rainy, icy days they'd had for several weeks.

They were almost back to the house when his phone vibrated in his pocket. Aunt Millie.

"Rowan, sweetheart, I need a favor."

Uh oh. This can't be good. "Your favors always seem to cause me grief." Especially when she called him sweetheart.

Her tone changed to super-sweet. *Nothing good is coming of this, I just know it.* "I hope you don't mind, but I might have to enter you in the drawing."

That sounded innocuous enough. "What drawing?"

"The entry period is over this evening, and we're short one man."

"What are you…" Oh, no. She meant the Love Drawing. "No. No way. Not a chance." Millie and her little old lady friends thought themselves the official matchmakers for the town. "Sorry. No."

There was a long pause. He opened his mouth to speak, then closed it, deciding to wait her out.

Bringing out the big guns, she sniffled.

Ah, geez. "You're not crying." He knew he'd lost by being the first to speak. He should know better than to think he could ever best the wily old woman.

Sniffling again, she managed to infuse a deep sadness into her voice. "It's fine, sweetheart, I'm sorry to have bothered you."

She was playing him like a fiddle, but he couldn't help himself. "You're not bothering me." He glanced down at Blue, who was more interested in watching a squirrel do a high wire act on the power line.

"I know you think it's silly, but the drawing means a lot to me and I would simply be *devastated* if we had to turn one of the ladies away because we didn't have enough men participating. I know it's asking a *lot*..." she sighed heavily. "Never mind. It *is* asking a lot and I should never have assumed you'd help me out like this." She sighed again. "I'll let you go..."

Rowan climbed the steps to his front porch. "Auntie, I'm not interested in dating anyone." He tugged Blue's leash and headed into the house.

"It's not dating. It's just so everyone has a partner to participate with. Most of the people don't end up dating, it's just a one-time event for the town."

"It sounds like torture." He couldn't think of anything he'd rather do less.

Her voice brightened. "It'll be fun, I promise. The drawing will be at the ball on Valentine's Day. It's at the rec center, starts at six o'clock. Then the winners are awarded their prizes after the scavenger hunt."

"I didn't say I would—"

She talked over him. "Oh, Rowan, sweetheart, you don't

know how happy this makes me, that you would do this for me." A fresh sniffle. "After all, I probably won't even be here to see next year's ball."

Yup, he'd been had by the master.

"You'll have so much fun. Each team does a weeklong scavenger hunt—"

Weeklong? What? "I thought this was just so everyone had a partner for the ball?"

There was a long hesitation. "No, sweetie, I said it was so everyone would have a partner for the *event*. The drawing is done at the ball, then there's a scavenger hunt for the teams. All the teams who complete the scavenger hunt get prizes."

He heard paper rustling. "I don't think I want to do this."

"Oh." There was another long pause. "Well, I'm sorry, dear, but I already entered your name into the drawing box. It's locked, I can't take it back out now."

Dread. That was the feeling winding its way up his chest. "Fine."

"You won't be sorry."

He already was.

Chapter Five

Saturday morning flew by. Sarah finished locking up the office and hurried to her car. Just enough time to grab a bite to eat and change clothes before heading to Corinne's new house. She assumed most of the heavy lifting was already done, so she'd help unpack and organize, or whatever Corinne needed her to do.

She dashed into her house, made quick work of changing her clothes, said hello to Harvey, then was back in the car, driving a little too fast, eating french fries with one hand and steering with the other.

Corinne's new driveway was full of trucks, so Sarah parked her car along the edge of the lawn. With a little shudder, she thought of her last move and hoped she never had to do it again. Moving was awful, no matter whether it was across the country or across town.

It was worth it, though. The two-story house was perfect for Corinne and Derek to start a family in. She could see Corinne planting flowers in front of the porch and Derek hanging a tire swing in the big oak tree for the kids.

Her father, Bill, and Corinne's husband, Derek, were on the front porch, wrestling with the refrigerator.

"We're gonna have to take the doors off to get it inside," Bill said.

Derek sighed and wiped his forehead. "I have no idea where the tools are."

Bill nodded in Sarah's direction. "Hey, sweetie, would you grab my toolbox out of the back of the truck?"

"Sure, Dad." She trotted over to the truck and looked in the bed. Nothing. She opened the door and checked the cab. No toolbox. "It's not in here," she yelled.

"Dang. I bet I took it out back at the old house so we could fit all those other boxes in the truck."

Sarah gestured to the house next door. "What about the neighbors?"

Derek shrugged. "I haven't seen anybody over there, but then again I've been a little busy."

"I'll go see if anyone's home." She went across the small front lawn and up the brick steps to a cozy front porch. She knocked on the screen door and waited. A second later, a dog barked, then footsteps came from the back of the house.

The door opened. "Yes? Oh. What are *you* doing here?" Then he smirked. "I see you *do* own a coat."

"Rowan." She wasn't any happier to see him than he was to see her, apparently. Giving herself a mental shake, she pointed to the house and said, "My friends are moving in next door and they have to take the doors off the fridge but all the tools are back at the old house. I was hoping you might have a screwdriver we could borrow. And for the record, I had no idea you lived here."

He stared her down for a moment, then nodded once. "I'll grab my tools and be over in a minute."

After an awkward pause, he closed the door.

"Alrighty then," she said to the door and walked back across the lawns.

Corinne appeared in the doorway. "How are we getting this inside?" Her face was tight, like she was trying not to cry.

Sarah went over to her and rubbed her arm. "It's okay. The jerk neighbor is bringing over some tools."

"What's wrong with the neighbor?" Her dad asked.

"He's an obnoxious, unfriendly know-it-all. Super annoying."

Her father's eyes widened and she knew Rowan had arrived. She felt a pang of embarrassment, but it was true. He was a jerk. Corinne put a palm to her face and went back inside, where Sarah's mom, Debbie, was arranging things in the kitchen.

Ignoring her, Rowan peered down into his toolbox. "Wasn't sure what you'd need. All these appliances are different."

Bill nodded. "Thanks. Bill Winchester." He stuck his hand out for a shake.

"Rowan Graham."

"Derek Baxter. I'm your new neighbor. Well, me and my wife Corinne."

Rowan shook hands with both men, then they set to removing the doors. Sarah scuttled past them into the house and found Corinne in the upstairs hallway, staring at the empty shelves of the open linen closet. "What are you doing?"

Corinne's chin trembled. "I have no idea. Everything's in boxes, I can't find anything, I thought I had everything marked and coded, but my lists are missing, and I can't find the instruction manual for the lawnmower."

Sarah put an arm around her shoulders. "Breathe. You don't need the lawnmower manual. Stop looking for it. The boxes are marked really well. Your lists are probably in the kitchen, and we'll get everything in order. It's okay."

"There's still stuff at the old house. Why? Why do we have So. Much. Stuff? There's like a million boxes and ninety percent of it is useless junk that I didn't need to pack and move." She looked hopeless.

"Honey, you're just tired and overwhelmed. It's okay. Let's focus on one thing at a time." Sympathy filled her heart. Poor Corinne probably hadn't slept in days, worrying about all the details of the move.

"Okay."

"Close your eyes. Deep breath. Where's the last place you saw the lists?"

Her eyes popped open. "The old house. On the kitchen counter beside the sink."

"Great! We'll take my dad's truck, go get your lists and grab a few more boxes. Sound good?" Sarah rubbed Corinne's arm.

"You're the best."

"I suck." She felt awful that she couldn't have come early to keep Corinne focused. "I should have taken today off so I could help the whole time."

"Yeah, you kind of do suck for that, but the upside is that you're fresh and can balance out my crazy." Corinne managed a genuine smile.

"See? Teamwork." Sarah held her hand up for a high five, which Corinne laughingly accepted.

Back downstairs, Derek and Rowan shimmied the doorless fridge into the kitchen while Bill directed them from the outside and Debbie steered them from the inside. Sarah said, "Can I get your keys, Dad? We're running back to the old house to get the lists and a few more boxes."

He handed her the keys. "Sure. Be careful."

She didn't relish driving the old F150. It was huge, for one, and for two, it wasn't the prettiest ride. Her dad had bought it new almost forty years earlier, and it had been put through the ringer. Every ding and dent told a story, mostly relating to her brother, Trent, and various baseballs through the years. Twenty minutes later, she pulled the beast in front of the old house. Thirty minutes after that, they headed back to the new house with Corinne's lists and the last few boxes. Sarah pulled in the driveway and turned the truck off.

Corinne leaned her head back against the seat. "Was this a mistake?"

"What do you mean?"

"I mean, now we have a mortgage. That seems so grown up and permanent. With a lease, we can leave after a year if we don't like it. If something breaks, all we do is call the landlord. Now it's all on us. And the property taxes! I think I'm going to be sick."

Sarah reached over and patted her leg. "You're going to be fine. Your mortgage is less than your rent, your taxes are escrowed with your mortgage payment, you can paint the walls any color you want, and you'll be building equity."

"No, I really want to throw up. We're locked in to this for twenty years. *Twenty years*, Sarah! We handed over our life savings." She bent forward, putting her head on her knees.

"It's called a down payment. And it's smart. You already have equity in the house, and it's *yours*."

"It looked so big when it was empty and now that all our stuff is in it I'm afraid it's not big enough if we start a family and I'm freaking out."

"It's the boxes. Optical illusion. This house is huge and you love it." She rubbed Corinne's back until she sat up and ran her hands over her face. "Once everything is in its place, you'll be able to relax."

Inside, the men were putting the refrigerator doors back on. Corinne watched their progress for a moment and promptly burst into tears.

Derek looked stricken as he rushed over. "What happened? Honey?" He pulled Corinne into a hug and looked over her head at Sarah.

"She's freaking out about being a homeowner." Sarah could relate. She'd had a similar panicked reaction when she bought her house. She didn't point out that Corinne had a partner to share the load with, and tried not to feel a little bitter that she'd done all her anxious crying alone.

Derek pulled back and put a finger under Corinne's chin, lifting her face to look at him. "I am *not* unmoving us. How about you call for pizza and we'll get the television hooked up."

Corinne nodded and wiped her face. "I do love this house."

Derek grinned at her. "I know you do. You also love pizza. Go call and sit down for a few minutes."

Sarah turned away, suddenly overwhelmed by something that wasn't quite jealousy or envy, just a whopping dose of wistfulness that she didn't have a happy marriage of her own. She'd had the marriage once, minus the happy. She shuddered. Nope, not letting her mind go to that dark place.

Back out on the front porch, Sarah pulled her coat tight, then held the front door open for her dad and Rowan to maneuver the clothes dryer inside.

Bill said, "This is the last of the appliances. Sarah, would you move my truck so we can get the U-Haul out? Just move it along the street." The street was a dead end that only serviced the few houses in this row.

"Sure." She made sure the doorway was clear, then shut it and hurried to the truck, glad the unpredictable February weather was decent for the move.

Putting the truck in reverse, she checked her mirrors and hit the gas. The truck inched backward out of the driveway. Keeping an eye on the passenger mirror so she didn't sideswipe Corinne's car, she cut the wheel and accelerated a little.

There was a sudden commotion at the house. It sounded like Rowan. Was he yelling "Stop!"? The truck jerked to a stop with a loud cracking noise.

Uh oh.

Sarah threw the truck into park and jumped out at the same time Rowan reached her door.

"What are you doing? I told you to stop," he yelled.

She snapped, "I couldn't hear what you were saying. I was watching Corinne's car."

He shook his head and went behind the truck, where he let out a few enthusiastic curses. "I just put this in."

Sarah looked at his mangled mailbox, lying on the ground, attached to a thick wooden post that was now splintered and split into two huge hunks, one of which now jutted dangerously out of the ground. The house numbers were intricately carved into the post, probably by hand. "I'm sorry."

Her dad came over. "Nice mailbox. Good solid post."

"Was," Rowan grumbled.

"You put it in yourself?" Bill squatted down and ran a finger over the carved numbers.

"Of course."

Bill nodded. "Good work."

The three of them stood, staring at the debris.

"I'm really sorry." Sarah was contrite. Jerk or not, this was totally her fault.

Rowan glared in her direction.

"I'll fix it."

At that, he snorted with derision. "You? Yeah, right. I'll just send you a bill." He stalked to his house, shaking his head.

Bill gestured to the mailbox. "Guess you better pick that up and put it on his porch."

While she lugged the awkward load to Rowan's front porch, her dad fished around in the cab of the truck and produced a roll of bright safety-orange duct tape he used to wind around the broken stump.

"Thanks, Dad."

His mouth quirked with a hint of a smile.

"Don't laugh at me."

"What? Me? Never." He jerked his head in the direction of Rowan's house. "He seems nice."

Sarah could only stare at her father in disbelief. "Nice? Are you kidding me? He's so obnoxious and he hates my guts."

Then, he did laugh. "A bit dramatic, don't you think?"

"I'm serious, Dad. He was there after I witnessed the accident and he gave me such a hard time."

"About what, exactly?"

Oh, no, she wasn't giving her dad a chance to get on Team Rowan. "About stuff that was none of his business."

"Such as?"

She heaved out a massive sigh. "Such as how stupid I was for standing out in the cold rain and for wearing thin clothes in the winter. Um, it's my freaking *work uniform*, what am I supposed to wear? And then I offered to sleep on the couch and he got so rude."

Bill chuckled.

"Not funny."

He wrapped his arm around her shoulders as they walked back to Corinne's house. "It kind of is."

"And now he's living right next door to my best friend, so I'm probably going to run into him from time to time."

"Well, as long as you don't run into him like you did his mailbox, you should be fine."

She poked him in the side. "You're mean."

He guffawed loudly as he opened the door for her to go inside the house.

Derek was in the laundry room just off the kitchen. "Hey Bill? Can I get a hand?"

"Coming!" Bill planted a kiss on her forehead and went to help Derek.

Debbie was unwrapping silverware and putting it in the drawer.

Corinne said, "Pizza's supposed to be here in fifteen minutes. I found a roll of paper towels for napkins, but no plates yet."

"Who needs plates for pizza, anyway?" Sarah slit the top of a box open. "Which cupboard do you want the cups and glasses in?"

Corinne pointed and Sarah began loading the drinkware into the cupboard.

The three women worked in silence, opening boxes, loading cupboards until the pizza arrived. Derek moved boxes from the kitchen table to the floor and they sat down to eat.

Sarah swallowed a bite of pizza. "I thought your brothers were helping," she said to Derek.

He answered, "They were here earlier. Helped get all the furniture moved. We started about four."

"Oh, wow."

Debbie asked, "Everything's here now? Nothing left at the other house?"

Corinne said, "I'm pretty sure we got everything, but we'll go over later so I can clean and double check the cabinets and closets to make sure we didn't leave anything behind. The landlord said the new tenants are moving in on Wednesday, so they want to get our walk through done tomorrow and get the keys back and all that good stuff."

"I hope you took a few days off work," Sarah said.

Corinne nodded. "We both took off Monday and Tuesday. I figured that'd give us three days to move, clean, unpack, and one day to lay in bed and do absolutely nothing."

"Maybe not *nothing*." Derek wiggled his eyebrows at her.

Sarah clapped her hands over her ears. "No, no, yuck, not in front of me, and *definitely* not in front of my parents!"

They all finished their pizza and got back to unloading boxes. The women finished the kitchen while Derek and Bill tackled a different area of the house.

Just before nine o'clock, Derek came back to the kitchen, triumphant. "All the appliances are installed and functional. Bed is assembled and I even found the sheets and blankets and made the bed so you don't have to worry about doing it later. *And* I found the towels and soap so we can get showers."

"You're the best." Corinne kissed him lightly.

Derek covered a yawn. "We should head over to the old house soon."

Bill stretched. "If you're done with me, I'm going home and sit on the recliner with a beer and watch some hockey."

"Have one for me. Thanks so much for helping, we really appreciate it." The two men shook hands, then Corinne gave Bill a hug.

"Thank you for helping, Bill," Corinne said.

"Anything for my extra daughter," he said with a wink.

It warmed Sarah's heart. Both of her parents had taken Corinne under their wings after her own parents moved across the country. Sarah hugged Corinne and Derek. "If you need anything else, call me. I'll help you clean the old house tomorrow, okay?"

Poor Corinne looked exhausted.

Debbie pulled on her coat and agreed. "We'll bring our carpet shampooer over right after church. I have plenty of paper towels and cleaning supplies to bring along. Text me if you need anything else." She gave Corinne a hug and a kiss on the cheek.

Sarah followed her parents outside.

Bill cast a sly glance next door. "I'm just saying. He's single, he's employed, he's nice…"

"He's ridiculous. And so are you." She kissed her fingertips and tapped his cheek with them.

Back home, Sarah turned on the television and found a Hallmark movie. She settled onto the couch with her favorite quilt and a bag of chips.

"You watching this?" she asked Harvey.

He didn't answer. He hated it when she talked over a movie.

"I can't believe these movies are so popular. Those kinds of coincidences just don't happen in real life."

Chapter Six

Two weeks later, Rowan had just come back from walking Blue when a sharp knock at the front door demanded his attention. He checked his watch. Who would be here at eight o'clock on a Friday night? A head full of gray curls covered with a clear rain bonnet answered his question.

He pulled the door open. "It's not raining."

Millie fixed him with a withering glare. "It's breezy and I just had my hair done this afternoon." Pulling off the bonnet, then her coat, she put them neatly across the back of the couch.

Her sudden appearance made him suspicious. "What's up?" He led her to the kitchen, where he poured a mug of hot water and handed her the small box of mint tea bags he kept around just for her.

"I can't stay long. I was just making sure you're still going to be at the ball tomorrow night."

He'd rather do anything else. Literally anything, up to and including a colonoscopy. "I said I'd go."

"I wasn't sure you'd remember."

Blue rested his head on her leg, patiently waiting for ear scratches.

Snorting, he said, "How could I forget? You've reminded me every day for the last two weeks. I'm impressed that you figured out how to text, by the way."

"Agnes's granddaughter taught us."

"Stella, right? The cute blonde?" He slid into the chair across from her.

Millie's eyes narrowed. "She's not your type."

That reaction piqued his curiosity. "You keep saying I need to go out and date. What's wrong with Stella?"

"Maybe she'll be your match for the ball." Her dry tone suggested it wasn't going to happen.

"Maybe you could rig it that way." He wiggled his eyebrows.

Millie's gaze darted away and she was suddenly very focused on bouncing her tea bag up and down in the mug. "I can't believe you'd suggest such a thing. The very notion."

Rowan's suspicion intensified at her reaction. What on earth was she up to? "I'm kidding. Is that all that brings you out here?"

Millie reached down and scratched Blue's head. "I suppose I should have called, but we just finished playing cards and it's almost right on my way home from Gertrude's house so I stopped in person."

Rowan shook his head. "I'm glad you stopped. Just wanted to make sure you weren't planning to hogtie me and throw me in your trunk to make sure I don't skip the ball."

"Don't be silly. I can't do those knots tight enough anymore, what with my arthritis." Her eyes danced with mischief as she looked at him over the rim of her mug.

He laughed. "I'll count myself lucky." Stretching to reach the junk drawer, he pulled out a deck of cards. "Wanna lose some money before you go home?"

"Not likely." Her supposedly arthritic hands expertly shuffled the deck of cards and dealt them out. "Wager a dollar?"

"Twenty," he challenged.

She shrugged. "Your loss."

It was just after nine when Rowan was a hundred bucks lighter and Millie was pulling her rain bonnet back on.

She gave him a kiss on the cheek. "I'll see you tomorrow at the ball." It was more of an order than a pleasantry.

"Yes, Auntie. I promise I'll be there. But I won't promise to like it." He closed the door and watched to make sure she got safely into her car. The things he did for that woman.

He let Blue out for one last potty break, then got ready for bed. He flipped off the bathroom light and snapped for Blue to move. He stood beside the bed, his hands on his hips while Blue pointedly ignored him. "You have a specially designed orthopedic bed right over there."

Blue's tail thumped against the comforter. He stretched out and flopped his head on Rowan's pillow.

"Oh, no you don't. Down."

Blue huffed a little, but jumped off the bed.

Rowan climbed under the covers and turned off the lamp.

Blue stood beside the bed.

"Stop staring at me. You're being creepy."

Blue stared.

"You have a nice warm bed. It's right behind you."

Blue whimpered once.

"Are you taking lessons from Aunt Millie on how to be manipulative?"

He whimpered again.

"Fine, get up here. But stay on your own side." Rowan had no idea why he even tried to keep the dog off his bed. It was a battle the dog won every time.

Blue leaped onto the bed and turned around in circles before curling up at the end of the bed.

"That's good. Stay down there."

In the morning, Blue was back to back with Rowan, sharing his pillow.

Rowan woke up and simply shook his head. "Such a bed hog." He scratched Blue's belly, ignoring the sense of dread in his own. Tonight was the night. The stupid ball. The even stupider Love Drawing.

At least it was only for this one event. He'd be a good partner, play nice, and they'd collect their prizes and go their separate ways.

Despite Millie's best meddlesome intentions, he wasn't going to find love. Not now, not ever.

Chapter Seven

Sarah kicked at the mountain of discarded dresses on her closet floor. She couldn't remember the last time she'd bought a dress, but apparently it was several styles and several sizes ago. She couldn't even go to the mall yet because it was only seven o'clock.

She consoled herself by eating half a row of Oreos for breakfast while Harvey ate a cricket. Washing down her breakfast with a flat soda, she went back to stare into the closet and lament her lack of choices.

At nine forty-five, she stood in the mostly-empty shopping mall, waiting for the metal grate to be lifted from the only store she knew of that had dresses like she had in mind. While she waited, she admired her classic French-tipped fingernails. At least she'd had the foresight to have her nails done the day prior.

The grate lifted and Sarah made a beeline for the rack of black dresses, and miraculously pulled a suitable option down, and even more miraculously, it was her size.

Although tempted to skip this step, she took it into the dressing room and was simultaneously glad and upset that she had. The dress was gorgeous on the hanger, awful on her frame.

"Gah!" She hastily took it back off and rehung it on the hanger.

Back on the floor, she flicked through the rest of the black dresses on the rack.

"Can I help you find anything?" The young sales clerk approached her.

"I need a dress for the Valentine's ball tonight. Do you have any other black cocktail dresses?"

The girl looked her up and down, as if sizing her up. "Does it have to be black?"

"Um… I… I was thinking black, but I guess I could look at something else." Not that she wanted to look at something else. She had a mission. Get a black dress. There was no need to complicate things.

With a nod, the girl said, "Follow me. I have just the thing."

Sarah followed her through racks of clothes toward the back of the store. She wasn't sure she wanted to take fashion advice from a girl with black lipstick and a chain that stretched from her nose ring to her earring, under a spiked rainbow of hair. The girl flipped a few hangers and pulled a dress off the rack. She held it out to Sarah. "Try this one."

"But it's so… red." She would never, ever, have picked this dress up. Her style leaned more toward neutral colors, and this was the exact opposite.

"See what you think when it's on."

Sarah reluctantly took the hanger and went to the dressing room. No way this was going to work. She slipped it on, afraid to look in the mirror. It was too bright, too loud, too low cut, too…

Perfect.

The fabric clung in the right places and correctly skimmed

others. The long sleeves would be warm enough, the v-neck didn't show too much, the waist was cinched in the exact right spot, and the skirt swirled and swished just above her knees. The bright red made her almost-black hair pop. She looked at the tag dangling from the sleeve. Holy crap, it was even on sale. She wasn't sure what she'd done to please the universe.

Sarah almost hated to take it off. As she did, she felt guilty for making assumptions about the girl. At the register, she said, "You've got a great eye."

The clerk gave a surprisingly shy smile and ripped the receipt off the printer. "Thanks. I'm studying fashion design, and I do personal styling on the side."

Sarah left and decided to press her luck at the shoe store. There, she found a pair of black high heels that didn't kill her feet. Jackpot. Maybe she should stop and buy a lottery ticket while she was on such a roll. Instead, she went through a drive through and got lunch on her way home.

At four o'clock, she opened the door to Corinne, who was armed with a massive tote bag full of makeup and curling irons and all manner of brushes.

"What on earth is all that for?"

"Hush. Where's this dress?" Without waiting for an answer, Corinne bustled into Sarah's bedroom, where the dress hung on the closet door in its plastic bag.

Corinne pulled the bag up to expose the dress. Holding out the skirt, she let out a low whistle. "This is gorgeous. I can't wait to see it on." Her gaze slid to Sarah. "I can't believe you bought a red dress."

"Me, either."

For the next hour, they giggled like teenagers while they spread out their curling irons and makeup all over Sarah's dresser and made each other up.

"I can't wait to see who you get matched with."

Sarah looked upward while Corinne swiped mascara on her lower lashes. "Eh, I'm not getting my hopes up. I didn't want to do this in the first place, and I still don't, so the bar is low. Someone who's not hideous, doesn't smell bad, and isn't obnoxious."

"Way to dream big." Corinne's tone was dry.

"No dreams here. I'm just hoping for someone I can be friendly with for the challenge. And someone who can help me win." She knew Corinne was hoping she'd end up with a love match, but Sarah held no such delusions.

"I can't wait to see what it is this year. All they'll say is it's the biggest event ever."

"I know. And Agnes, who normally can't shut up, has been really tight-lipped about the prizes, too." If the Ladies' Society had sworn themselves to secrecy, that meant they had something big up their sleeves.

Corinne smoothed one of Sarah's unruly curls around the hot iron. "I know! I couldn't get anything out of her. I even tried bribing her with pie."

"She probably gets all the fresh pie she wants from Ruth."

"Yup, that's what she said." Corinne spritzed hairspray.

"If worse comes to worst, I'll ditch him and hang with you guys."

"And ruin *my* Valentine's? No thanks," Corinne joked.

"Please. You barfy lovebirds have Valentine's every day. It's revolting."

"It is, isn't it?" Corinne and Derek had both been through a lot before they found each other. Then, the day they met, it was love at first sight and they'd been together ever since. If Sarah didn't love them both so much, she'd be disgusted.

The final curl tamed, they switched places. Sarah did Corinne's makeup, then flat-ironed her gorgeous, thick, blonde hair.

"Okay, big reveal!" They laughed and scurried to Sarah's bathroom, where her huge mirror hung over the sink.

"Face this way." They walked sideways into the bathroom, their backs to the mirror.

In unison, they said, "One… Two… Three!" and turned.

Corinne was first to speak. "Daaaaaaaaaaaamn, we are *fine*."

Sarah had to agree. Her own black shoulder length hair danced in the tiny corkscrew curls Corinne had painstakingly created. Her eyes were simply done, just some eyeliner and mascara, keeping the focus on her bright red lips. She'd balked at the color, but in the end, she had to admit it was perfect. Today was all about the color red, which was appropriate, she supposed.

Corinne went to the guest bedroom to change, and Sarah pulled her red dress off the hanger and slipped it on. It felt just as great as it had in the store. She decided it was a miracle dress, because she hated shopping, hated dresses, and normally hated the way she looked in anything fitted.

But this was perfect. She slipped on her black heels, classic, simple, and sky high. Then she opened her little-used jewelry box and secured a double-strand of pearls around her neck, then a matching pearl bracelet on top of the red sleeve at her wrist.

Turning one last time, she stood in front of the full length mirror and blinked a few times. Objectively, she looked fantastic.

Corinne tapped on her door.

"Come on in."

The door popped open.

"Oh, Sarah. You're stunning." Corinne's reverent tone made her blush.

"Thanks." She turned to take in her friend's own red carpet-worthy appearance. "Wow." Corinne was in a floor-length black number with tiny sequins that caught the light every time she moved. "Derek's going to flip out."

"I hope so." She nervously smoothed her hands down the front of her dress. "It seems so silly to be nervous about him seeing me. He sees me every day."

"Not like this."

After a moment, they both burst out laughing.

"Okay, let's go," Sarah said.

They took Corinne's car to the community center where the ball was being held. Derek rode with Rowan so he and Corinne only had one car at the center.

Sliding into a parking space, Corinne dropped her keys into her tiny sequined purse and took a deep breath. "Here we go."

They went into the community center, and Sarah could tell the instant Derek saw Corinne. He was with a group of friends, holding a drink in one hand. He was talking and stopped mid-sentence. Maybe even mid-word. His eyes went huge, he stood stock still, just gaping at Corinne.

It was so beautiful it almost made Sarah want to cry.

Someone walked between them, breaking their line of sight and thus, the spell.

"I'd say he thinks you look amazing." Sarah nudged Corinne and they crossed the room to where Derek stood with his friends. Including Rowan, of all people.

She gave him a cool nod, which he returned.

The DJ played a nice mix of dance music, and the decorations were simple and elegant, tiny white lights twinkling overhead, filmy white curtains around the perimeter of the room, giving it a cozy, warm feeling. Half the room was open for dancing, the other half had white- covered tables and white candles protected by tall vases so they could enjoy the soft glow without danger of catching anyone on fire.

At seven on the dot, Agnes took the microphone on the tiny stage at the front of the room. There was a table on the stage, with two wooden boxes, where they traditionally split the entries between the men and women.

"Welcome, everyone!"

The crowd clapped and cheered for Agnes to continue.

"It's time for our Love Drawing. This year, as in every past year, the Hickory Hollow Ladies' Society has taken great care to make sure we have an even number of single ladies and single gentlemen to match up. This year's event for the couples we're about to match will be a weeklong scavenger hunt." She paused for effect.

"Teams will have ten challenges, all sponsored by local businesses. The challenges are *not* the same for all teams, since we have an abundance of businesses who are graciously participating. All the businesses are listed on the back of the programs on the table. Please patronize these establishments generously and often."

Sarah felt a little rush of anticipation. As much as she'd dreaded the event, now that it was happening, she hoped more than anything to have some fun.

Agnes continued. "I'm sure I don't have to tell you that this is for fun. If your partner is anything less than cooperative and kind, let us know immediately. It will not be tolerated." She cast a stern look around the room.

Sarah stifled a smile. None of the men in this room would dare cross Agnes or the Ladies' Society. While they couldn't officially do anything, they had ways of making a person very, very uncomfortable. Just ask the disgraced former mayor.

"This is all in good fun. When a team completes a challenge, they will be given a token. Once a team has collected their ten scavenger tokens, they will be entered into the grand prize drawing." She cleared her throat and paused until the room was silent. "We are so excited to announce this year's top prizes. Without further ado, they are... Third place. This prize is a thousand dollars in cash, sponsored by Bert and Dolly Myers of Myers Insurance Agency."

A murmur ran through the crowd. Sarah grabbed Corinne's hand. If that was the *third* place prize, the grand prize must be a doozy.

Agnes was clearly pleased with the crowd's reaction. "The second place prize is not one, but two thousand dollars, sponsored by Stewart and Jody Caretti of Caretti's Coffee Shop."

The entire audience hung on her every word. Sarah felt her eyes go wide. These were huge prizes. She could hardly wait to see what the grand prize was.

Agnes cleared her throat again and opened an envelope slowly, purely for effect. The tearing sound carried through the mic and filled the room.

"And the grand prize, sponsored by Toby and Phyllis Warner of Hickory Hollow Travel," she paused and slowly looked from one side of the room to the other, sweeping her gaze across all the eager faces. "Is an all-expense-paid trip for two, valued at Seven. Thousand. Dollars!"

The room erupted with gasps and cheers and excited chatter. Sarah's mouth dropped open as she applauded. It was the biggest prize the Ladies' Society had ever secured. When the cheering subsided, she continued.

"I hope the winners have their passports."

More gasps. Sarah leaned forward, anticipating Agnes's next words.

"There will be a choice of four *international* destinations that the winning team can choose from. They wanted me to be sure to mention that the prize includes airfare, all activities, meals, and even a little spending money. Let's all thank Hickory

Hollow Travel for this generous grand prize package. Toby, Phyllis, we're so grateful."

A huge round of applause. Sarah's hands hurt as she clapped, hard. This was going to be fun. Maybe she'd even come out of it with a new friend. Corinne leaned over and said, "If you win and the guy is a weirdo, you're taking me."

Sarah grinned at her. "Absolutely."

"And now! The moment you've all been waiting for! Millie, Ruth, Gertie, please join me on stage and we'll draw our matches!"

Murmurs ran through the crowd as the ladies made their way onto the stage. The ladies had outdone themselves with this year's prizes. Millie and Gertrude took their places behind one box, while Agnes and Ruth stood behind the other. With a dramatic flourish, they opened both boxes in a synchronized motion. Millie pulled out a card and announced, "Our first lady is Jessica Cooper."

Sarah's hands pressed against her stomach, trying to contain the rush of butterflies.

Agnes pulled a card out of the second box. "And our first gentleman is Jeremy Conrad. Look at that, you even have matching initials. Must be fate."

Jessica and Jeremy met in front of the stage, shook hands, and went to stand off to the side.

Sarah's mind wandered as each name was drawn and the eligible people dwindled. She glanced over the remaining men. As she looked, Rowan caught her attention. He was watching the stage, attentive, as Millie called Stella Pennington's name. Agnes announced her match. Jon something-or-other.

Rowan looked mildly disappointed.

Interesting.

More names were called until there were only four people

still waiting to be matched. Only two men. Danny Winters…
and Rowan. Had the universe really given Sarah such an
awesome dress, only to waste it on Rowan? It couldn't be so
cruel. Sarah grabbed Corinne's hand and muttered, "Please let
me get Danny, please let me get Danny."

"Angela Smith."

"Please please please…"

"Danny Winters."

Her stomach dropped. "You've got to be kidding me."

Millie seemed to have a little trouble picking the last card
out of the box. "Sarah Winchester."

Agnes grinned as she waved the last card and announced,
"Rowan Graham."

Sarah gave Corinne's hand one last desperate squeeze,
gritted her teeth and met Rowan in front of the stage. Sarah
noticed a look pass between Agnes and Millie. Those old bats
were up to something. She and Rowan gave each other a terse
nod and joined the other couples, politely applauding with the
rest of the crowd.

In all, there were twenty couples. As was customary, the
dance floor cleared, and the new couples went out for the first
dance.

Sarah awkwardly put her hand on Rowan's shoulder and
put her other hand in his. Jewel's song, "You Were Meant for
Me" blared through the community center's ancient sound
system, giving the evening an authentic high school prom feel,
complete with disappointment.

Sarah couldn't stand the silence between them. "So."

"So."

"Am I crazy for thinking this was a setup?"

Rowan grinned, an actual, genuine smile. "Surely you
aren't suggesting Millie could be capable of rigging a drawing?
Or Gertie and Ruth? Agnes?"

She smiled back. "Agnes? Without question. Millie? Yes. Gertie and Ruth? I'd guess innocent bystanders at best, complicit at worst."

The camaraderie faded quickly, leaving them in another awkward pocket of silence.

Rowan broke first. "Sorry you got stuck with me. I'm not exactly a willing participant."

"Surely you aren't suggesting your sweet aunt Millie was able to strong arm you into entering the Love Drawing."

"Strong arm? No. Guilt? Yes."

Sarah looked directly at him for the first time. His eyes were bluer than she'd thought. His jaw sported a fashionable amount of stubble. He wasn't bad looking, for a jerk. "Wow. What's she got on you? Must be epic if you agreed to be a part of this. Or were you going to be a willing participant if you happened to get matched up with Stella Pennington?"

He looked away.

Ah. She'd hit the bullseye. "Sorry to disappoint." She tried to keep the annoyance out of her voice, but failed miserably. Focusing on a fuzzball on his jacket, she pushed away the thoughts that threatened to overtake her. It was high school all over again. This stupid dance, these stupid songs, getting her stupid hopes up, buying a stupid dress... While her date stared wistfully at the stupid blonde across the room dancing with someone else.

Yup. It was déjà vu. And it sucked.

The song ended and she pushed back from him. "Excuse me. Ladies' room."

Replaying an almost-twenty-year-old scene, Sarah's heels clacked against the floor, the same rapid staccato as she fled to the restroom. The same click as she locked the stall door. The same giggling from other people in the restroom. The same echoing voices as they left her alone and went back to their party. The same crappy lighting. The same sigh as she put her hands on the same cold metal stall door and rested her same forehead against it.

At least something was different. She had boobs this time. The thought made her laugh and push back from the door. Taking a deep breath, she left the stall and stopped to fix her makeup.

No. Something else was different about this night. She had no hopes or expectations from her date this time. No feelings – good ones, anyway, and no wistful romantic notions.

There would be a different ending to this night, too. She wasn't going to shed one single tear. Instead, she'd go out, dance her new heels off, and do this awesome dress proud.

Chapter Eight

What just happened? Rowan watched Sarah hurry to the bathroom, more than a little confused. One minute, they were dancing, and the next she was making a beeline for the bathroom. He hoped she hadn't eaten anything bad.

"Hey, neighbor." Derek came up alongside him and handed him a plastic cup of punch. "Sorry I couldn't spike it. Ruth was watching."

Rowan took the cup. "Too bad."

"What happened with Sarah? Corinne saw her heading to the bathroom and took off after her."

"I have no idea."

Derek held up his plastic cup and tipped it toward Rowan's. "To women. May we someday understand something – *anything* – about them."

Rowan tapped the lip of his cup to Derek's. "Hear, hear."

"Sarah's a great girl. I know you two had some issues with the mailbox and all, but maybe go easy on her, at least tonight, okay?"

He looked up from his drink, surprised. "I don't have a

problem with Sarah." Okay, they hadn't gotten off to the best start, but he didn't wish her any ill.

Derek put a hand on his shoulder. "Does she know that?"

Corinne slid up beside Derek, giving Rowan the slightest indecipherable glance. Sarah arrived behind her, more subdued than he'd ever seen her. Her hands were clasped in front of her, and although her chin was high, her gaze was on the floor.

What had he said or done to upset her? He couldn't come up with a single thing. Or was she just that disappointed and disgusted that she'd ended up with him?

Ouch.

He supposed the best approach would be to grin and bear it until the merciful end.

The microphone screeched, then broadcast Agnes's throat-clearing. "Ladies and gentlemen, if we could have our couples – er, our teams – front and center, we'll hand out the scavenger hunt packets."

Rowan and Sarah walked to the stage, ending up at the back of the group. Stella and Jon stood right in front of them. Looking over at Sarah, he caught her glaring holes into the back of Stella's head. Ah. Mystery solved. At least that was one thing he could clear up. As pretty as Stella was, he doubted she'd make a good partner. He got the impression she was a bit spoiled, and probably enjoyed drama a bit more than he did. Just a hunch.

Rowan took their envelope from Millie, who winked. "Fancy that, the two of you being matched up together. You make such a nice couple."

"Team," Sarah corrected. "Fancy that, indeed. A more suspicious person might think the drawing wasn't actually random."

Millie was unflappable. "Don't be silly, dear, it's all in the luck of the draw."

"Luck." The sarcastic word was under Sarah's breath, but he heard it.

"Let's go sit down and check out our packet." Rowan had heard the tone in Millie's voice, and it left him no doubt that she'd made sure he and Sarah were matched. At least he and his partner completely agreed on that point. They'd been set up. *Why* they'd been set up, he didn't know, and at this point, it didn't matter. It wasn't like they could expose the scandal and demand a new drawing.

Glancing around, the other teams seemed to be having a good time. Except Stella and Jon, who were arguing. Stella yelled and pointed her finger at Jon, who looked rather embarrassed.

Rowan picked a table far away from that scene and sat with his back to them. Did he call that one or what? He didn't want Sarah to think he cared what they were doing. Because he didn't. Truth be told, if he was stuck doing this, he wasn't disappointed to be doing it with Sarah. At least they already knew each other, and as much as she annoyed him, she was genuine.

And to be honest, he annoyed her, too, so any entanglement was unlikely. It was a relief, really. No pressure to impress her.

He opened the envelope and pulled out a stack of smaller envelopes. Each one held an index card with a business name and address. Interesting.

Sarah picked up a folded sheet of paper and skimmed down over it. "We'll get instructions and complete a challenge at each location. After we complete the challenge, we'll get a token. We should keep the tokens in the individual envelopes provided. Lost or stolen tokens will not be replaced." She glanced over. "What are the businesses we got?"

"It's quite a mix. Hardware store, grocery store, paintball course, pet shop, a bunch of others." He surprised himself by actually looking forward to the challenges. All he did was go to work and go home. It'd be nice to have a change of scenery.

"Oh. Should be fun, huh? I wonder what the challenges are."

"I don't know." He wondered that, too. The businesses were all so different that the challenges almost had to be customized to each site. Hopefully Millie and Agnes hadn't rigged those, too.

"Should we sort them somehow? Maybe by hours or location?" She flipped the paper over. "Never mind, we have a schedule."

He leaned over and looked at the paper with her. Shoulder to shoulder, he caught the sweet scent of her shampoo. "Looks like we're completely booked for the next week, huh."

"Looks like it."

A shrill voice rose over the dull roar of conversations. "Attention, please." He glanced at Sarah before turning to see what was going on. Stella stood on her chair and waved her arms. He hoped her heels didn't poke holes in the upholstery, or the Ladies' Society would probably end up paying for it.

Stella yelled, "If anyone would like to switch partners, come see me. In fact, maybe we should just redo the whole sham drawing."

Agnes made a beeline for her granddaughter. "Stella, get down. What's the problem?"

Stella jumped down from the chair. "I want a different partner."

Through clenched teeth, Agnes said, "It doesn't work that way, unless you can find a team that's willing to switch partners."

Stella's gaze lasered onto Rowan. "What about you guys? Let's swap."

He jerked up straight in his chair. What was happening? He looked over at Sarah. She unnecessarily shuffled the envelopes, completely avoiding his eyes. Without a doubt in his mind, he knew she was sure he was going to suggest they change teams. Is that really what she thought of him?

Had he given her reason to think anything else?

"Nope, we're good."

Sarah stopped organizing the envelopes and looked up at him, her eyes wide. He reached over and lightly touched her arm. Stella moved on to another team and he leaned over. "I'm not disappointed you're my partner, Sarah."

After this display, he was relieved he hadn't been paired with Stella. He didn't have the patience for that level of drama.

In the end, Stella and Jon couldn't convince another team to swap, so they had to decide to cooperate or be disqualified. Initially they agreed to cooperate, but after another dramatic scene involving a knocked-over chair and "spilled" glass of red punch, they were disqualified.

Rowan and Sarah danced a few times, including a conga line and the chicken dance, before the evening wound down. Rowan followed her to a table where Corinne and Derek were sitting.

"We can give you a ride home," Corinne said with a yawn.

Rowan spoke up. "Actually, I can take you if it's okay. We can plan our strategy."

Derek laughed. "Sow discord in the other teams. Get them all disqualified."

Sarah chuckled at that, then turned to Rowan. "Are you sure you don't mind taking me home?"

"I don't." He stifled his own yawn. "Let's get your coat."

Derek jumped up. "I'll go warm your chariot, milady."

"Good idea. I'll do that, too. Warm up the Jeep." Rowan wondered if it sounded as awkward to them as it did to his own ears.

Rowan caught Derek grinning as they walked outside into the brisk night together. "Yes?"

"I gotta tell you, I thought you'd jump at the chance to team up with Stella."

"I would never have done that to Sarah. In spite of what she thinks, I'm not a complete jerk." They parted ways and went to their respective cars.

Rowan got in his Jeep Wrangler, turned the heater on full blast, and picked a stack of receipts, some wrappers, and a pair of gloves off the front seat and set it all in the back. The windshield fogged, then cleared as the blowing air warmed up.

He was just about to drive around to pick Sarah up when he saw her come out the huge double doors with Corinne. They hugged and Sarah looked around to find his car. Rowan jumped out of the Jeep and walked toward her, and it occurred to him that he hadn't thought to compliment her. She looked amazing.

Her inky black hair was curled, the ends skimming her shoulders. Her bright red lips matched her bright red dress, which clung nicely to her figure. She'd obviously put in a lot of effort, and ended up stuck with him. He wondered who she'd been hoping to be matched with.

Opening the passenger door, he helped her in and waited until she adjusted her skirt before closing the door.

He slid into the driver's seat.

"Oh, no!" Sarah looked panicked. "The envelope. I didn't grab the envelope. Did you?"

"No, but I'll run in and get it. Be right back." Rowan jogged back into the mostly-empty building and retrieved their envelope from the table.

Millie's voice came from behind him. "That wasn't so bad, now was it?"

"I didn't die, so I guess not."

"So dramatic." She playfully swatted his arm. "Where is Sarah?"

"In the Jeep. We forgot the envelope."

"She's a nice girl."

"Auntie. Stop. We're teammates and maybe by the end of this, we'll be friends."

"Only if you keep your head out of your behind. Quit wasting time with me and get back to your girl."

With a dramatic sigh, he planted a kiss on Millie's forehead. "My *partner*. Good night."

Millie waved him away. Her smile seemed… triumphant. Smug. He wasn't sure what to make of it. He pushed back through the heavy doors, into the cold night, and trotted back to get into his vehicle.

He handed the envelope to Sarah. She pulled the itinerary out and looked over it. "This is a big challenge. We have one stop every night of the week, then Saturday is a full day of it."

"Anything tomorrow?"

"Nope, it starts on Monday."

"Maybe we should get together tomorrow afternoon and make our plan."

She raised an eyebrow. "Plan?"

"This will surprise you, but I've been accused of being a bit of a control freak. I like to know where I'm going and when."

"Yeah, I'm more of a go with the flow kind of girl."

They pulled into Sarah's driveway and an unexpected pang of disappointment poked his chest. Talking about the challenge with Sarah was fun. Maybe this wouldn't completely suck after all.

Chapter Nine

Sarah slid the papers back into the envelope as Rowan went around the front of the vehicle to open her door. At first, she hadn't been happy they'd been matched, but maybe it wouldn't be so bad. And maybe he wasn't as disappointed as she'd feared. After all, he'd turned down the chance to team up with Stella instead of her. Of course, Stella was a drama llama, and it's not like the challenge was romantic.

He opened the door and gave her a hand to help her out. "You don't have to walk me to my door."

"I do. Millie's probably in the bushes with binoculars, and if I don't see you safely inside, she'll box my ears."

Sarah laughed. Who knew he actually had a sense of humor? "It's funny because it's true." She pulled her keys out of her tiny purse. "Do you want to hang onto the envelope, or what do you want to do with it?"

"Since it's in your hand, why don't you keep it and we'll go through it tomorrow."

"Sure. Did you want to come over after lunch?"

He nodded. "Yeah. Sounds good. I'll come over around 1? 1:30?"

"Okay." She unlocked her door and hesitated. "I think this'll be fun."

Rowan nodded and she saw him swallow hard. His brow furrowed a little and he shoved his hands in his pockets. He took a step back, then his words came out in a rush. "I should have said so earlier, but you look beautiful tonight, Sarah. Happy, uh, Valentine's Day."

With that, he cleared his throat and turned toward his car.

"Thanks," she barely squeaked out. Where did *that* come from?

He gave her a small wave, then it seemed like he was in a hurry to leave. She returned his wave, then went inside. She dropped her purse on the side table and peeked out the window, watching the lights of Rowan's Jeep until he turned the corner. "Harvey, have I got a story for you."

The turtle listened as she related the whole story while she changed for bed. Standing in the living room doorway in her pajamas, her toothbrush waving in one hand, she shook her head. "Can you believe that? Those old ladies absolutely rigged the drawing. I hate to get my hopes up… not that I think there's anything romantic, but I can almost see us getting through this week without wanting to kill each other." She paused, thoughtful. "Maybe that was actually Rowan's twin brother or a cyborg replacement or something. He was nice and funny. Not himself at all."

Harvey didn't offer any comment.

She shoved the toothbrush back in her mouth and went back to the bathroom to rinse. She wiped her mouth with the towel, then cleaned the makeup off her face and put moisturizer on. Back in the living room, she put a carrot top in Harvey's cage. "You're out of crickets."

Harvey's neck stretched out, then retracted back into his shell.

"Rowan's coming over tomorrow, so be sure to get a good look and let me know what you think."

Harvey pulled his legs into his shell.

"Or ignore me, whatever."

She flitted around the living room, picking up a half-folded basket of laundry and taking it to the bedroom. She straightened the mishmash of fabrics hanging over the edge of her quilting basket. Magazines – her guilty pleasure – were strewn across pretty much every flat surface. Every time she went into a store, she came home with more magazines so she could keep up with celebrity gossip.

Piling them neatly in a basket beside the couch, she decided the living room was presentable. Next, she tackled the kitchen, putting away the toaster, wiping down the counters, and sorting the piles of mail that seemed to congregate and multiply on the kitchen table. She ended up with a stack of trash and only three envelopes to keep.

She straightened the tablecloth, then set the challenge packet in the middle. One last look around, and she deemed the kitchen guest-worthy. As for the rest of the house, she'd keep the doors closed. It wasn't like he'd need a tour.

Climbing into bed, Sarah pulled the thick comforter up to her chin. What she'd imagined would be the worst case scenario, being matched with Rowan, didn't seem so bad. So far.

Morning came, deceptively clear and bright, which belied the freezing temperature. She went along to church, and then lunch, with her parents.

"Why do you keep checking your watch?" Debbie asked.

Bill smirked into his coffee cup. "I bet it has something to do with a certain young man."

Sarah kicked his foot lightly under the table. "I'm meeting Rowan. We're going over our challenge strategy."

"Quite a coincidence that you two got matched up." Debbie's wry expression made it clear she didn't think it was a coincidence at all.

"It doesn't make any sense why Millie and Agnes would have wanted to put us together, though. Millie saw how much we annoyed each other the night of the accident. Maybe she's a sadist."

Debbie took a bite of her pickle and looked skyward, contemplating the suggestion. "Millie? I doubt it. Agnes? I could totally see that."

Bill chuckled. "They're two peas in a pod. Maybe Millie thought if you two brought out the worst in each other, you could bring out the best, too."

"Or maybe," Debbie added, "Millie was just glad to see Rowan having *any* kind of reaction to someone. He seems very closed off and private."

"I don't know, he's very close with Millie and he's getting along great with Derek. He got along fine with Dad, too."

Bill agreed. "He did, but it was all very superficial."

"Oh, geez. What, was he supposed to impart his deepest, darkest secrets and wildest dreams over installing a fridge?"

"Of course not. That's what football's for."

"Football season is over until August." Sarah knew her dad was still riding the high after his team won the Super Bowl a few weeks earlier.

"Baseball will do in a pinch."

"You're a goofball, and I gotta go." She slid out of the booth and leaned over to kiss each of her parents on the cheek. "Thanks for lunch. Love you."

As soon as she got home, she lit a well-used scented candle in the kitchen and went to change into jeans and a sweatshirt.

Padding through the house in her fuzzy socks, she double checked to make sure there were no huge messes.

At five after one, she heard Rowan's Jeep pull into the driveway. She peeked out the window and was surprised to see how bright orange it was. In the dim lights last night, it hadn't seemed so colorful. It seemed so unlike him. She would have expected him to drive something black. With lots of chrome.

"Okay, Harvey, get ready."

Harvey stared out of his glass enclosure.

Rowan knocked. Sarah counted to ten, smoothed her unruly curls, which was pointless, and opened the door. "Hey, come on in."

"Smells good in here."

"Caramel apple candle. It's my favorite."

He looked around the living room, then walked over to Harvey's tank. He put a finger on the glass. "Hey, buddy." To Sarah, he said, "This is cool, what all do you have in here?"

Who is this guy?? Sarah was caught off guard – again – by Rowan acting like a normal human being. Better than normal, actually, because most people completely ignored Harvey. "Just the one turtle. Harvey. He likes his space."

"Hi, Harvey. Nice place." He glanced at Sarah, then back to the tank. "This is great. I had tropical fish a long time ago, but they were too hard to take care of. I couldn't get the temperature regulated enough, so I ended up giving the fish away. I was afraid I'd hurt them."

Well, crap. That went straight to the old heartstrings, didn't it? "Fish are hard. Harvey's pretty easy."

"What's he eat?"

Actual interest? She wouldn't have guessed in a million years that they'd be having this conversation. "Veggies, crickets, and sometimes I get him these tiny little feeder fish. Otherwise, he gets pellets."

"Very cool."

"Thanks." It pleased her greatly that he liked her turtle and didn't act like it was weird. Just because it wasn't your standard dog or cat didn't mean he wasn't a great pet.

"Does he ever come out and walk around?"

Okay, *now* he'd probably think she was nuts. "Um, yeah. Sometimes." She fidgeted with the hem of her sweatshirt. "I got these bumpers that snap onto the edges of the kitchen table so he can walk around without falling off, and I don't have to worry about him getting lost or, my worst nightmare, stepped on."

"That's a great idea." He sounded sincere.

Sarah blinked. She'd have to be careful or she might actually start to like this guy. "I have the packet in the kitchen."

Rowan followed her. He sat at the table and opened the packet. He spread the envelopes on the table and pulled out the schedule.

"Do you want anything to drink? I have Pepsi, water, iced tea, hot tea, or coffee."

"Whatever you're having is fine."

"Hot tea it is." She poured two mugs of hot water and set a basket of tea bags on the table. "Hopefully we have decent weather this week. Are any of the stops outdoors?" she asked as she sat down.

"Not sure. Tomorrow night's stop is at six at the hardware store, so that'll be inside."

"What on earth would they have us do at the hardware store?"

"I can tell you right now, if it's hardware trivia, we're golden." He gave her a half-smile that caught her off guard. He was a completely different man from the one who'd been a jerk after the accident.

"That's a pretty random trivia specialty, isn't it? Why hardware?"

"I'm a carpenter. Soooo…"

"I had no idea." She considered for a moment. "I'm not sure what I thought you did. Maybe customer service since you're usually grumpy."

"Hey, now." He looked down. She couldn't be sure, but it looked like he might have blushed a little.

She laughed. "Kidding. So what do you make, Mr. Carpenter?"

"I work in a cabinet factory to pay the bills, and I make some custom furniture on the side." He gave her a sly look. "Custom mailbox posts…"

She groaned. "You're never going to forgive me for that, are you?"

"Two days. That's how long my hand-carved post lasted." He held up two fingers. "Two."

"Back to the custom furniture. Tell me more about that. What do you make? Besides mailbox posts?"

"Porch swings, tables, chairs, things like that."

"I'll have to remember that. My porch swing needs replaced when it gets warm out. Right after I moved in, the beams it was anchored to rotted out and it fell and smashed. I had the beams fixed but I haven't replaced the swing yet. Actually, the whole porch was fixed. Ripped it off and started from scratch. So the porch is good now. But I still have no swing." She turned her attention to her mug, realizing fifty words ago that she'd been rambling.

Rowan looked up from the envelopes, his blue eyes dancing with amusement. "And what do you do? Elementary school teacher, since you're always so perky and distractible?"

"Ha, no. I'm an MRI technician."

"MRI as in the scan for broken bones and concussions and stuff?"

"Basically."

"Do you like your job?"

The question caught her off guard. No one ever asks that. "I do. I was originally going to go into nursing, but one semester of nursing school convinced me to take a different path. I'm not cut out for dealing with blood and other bodily fluids."

"Have you ever had someone freak out in the tube thing?"

One patient immediately came to mind, because they eventually had to call security to subdue him. Thankfully, he was a very unusual case. "Pretty much on a daily basis. They keep talking about upgrading to an open MRI machine, but of course those things are a bazillion dollars, so I don't think it'll ever happen."

Rowan shuffled the envelopes absently, then spread them out again. "I don't think I'd like being put into one of those machines."

"Most people don't."

"Have you ever been in one? Just to see what it's like for your patients?"

"Of course. And I don't like it, either."

He looked down at the envelopes. "I'm really curious about these businesses. They're all so different. It's great they all agreed to be involved in this."

"You know the Ladies' Society, they're hard to refuse. Just ask either of us, right?" They lapsed into an awkward silence that stretched until Sarah couldn't stand it anymore. "So tomorrow night. Are we meeting at the hardware store or do you want me to pick you up or what?" She lifted her hands in question.

"We have to be there at six. When do you get home?"

"I'm home by a quarter after five. You?"

"Quarter til six, usually, but I'll try to get home a little sooner this week. Five thirty shouldn't be a problem. We should probably exchange numbers."

Sarah pulled out her phone, tapped a few times to bring up a new contact, and Rowan did the same. They traded phones and entered their numbers.

When Sarah was done, she slid his phone back and said, "After work, I'll come home, get changed, and pick you up by five forty-five. That work?"

"Sounds like a plan." He tapped the stack of envelopes. "I think it'll be fun."

As much as she hated to bring it up, she still felt guilty and wanted to make sure he wasn't still upset. "You know, I would have replaced your mailbox."

He almost smiled. "I already fixed it."

"I know. Corinne saw you putting the new one in. You didn't give me a chance to take care of it."

Shrugging, he said, "I wanted it done right away. Unfinished projects bug me."

"How much do I owe you?"

"Nothing. I had the extra lumber in the garage, and the mailbox itself was fine, so it didn't cost me anything."

"But all that time you put into carving the design, I still feel awful."

"Don't worry about it. The numbers were crooked anyway." He stood and pulled his coat on. "I'll see you tomorrow evening."

"You got it." She rose and followed him through the living room.

He paused and waved to the tank. "Bye, Harvey."

If her fluttering pulse was any indication, she was in trouble. It wouldn't be hard to develop a serious crush on a man with eyes that blue who talked to her turtle.

Chapter Ten

As Rowan drove home, an unfamiliar feeling settled in his gut. He chose to ignore it until late that night, when it dawned on him what it was. Anticipation. He was looking forward to the challenge. He was looking forward to spending more time with Sarah. He was looking forward to being out of the house. Out of his comfort zone.

On Monday, work dragged on twice as long as usual. His attention wandered.

"What's got into you?" Mack Beasley nudged his arm. "Maybe watch the line instead of the clock."

"Yeah, yeah." Rowan slid a cabinet door down the line. That was rich. If Mack watched the line half as much as he ran his mouth, he'd get a lot more work done.

"Heard you got yourself a girlfriend at the dance Saturday night." He wiggled his eyebrows.

Rowan had no desire to talk to Mack about the weather, let alone talk to him about anything even remotely personal. The guy was a pig who'd been told more than once to be respectful to women. It always went in one ear and out the other. Rowan inspected another cabinet door and slid it down the line to Mack.

"Also heard you could have swapped her for Stella Pennington. What's the matter with you, turning down a set of cans like that?" He grabbed his own impressive boobs for emphasis. "I hear she's wild in the sack, too. Crazy chicks usually are."

Rowan shook his head and brushed a speck of sawdust off the next cabinet door.

Mack made an appreciative grunt. "Sarah's got a decent rack, I guess."

Rowan's jaw clenched. "Shut up."

"I'd do her for sure." He jutted his hips forward and back a few times, laughing.

Rowan shoved the next cabinet door with more force than necessary. He could easily imagine picking it up and breaking it over Mack's thick head. The man was a walking, talking caricature of the chauvinist pig stereotype.

Mack guffawed. "I'd grab that hair and bend her over until she begged for it."

The next cabinet door was taking forever to reach Rowan's station. It gave him too much time to think about Mack's disgusting words.

"Seems kinda desperate, too. Bet you didn't even have to buy dinner to get her legs op—"

Mack was on the floor and the foreman dragged Rowan backwards before he could finish his sentence. Rowan held his hands up and stepped back. "Sorry. I'm good." He was keenly aware of the dozens of pairs of eyes watching with interest.

The foreman shoved his shoulder mildly. "You know better than to let Mack's mouth get to you. We gonna have any more trouble?"

"No." The only thing Rowan felt bad about was causing the

foreman to step in. He hated to be the cause of any grief. No matter how much Mack deserved it.

"Get back to work."

Mack scrambled to his feet, glaring at Rowan. "I could have you arrested, asshole."

The foreman stepped between them. "Carl! Switch places with Big Mouth."

Mack scowled at the insult, but slunk over to his new spot without further incident.

The scene was over and everyone went back to their drama-free existence. Rowan worked beside Carl, while Mack griped to his new linemate, loud enough for Rowan to hear.

"That guy's a jerk," Carl offered.

"I know. I shouldn't've let him bother me."

"It's a wonder nobody's knocked all his teeth out yet." Carl pulled a door from Rowan's spot.

Rowan grinned a little at that. He wouldn't be the guy to do it, but he wouldn't step in to stop it, either.

After that, the day went a little faster. Carl was chatty, in a good way. He talked about his son in college, his daughter in high school, and his wife, the elementary school music teacher, whom he obviously adored.

Rowan did a lot of nodding and very little commenting.

At five, he clocked out and made a beeline for the parking lot, hoping to miss the mass exodus of workers escaping and the next shift coming in. He hit the gas a little hard to get home by five thirty, but he did. After the fastest shower ever, he dried off and dressed, shoved his feet in his shoes and ran a hand through his hair. A knock on the door let him know time was up.

Grabbing his coat, he opened the door and grinned. Sarah was bundled up, a red knit hat pulled down to her eyes.

"You cold?" The temperature hovered around thirty degrees, but it felt mild to him.

"Freezing. And I have it on good authority that you should wear heavy clothes when it's cold outside."

"Excellent advice. Might save your life sometime."

They got in her car and buckled up.

When they merged onto the highway, he asked, "Did you bring the envelope?"

"It's on the back seat. I only brought the envelope for the hardware store, not the whole packet. But I'm thinking from now on I'll just keep it all together. I'm paranoid I'll lose something."

They pulled into the Hannigan's Hardware parking lot and found an empty space a few rows away from the entrance.

"Busy place." Rowan pointed to the car beside theirs. "I think that's Mike Flynn's car. I wonder if more than one team is doing this challenge tonight?"

"I guess we'll see." Sarah leaned into the back seat, grabbed the envelope and they went into the hardware store.

"Hey, guys." Avery Hannigan waved at Sarah.

"Avery! I heard you were back in town." Sarah grabbed her in a hug. "Why weren't you in the Love Drawing?"

"Because I got lucky." She jerked her head slightly toward Rowan and lowered her voice. "Guess you did, too, huh?"

Rowan hid a smile.

"We'll have to catch up."

Avery agreed. "We'll do lunch next week, for sure."

"Right on time!" James Hannigan, proud owner of the hardware store, and Avery's dad, showed them to a table in the back. Mike and Juanita Collins, another team matched at the ball, were already seated and waiting. "All right, folks, here's your challenge. Each team is going to build a pinewood derby car, and when you're done, we'll race. Both teams get the token, winning team gets bragging rights. You have one hour to build your car, you can test it as many times as you like." He pointed to the long strip of curved wood that served as the track. "No searching the internet for tips. We'll flip a coin for lane choice at exactly seven o'clock. Here are your kits. Good luck."

James disappeared into the aisles.

"What the heck is a pinewood derby car?" Sarah asked.

Rowan grinned. This was right up his alley. "We made these in Boy Scouts." He still had the pinewood derby trophy he'd won when he was a kid. He opened the package and dumped out a block of wood shaped like a car body, and a multitude of tiny car pieces, including tires, rods, little round metal pieces, and a tube of superglue.

He expertly grabbed the pieces, attached the tires to the car, then spun them to make sure they worked. He got up and ran the car down the track, then sat down and glued a weight to the bottom. When it was secure, he tested the car again.

"What can I do?" Sarah asked when he sat back down.

"Um, nothing yet." He was in the zone, manipulating the block of wood in his hands. They were definitely going to win this challenge.

"What are you doing?"

He attached another weight. "Putting weights on the car."

"Why?"

He glanced up at her. "So it goes faster. Obviously."

She sat back in her seat and let him work.

Rowan tested the car again, pleased with the increased speed.

Adding more weights, he half-watched as Mike tested their car. Rowan tried not to smile. His was definitely faster. And would be faster yet after he finished. Flipping the car over, he strategically placed the last weights near the front wheels.

"There's stickers and markers in here." Sarah rifled through a small plastic bin and held up a red marker.

"We can mark it, but be careful. Don't push the marker down too hard. The wood's really soft so it'll make dents. Here, let me." He picked up a green marker and wrote R & S on the roof of the car.

"Here, how about this sticker for the hood?" She held it out to him. "It's a lightning bolt. For extra speed."

"No stickers." Anything else would throw off the balance. His car was perfect, and he could pretty much guarantee it was winning.

She dropped the sticker back into the bin and checked her watch.

Rowan glanced over at Mike and Juanita, hunched shoulder to shoulder over their ridiculous car. The whole thing was covered in stickers. A pile of unused weights lay beside the markers they'd used to color the entire body in some sort of swirly rainbow design. No way it was going to beat his car.

At seven on the dot, James reappeared. "Okay, here's the coin." He showed them both sides. "Sarah, call it." He flipped the coin.

"Tails," she said as it spun through the air.

"Heads," James said, after checking the coin. "Juanita, which lane would you like?"

"That one." She pointed to the lane closest to them.

Rowan stifled a groan. It was the lane he would have chosen. "Always pick heads," he muttered to Sarah, who seemed not to hear.

James motioned for the guys to put the cars at the starting line. "We'll do best three out of five. Jumping the gun gives the other team an automatic win for that round. I'll count 1 – 2 – 3 – GO. Go on go. Got it?"

"Got it," Mike and Rowan said in unison.

"1 – 2 – 3 – GO!"

Rowan let go of his car. It easily sailed past Mike's and came to rest against the bumper at the end of the track.

"Winner of round one, Rowan and Sarah."

Rowan held his hand up for a high five. Sarah lightly tapped it with her fingertips.

They easily won rounds two and three as well.

Mike and Juanita congratulated them and shook their hands. James gave them their tokens and another handshake before they pulled their coats on and went to the car.

"That was fun." For the first time in a long time, Rowan felt almost giddy. He'd gotten out of his comfort zone and enjoyed himself. Mainly by winning. It felt good to win, even if the only prize was bragging rights.

"Hm." Sarah backed out of the parking space.

"You want to get something to eat?"

"Sure."

"Just want to grab something at Sheetz?"

"Sure."

He wasn't sure if she was just concentrating on driving, or if something was bothering her. It *was* full dark, and a lot of people didn't like night driving. He guessed that was it.

Sarah pulled up to a gas pump at Sheetz. She didn't say anything as she got out and pumped gas, nor when she got back in and pulled to a parking spot close to the door.

"Low on gas, huh?"

"Not anymore." She jumped out of the car.

He got out and hurried to the sidewalk so he could pull the door open for her, but she beat him to it. She went directly to the ordering kiosk and poked the screen with a fair amount of force.

"Everything okay?" They'd won, why wasn't she happy about it?

"Yup." She tore her slip off the machine and went to the soda fountain.

Rowan ordered his food and went to get his drink. Sarah was already in line to pay when he caught up with her. "Hey, I was going to get your food if you want."

"I think I can handle getting my own supper."

"Yeah…?" He was starting to think maybe she was upset about something.

She stepped up to the counter, had her rewards card scanned, paid for her order, then walked away without looking back.

Yup, she was upset.

Crap.

About what?

He paid and followed her to the table she'd sat down at. Maybe she'd gotten an upsetting text or something. "Care to tell me what's wrong?"

She finally fixed her gaze on him, and he was immediately sure he preferred being ignored. "We're supposed to be a *team*. This is supposed to be *fun*."

"That was fun. We won."

"*We* didn't win, Rowan. *You* won." She pointed at his chest for emphasis.

"What are you talking about?" This. This is why he wanted to be single. Women didn't make any sense. She was right there next to him the entire time.

"You acted like my questions were stupid, you wouldn't let me touch the car, and you wouldn't let me put stickers on it."

He tried explaining his reasoning again. "Stickers would have thrown off the balance. I let you put the design on the roof."

"Oh, we're rewriting history now? *You* put *your* design on the roof. You wouldn't even use the color I wanted."

"Come on, Sarah, you're acting like I did the whole thing myself."

She glared at him with one raised eyebrow, in utter disbelief, like he'd sprouted another head, one that was even stupider than the one he already had.

Annoyed, he snapped, "We won, isn't that the whole point?"

Her eyes narrowed. "You really think that's the whole point? Just to win?"

"So you wanted to lose?"

She opened her mouth to answer, then snapped it shut as her order number was called over the loudspeaker.

Instead of rejoining him at the table, she went to her car. He was pretty sure she was seriously considering leaving him behind.

His number was called and he went to the car with his bag.

"I'm missing something here."

"What does the word *team* mean to you?"

He didn't answer as she backed carefully out of the parking space and left the parking lot. When they were on the road, he said, "This is supposed to be fun. Losing isn't fun for me."

"Sitting there being ignored isn't fun for me. Not participating isn't fun for me. Being shot down when I suggest something isn't fun for me."

He pulled in a long breath and let it out slowly. Staring out the window at the blackness, he supposed he could admit that he'd taken over this challenge. "I wasn't trying to ignore you or shoot you down. I was focused on winning, and I apologize. If we're not in this to win the challenges, that's fine. Now I know."

She made a disgusted snorting noise. "You were doing so well, then you had to go and mess it up. It's not about winning or losing. Of course I want to win, but I want to win *as a team*, Rowan. I can't believe you can't grasp such a simple concept."

They were in his driveway. He didn't want her to leave angry. "Sarah."

"Don't. It's fine. I'll see you tomorrow at the same time." She waved him off.

"Sarah. Hey." He waited for her to turn and look at him. This called for an apology, to keep the peace. "I'm sorry. I'll reign in my competitive streak and let you do more of the work."

"Let me? That's *so generous* of you." The sarcasm positively dripped off her words.

"Obviously I'm not saying anything right. I'll see you tomorrow night."

He got out of the car and went inside. One epic failure of a day down, five more to go.

Chapter Eleven

Sarah threw the bag on the kitchen table. What a crappy night. If this was what the rest of the week was going to look like, she was tapping out. There was no sense making each other miserable for a one in nineteen chance to win a prize. And if they did win? She couldn't even fathom being trapped on an international flight with him.

She went to bed and woke up Tuesday morning still annoyed. She grumped her way through the day and arrived at Rowan's house at five forty-five. Instead of going to the door, she sat in the car and waited.

Rowan got in the car and gave her an unsure smile. "Bowling alley, right?"

"Yup." She decided to check her attitude and make the best of it. If tonight was ruined, it would be because of Rowan, not her. "I haven't been bowling in ages. You?"

"Years."

The drive to the bowling alley was supremely awkward, but at least it was quick. Sarah pulled into a parking space and practically dove out of the car to change the scenery.

Rowan held open the heavy glass door for her. Inside, they

met another team, Chad and Stephanie, and they all got their complimentary rental shoes and selected their balls. Rowan's was white with scuff marks, hers was sparkly purple.

A bored teenage bowling alley employee pointed from his station behind the counter. "Use the two far lanes. You can either have one person bowl for your team, or you have to take turns."

Chad smirked. "I'll bowl for us. I was in a league in college."

Sarah glanced at Rowan, waiting to hear his level of expertise on this, too.

"You want to go first?" he asked her.

Her eyes widened. "You want to take turns?"

"Yup." He shrugged. "I'm trainable."

Pleasantly surprised, she took it as a sincere apology and let go of her annoyance. "Thanks."

They got settled in on their lanes and Chad took his spot while Sarah took hers. Chad's roll knocked down nine pins. Sarah's rolled wide and dropped into the gutter. Chad's second roll knocked down the remaining pin, while Sarah managed to knock down five of hers.

Chad laughed and said, "Like taking candy from a baby."

Sarah tried not to be annoyed at his trash talk, but it didn't feel like companionable joking. It felt like he actually thought he was something super special. Blech.

Rowan lined up for his turn. Chad's roll was a strike. Rowan's knocked down eight pins, leaving a seven – ten split, which he failed to clean up on his second roll.

"Dang."

Chad got his second strike, and Sarah knocked down nine pins.

Chad's cocky dance was ridiculous. She rolled her eyes at Rowan, who gave her a look that was total agreement. That.

Right there. They were a team. Screw Chad and his stupid dance. They were going to have fun.

Chad's next roll only took down four pins and Rowan got a strike. He pumped his arms in the air and Sarah gave him a high five. "Nice!"

"Big deal, I'm still ahead by a mile."

Stephanie scrolled through her phone.

Half an hour later, the score was tied, thanks to a string of strikes, courtesy of Rowan.

Chad lined up beside Sarah for the last round. She patted her ball and said to it, "Come on, baby. Give me a strike." She pulled back, then swung forward and released the ball. It rolled straight down the middle, fast and sure, striking the first pin. Pins flew, knocking each other down, all except one pin that teetered and tottered and wobbled precariously.

Sarah clasped her hands and jumped up and down. "Come on, come on." The pin stopped wobbling and landed on its base, standing upright.

All Chad's pins fell.

With a sigh, she turned around, expecting to see disappointment or annoyance. Instead, Rowan's hands were up for a double high five. "So close."

"WOOO! In your face!" Chad snatched the token from the employee and waved it at them. "Suck it, you lose!"

Sarah ignored him and followed Rowan over to the bench, where they took off their rental shoes. The employee came over and handed Sarah their token. "Thanks." She put it in her purse, then pulled out a clean pair of socks. She changed socks, then put her sneakers on.

"Paranoid about foot germs?"

"You never know."

Chad and Stephanie headed out.

Sarah watched Rowan watch them leave. She said, "I guess

I should have let you bowl for us. It's been a while, but I expected to do better."

"No. You were right. It was a lot more fun working together as a team." He shook his head and gestured to the now-empty doorway. "I'm really sorry about last night. Please tell me I wasn't that much of an ass."

She snort-laughed. "Nobody's *that* much of an ass."

He nodded in agreement. "When you were up, I kept looking over at Stephanie, bored out of her mind, all by herself, and thinking that must have been how you felt last night. It won't happen again, Sarah."

Wow. She never expected him to not only understand what she'd been trying to tell him, but take it completely to heart. "Thanks. Sorry my last roll wasn't a strike." She hated that Chad won.

He held up her coat for her to slip on. "It would have been nice to beat him, but this was fun. I'm glad you called me on my stuff last night. I don't want to be that guy."

"Well. I'm glad you acknowledged your stuff." She grinned and grabbed the front of his coat, looking up at him. "And you're right. This was fun." She pulled her phone out of her back pocket. "Let's commemorate the occasion with a selfie."

He obliged, hunkering down and smiling while she snapped a few photos and texted them to him. When she was done, he asked, "Hungry?"

"Starving."

"Cracker Barrel?"

"Absolutely."

She led Rowan out of the bowling alley, enjoying the feel of his hand on her back as they went out.

The Cracker Barrel parking lot was nearly empty, so they were led directly to a table in front of the fireplace. "This is nice and toasty."

Rowan nodded. "I should use my fireplace more often."

"I wish I had one. They're so cozy."

"A lot of maintenance. But yeah, it's nice to sit in front of a fire when it's really cold out."

"Especially when it's snowing. Or Christmas." Sarah looked at Rowan over her menu.

He glanced up and caught her gaze. "Speaking of which, did you see it's supposed to snow later this week?"

"I did. Hopefully we don't get the foot of snow they're calling for." She hated driving in the snow.

He shrugged. "It'll change. It always does."

They ordered their food and the waiter brought their drinks. They hadn't even begun another conversation when their food arrived.

She smiled at the waiter. "Wow, that was fast. Thanks."

"What's tomorrow night's stop?" Rowan asked.

"Art studio."

He made a face. "Great. Definitely not my area of expertise."

"If you're a carpenter, you have to have some artistic abilities. You can't make things in any medium without being creative. Especially those carvings you did."

"It's not the same as painting a picture or drawing something."

"Eh, I think it uses some of the same skill set, doesn't it?" She dug into her pancakes. Yum. Nothing better than breakfast for dinner.

"Maybe." He didn't sound convinced.

"I wonder what they'll make us do. Maybe we'll have to sketch a nude model. We'll have to draw some guy's junk." She laughed at Rowan's horrified expression. "Guess you're hoping that's not it, huh?"

"Oh, please, no. I'm going to have nightmares tonight."

"Maybe we'll have to be covered in paint and roll around on a massive canvas."

"That's not any better. Maybe we should stop speculating. It's making me nauseous."

Sarah laughed again. "I think it's mostly a ceramics place, maybe we'll just have to paint a mug or something."

"I could handle that."

"Me, too. I can always use a new mug."

They finished their meals in companionable quiet, with the crackling fire and clinking sounds from the kitchen filling the silence.

When Sarah dropped Rowan off at his house, she put a hand on his arm before he got out of the car. "Tonight was a lot of fun. This is what I was hoping for out of this."

He nodded. "Yeah. I'm on board from now on. Go Team." He pumped his fist in the air, then got out of the car and went inside.

When Sarah got home, she was surprised to see she had a text from Rowan.

We need a team name.

She showed the message to Harvey. "Look at that. He's getting into the spirit. Tonight went a lot better than last night. I'll fill you in once I put my jammies on."

Chapter Twelve

Rowan laughed at the texts rolling in. Blue lay on the couch with his head in Rowan's lap.

Team SarRow?

Team Rowah?

Team Winchester-Graham?

Team Chad Sucks?

He texted back,

That one for sure.

Maybe Team Chucks so nobody knows what we're talking about LOL

His head fell back against the cushion as he laughed.

Perfect. Go Team Chucks.

Even Blue thumped his tail in agreement.

He could hardly wait to see what Wednesday night's challenge brought.

It took forever for Wednesday evening to roll around. When Sarah picked him up, he was out the door before she was all the way in the driveway. He got in the car. "I was tempted to make us t-shirts."

She squealed and clapped her hands. "Team Chucks shirts? That would be awesome."

They got to The Color Wheel, and were both surprised to find the parking lot mostly full. In the lobby, a perky woman in a black apron with a bright business logo greeted them. "Hang your coats up over there, then you'll be in the classroom on the right."

Rowan hung their coats and followed Sarah into the classroom, past shelves of unpainted ceramic mugs, bowls, plates, and figurines. The classroom was full of tables, each set up with two chairs, two easels, two canvasses, and two sets of markers. And two blindfolds. He raised an eyebrow. "I'm not too sure about this."

"It'll be fun." She led him to a table near the front of the room.

A few minutes later, it seemed like all twenty – well, nineteen – teams were present. A different woman in an apron went to the front of the room and greeted everyone.

"What we're going to do is blind art. One person will be blindfolded. Your partner will be given a picture that you are to duplicate, but they cannot directly name what it is. Instead, you must describe the items." She held up a picture of a kite. "For instance, you might say this is a diamond shape at the top of the page. The blindfolded player must draw the object using those descriptions. We'll have fifteen minutes to draw. Then we'll swap and the second person will be blindfolded and draw. Any questions so far?"

"Do we get wine?" one of the guys called from the back.

Everyone chuckled.

"Afterwards," she answered. "Once both drawings are done, you can have a glass of wine and some refreshments while we have our other class come in and vote for the best drawings. We've given the other class three pennies each, so they can vote for their favorite three drawings. The team that gets the most combined votes is the winner. Okay, decide who gets blindfolded first."

Rowan sighed. "Can I go first and get this over with?"

"Sure. Get a good look at your supplies. I don't think I can help you once we start."

"Got it." He pulled the silky blindfold over his eyes and felt like a complete idiot.

"They're handing out the cards now. Looks like almost everyone has one. Okay, she's heading back up front." Sarah gave him a running commentary, which he appreciated. It was a silly little thing, but he didn't like the feeling of being vulnerable even though he could easily rip the blindfold off.

The woman spoke again. "Setting the timer for fifteen minutes. Try to get as many details as you can. Remember, you can't specifically say what the object is. Ready, set, go!"

Sarah said, "Oh, crap. Okay, there's a brown thing that's tall. Draw a tall brown line along the left side of the canvas."

"Brown?"

"Wait. Use that marker. Nope, next one. Next one. Good."

He uncapped the marker and put his finger on the top of the canvas. "Line from top to bottom?"

"Yes. Great."

He drew a line straight down.

"Now draw a bunch of shorter lines up and down between that line and the left edge of the canvas."

He tried to envision what would be tall and brown with lines. "Am I making a tree?"

Her little gasp gave it away. "I can't say."

"You didn't." He grinned and made some streaks that were probably more or less along the trunk of what he assumed was a tree.

"Now make a horizontal line come out of the first brown line, about two or three inches from the bottom of the canvas."

"Like a branch?"

"Sure. It should stick out about seven or eight inches to the right of the vertical line."

Rowan guessed where his tree trunk started, then drew a line straight out and hooked it back and drew a line connecting his branch to his tree. "How's that?"

"You're fabulous. Now we're going to use a different marker and make a circle on top of the horizontal line you just made."

"Circle?"

"Yup."

Now he was confused. A bird wouldn't be a circle, would it? Oh, well. He picked up another marker and tried to visualize where the branch was. He drew a circle.

"Perfect. Now at the sides of the circle, we're going to draw triangle-ish shapes."

He laughed. "Like wings?"

"Sure."

He made two half-triangles where he thought the sides of the circle were. "Now what?"

"Um, we need two dots near the top center of the circle, then a triangle with the long side at the top and the pointy side down right under the dots."

"Like eyes and a beak?"

"Sure."

He grabbed a different marker and drew dots and a triangle.

"Now we need to make little upside down pitchforky things at the bottom of the circle."

"Pitchforky things?"

"Yup."

"Like bird feet?"

"Sure."

He guessed where the bottom of his bird was and drew two legs. "Now what?"

"At the very top of the canvas there are green... um... swirly shapes? Like a bunch of random... shapes. At the top of the brown part you drew first."

"Leaves?"

"Sure."

He picked another marker and made some ovalish shapes all over the top inch of the canvas. "Now what?"

The woman at the front of the room called out, "Time!"

Rowan pulled his blindfold off to behold his masterpiece and burst out laughing. It was recognizable, he'd give it that, but the wings weren't touching the circle, and the eyes were floating well above the head. The legs were way off center. "Poor thing."

Sarah giggled. "I'm not saying anything, mine is going to be awful."

After the laughter died down, the woman had them switch roles.

"Handing out cards," Rowan told Sarah. She clutched a fistful of markers.

"She's heading back up front. Almost ready."

The woman set the timer and Rowan looked at his card. It was harder to describe it than he thought it'd be.

"Okay. There are two circles, both at the bottom, with probably two inches between them. Circles are about three inches in diameter."

"Oh, geez. Okay." She reached out hesitantly and made some circles on the canvas.

"I have no freaking idea how to describe this. Okay. Above the first circle is a line that comes down to the center of the circle, then goes straight back to the center of the second circle."

"What?"

"Sorry, this is a lot harder than it looks. Um, wait. We'll do something else first. Both circles have lines all the way through them, like pie wedges."

"Ooooh!" Sarah shook a fist. "Spokes. It's a bike, isn't it?"

"Sure." He had no idea how she'd guessed correctly from his mangled description.

"Spokes. I can do spokes."

"Perfect." He watched as she made lines on the canvas. "Now go above the first circle and draw a line with two bent lines on the ends."

"Handlebars. Got it." She made some lines on her picture.

"Now straight down to the center of the first circle, good, then straight back to the second wheel, then up, stop. Right where you're at you want to draw a triangle."

"Triangle?" She bit her lower lip as if she was confused, then smiled. "A seat."

"Sure." Dang, she was so much better at this than he was.

"Now go straight from your triangle back to the line over the front circle."

The woman at the front called, "Time!"

Sarah pulled off her blindfold and laughed. "Oh, that's horrible. It looks like a preschooler drew it."

"It's brilliant. Like a Picasso." It did resemble a bike, even if the parts weren't all attached. He was impressed with how well they'd both done. Okay, the art itself was crap, but they'd nailed working as a team.

"I'm not cutting off my ear."

Rowan snickered. "Wasn't that Van Gogh?"

"Oh, yeah."

"Alright, everyone, please write your name on the back of your canvas, then bring it up here and put it along this wall."

They did as she instructed, putting their artwork on a narrow ledge on the wall. Under the ledge were long tables holding jars for the votes.

"Okay, everyone, grab some snacks and head back to your seats and we'll invite the other class in."

A second employee opened the classroom door and let the other class in. Rowan put his arm around the back of Sarah's chair as they watched the other class come in and make one pass in front of the artwork, then form a line to circle back and cast their votes.

The first penny clinked into a glass jar. Everyone watched as, one by one, the other people dropped their pennies into the jars.

He leaned close to her ear. A stray curl tickled his cheek. "This is more nerve wracking than I thought it would be."

"No kidding. I feel all jittery." Her voice dropped to a whisper. "Some of them are really bad, I can't even tell what they are. At least you can tell what ours are."

"I'm hanging mine in the middle of my living room. I might even get one of those art spotlight things to shine on it."

Sarah giggled, and he decided it was a sound he wanted to hear more often.

The last of the voters left the room and the two women with aprons counted the pennies. When they were done counting, they added the team's paintings together.

"Great job, everyone." The instructor clapped and gave them a big smile. "To thank you all for your participation tonight, we're giving each team a buy one, get one free coupon for any of our classes or workshops. Now, our third place winning team will receive a gift certificate for twenty-five dollars. That team is Diana and Bud."

Everyone clapped as they went up front to claim their prize.

"Second place wins a fifty dollar gift certificate. Shelly and Corey."

More applause as they were given their certificate.

"And now, the first place team, winning by a landslide, receives a one hundred dollar gift certificate. Congratulations to our first place team, Sarah and Rowan."

Sarah's mouth dropped open. "No way!"

Rowan stood and grabbed her hand, practically pulling her to her feet so they could accept their certificate. Sarah bounced on her heels beside him, grinning from ear to ear. "This was so fun!" She hugged both the ladies before they went back to their seats.

"Thank you all so much for coming. It's been a blast, and we hope to see you all back for a class where you can see what you're doing. Your artwork is yours to take."

The room cleared out. Sarah clutched Rowan's hand as they stood in the not-quite-a-line to take their canvasses. "I can't believe we won." She convinced Rowan to take a selfie with their artwork.

"Congrats," came the sarcastic voice of none other than Chad.

Rowan gave Sarah's hand a little squeeze. "Team Chucks."

"Team Chucks," she answered.

"That doesn't even make any sense," Chad muttered as he sneered at them. He snatched one of the unrecognizable messes.

Sarah pushed her face against Rowan's arm, trying not to laugh. He dropped her hand and put his arm around her.

On their way to her car with their terrible pictures, Rowan shook his head. He never would have believed anyone who told him he'd have a great time while being blindfolded at an art studio. But here he was, on one of the best dates ever.

Wait.

Date?

Chapter Thirteen

Sarah pulled out of the parking lot and hung a left. "You hungry?"

"Uh, not really, I… um."

She glanced over. He looked a little green. "Are you feeling okay? Do you need me to stop at CVS or anything?"

"No, I guess it just kinda came on all of a sudden."

"Did you need food? Or just go home?"

"Home, please."

Sarah guessed he was having stomach issues. Remembering the last time she was stuck in a car and had to go to the bathroom desperately, she drove a little faster than she might have otherwise, and didn't ask any more questions.

"I'm sorry you're not feeling well," she said as he got out of the car. "Hopefully you're better for tomorrow."

"Yeah, I'm sure it'll be fine. Sorry. Thanks." He gave a little wave and hurried into his house.

He'd left his artwork in the back seat.

Back at home, she made herself a sandwich and a bowl of soup and sat in the living room filling Harvey in. "Tonight was great. Well, up until Rowan got sick. Not really *sick*, but he just got really quiet all of a sudden and wanted to get home. I'm betting he made a beeline for the bathroom as soon as he got inside. I'll text him after I'm done eating and make sure he's doing okay. Stomach stuff is the worst."

Harvey stood on the rock ledge in his tank, listening intently.

"That's his picture on the left. Mine's on the right. I think we did an amazing job of teamwork this time. We even won the challenge and got a gift certificate for a hundred dollars to use at the studio. I thought it might be fun to go back after the challenge is over and paint mugs or something. I can always use more mugs."

She finished her food and carried the dirty dishes to the kitchen and loaded them in the dishwasher. It was nearly full, so she threw in some detergent and started the wash cycle before going back to curl up on the couch.

Picking up her phone, she texted Rowan.

> Hope you're feeling better.

She waited a few minutes, but there was no reply. A few old *Friends* reruns later, she was ready for bed. Her fingers itched to send him another text, but she resisted and went to sleep.

Thursday morning, she checked her phone every two minutes, but he didn't reply. When she got to work, she couldn't stand it anymore, so she sent another text before she got out of her car.

> Hope you're feeling good today. Tonight is the tattoo shop!!! Pick you up at 5:45 unless I hear otherwise. Have a great day.

She hesitated over the long message. Was it too much? Would he read too much into it? She tapped the button to send the message.

She was hanging up her coat when her phone vibrated.

Feeling better. See you tonight.

Tucking her phone into her pocket, she smiled. Now she could get on with her day without creating unnecessary imaginary drama. Not that she was prone to do such a thing.

"How's the challenge going?" Becky asked.

"So far, so good. Rowan and I are getting along, the challenges have been fun, and we won a hundred dollar gift certificate to The Color Wheel."

"I bet he was thrilled with that."

Sarah shrugged and pulled up the day's schedule. "He had fun. I'm sure it wasn't his first choice of activity, but he was a good sport."

"What did you have to do?"

Sarah filled her in on the art challenge, then had to start over when Julie came in and wanted all the details, too.

Before three o'clock, the last patient was done and gone. Becky looked around at the empty waiting room and said, "Why don't you both go ahead and go? I have some paperwork I can finish up, but there's no reason we all have to hang around and twiddle our thumbs."

"You don't have to tell me twice." Sarah grabbed her coat. "Now I can stop and pick up some crickets for Harvey."

Julie made a face. "That's so gross."

"At least he doesn't eat feeder mice."

"Stop, you're going to make me barf."

Laughing, Sarah picked up her purse. "Thanks, Bec. See you in the morning."

"Have fun tonight."

Outside, the temperature had dropped since the morning. She pulled her coat tight and scurried to the car. Getting inside didn't help much, but it did block the biting wind.

She pulled her knit hat down and straightened her gloves, then drove away from the hospital and into town. In the pet shop, she stopped at a display of dog toys.

"Can I help you find something?" A skinny balding man with thick glasses came over.

"Um, I want to get a dog toy."

"Sure. What kind of toys does the dog like?"

"I don't know. It's for a friend. Well, a friend's dog."

"Ah. What kind of dog?"

"Medium? It's black."

The man blinked a few times, then nodded. "Well, there are different toys for different kinds of dogs." He pointed to a row of chew toys.

"I'm sorry, I don't know much about dogs." She felt stupid, wishing she hadn't been possessed by the urge to get something for Blue. Looking around, she spotted a display of flea medication. She pointed to one of the boxes. "That's the kind of dog. Right there. Blue looks exactly like that dog."

The man smiled and nodded enthusiastically. "That's a German Shepherd." He turned back to the toy display and picked up what looked like a tire. "This is a good one for extreme chewers like Shepherds and Labradors. It's puncture resistant, and it has lots of textures for the dog to enjoy. I've gotten excellent feedback about this toy."

Extreme chewers? Puncture resistant? Dogs were way more complicated than turtles. "Okay, great. I'll take it."

"Did you need anything else today?"

"Crickets. For my turtle," she added, just in case he thought she was dumb enough to buy crickets for a dog.

"Size?"

"Small."

"I'll be right back with those."

While he went in the back to get her crickets, Sarah walked up and down the aisles, not looking at anything in particular.

When he came back, she paid for the crickets and the tire. He handed her her receipt, then paused. "Are you on the scavenger hunt thing the Ladies' Society set up?"

"Oh, yes. I think we stop in here on Saturday."

He smiled brightly. "Great. We've had a couple of teams already. It's a wonderful boost for local businesses."

"I'm so glad. I'll be sure to let Agnes know you said so."

Sarah got home and hurried inside. The air was so cold it hurt her face.

"Good thing you have your heat lamp, little dude. It's freezing outside." She changed and got ready to pick Rowan up.

"Do you think it's weird that I bought Blue a toy? That's not weird, right? I mean, I was right there. If I made a special trip, *that* would be weird, but since I was already there, it's okay, right?"

Harvey slipped into the water and swam to the far side of the tank.

"Great. You're saying it's weird."

Harvey refused to respond.

"You're not very helpful."

She checked the time and got her coat and steeled herself to head back out into the bitter cold. "I'm ready for spring. Okay, Harvey, have a good evening."

She pulled into Rowan's driveway a few minutes early and went to knock on the door. Blue barked like crazy until Rowan opened the door and let her inside.

"Hi, sorry I'm early."

"No, come on in."

"I left the car running, but I wanted to pop in and give Blue a present, if it's okay with you."

Hearing his name, Blue's butt dropped to the floor and his tail swished back and forth, his ears perked forward in anticipation.

"What is it?"

She pulled the tire out of the bag. "The guy at the pet store said it's a good toy for breeds like Blue."

Blue's tail thumped harder.

Rowan smiled, seeming enthusiastic about the toy. "Hey, that's great. He just destroyed one of those and I hadn't gotten around to replacing it. What do I owe you?"

"Oh. Nothing, I got off work a little early so I stopped to get Harvey crickets and I just saw it so I thought Blue might like it and I got it but I don't expect you to pay me for it. I mean, it was just an impulse buy. No big deal." She clamped her lips shut to stop the rambling. "Here you go, Blue."

Blue's front paws danced.

Rowan warned, "Nice, Blue."

Blue gingerly stretched forward and took the toy in his teeth. As soon as Sarah let go, he took off running down the hallway.

"He'll put it in the bedroom and bring it back out later. He has a whole system."

"Gotcha."

"I'll grab my shoes then we can go." He went down the hallway Blue had gone down.

Sarah took the opportunity to look around. The front door opened into a small entryway. There was a coat closet to her left with the hallway next to it. A large archway led to the living room on the right. The kitchen lay straight ahead, with a shotgun style back door. She could see a large yard beyond the door, and a wooden fence at the back of the yard.

His living room was cozy. A massive television dominated one wall, and a large stone fireplace dominated the adjacent wall. Picture frames lined the wooden mantle. She fought the urge to cross the room and see who was in them.

"Okay, ready."

Startled, she practically yelled, "Great!"

Rowan opened the closet and got his coat, then they went out to her car.

Sarah backed out of his driveway and said, "I wonder what kind of challenge they'll have at a tattoo shop. That seems like an odd place."

"Yeah, I've been trying to figure that out, too."

Twenty minutes later, they found out.

A woman with a tattoo that drew the eye well into her ample cleavage greeted them. Sarah could barely pull her eyes from the lightning bolts disappearing down her shirt. She focused on the wall instead, where framed tattoos made a border around the room.

"I'm Kit. I'll be doing either a piercing or a tattoo for your challenge. You pick."

"Wait, what?" Sarah froze.

The woman's nose ring shifted as she grinned. "It's a henna tattoo. But there's a catch."

Sarah looked at Rowan and back to the woman. "That sounds ominous."

"If you get the piercing, you pick the location and the jewelry. If you pick the henna tattoo, I pick the location *and* the artwork."

Sarah asked, "How long does it last?"

"Anywhere up to three weeks."

"You wouldn't... like... put it on my face or something,

would you?" She didn't want to insult Kit, who had a spray of stars tattooed over her temple.

The woman shrugged. "That's the deal. Who's going first?"

Sarah swallowed hard. Either this woman had some wicked dry humor, or she was serious. "I guess I'll go first. Rowan?"

"I think I'm getting my nipples pierced."

She gave him an open-mouthed stare.

"Kidding. I'll get the tattoo. What are you doing?"

"I'm not sure. I had thought about getting a stud in the top of my ear, but I think I'll do the tattoo instead."

Rowan pointed at a picture on the wall. "There's a fancy sea turtle."

"That would be awesome."

"Sorry, you don't choose." Kit told them. "Let's go over here."

They followed her to a padded table covered with a paper sheet. Just like a doctor's office, but hopefully not as unpleasant.

She turned around and looked Sarah up and down, then reached over and grabbed her chin and turned her face to the left and to the right, then tapped a spot on her neck. "Perfect."

Sarah's heart pounded. Was this woman actually going to give her a neck tattoo? That would last for three weeks?

"Have a seat."

"Um…"

"Pull up your sleeves." Sleeves? For a neck tattoo?

Sarah did as Kit asked. Kit sat on a stool and examined both of her forearms. "Okay. No peeking." Rowan sat on her other side, so she focused on him.

"You're fine," he encouraged. "No needles with this tattoo."

"At least it's not on my face. I don't think they'd appreciate that at work."

Kit chuckled. "I wouldn't do that to you."

It felt like forever, with odd cold and wet sensations on her arm, before Kit announced that she could look, but it was only ten minutes or so. "You can look, but don't touch it. The paste needs to dry for about ten minutes. Your turn, big boy."

Rowan held his arm out.

"Nope. Lay on this table, face down."

"What?" He looked panicked. "Why?"

Kit patted the table and Rowan eventually laid down. She pushed his shirt up over his back.

"You're giving me a tramp stamp?"

Kit laughed. "Not quite."

Sarah tried not to laugh. "I can't wait to see this."

Kit worked along Rowan's side, then scooted her stool back so Sarah could see. "What do you think?"

"Oooh, that's really cool." Kit had done a tribal design with swirls and rounded lines ending in sharp points.

Kit went back over to Sarah and sprayed something on her design. "Lemon juice to help set the paste. It'll dry in about five minutes."

"Then what?"

"Once you're both dry, we'll leave the paste on. It'll flake off on its own overnight, then you can wash whatever's left off in the shower in the morning."

Rowan tried to peer down his side. "I don't want to move and mess it up, but I want to see it."

Sarah pulled her phone out and snapped a picture, then texted it to him. "How's that?"

Rowan's eyebrows rose as he nodded. "Not bad."

Kit sprayed the lemon juice on Rowan's paste. "Five minutes and you'll be ready to go. Let me grab your tokens."

A few minutes later, she came back and helped Sarah off the table, then handed her the token. "You guys did great."

She reached over and adjusted Rowan's shirt over the paste and when he was up, led them back to the front.

"Thanks, Kit, the turtle is awesome. I love it."

Kit winked. "If you decide to make it permanent, come see me."

When Sarah lifted her phone to take a selfie, Kit offered to take it and got a good picture of them and their not-quite-tattoos.

Back out in the car, Sarah debated whether to pull down her sleeve. She didn't want to smudge the paste, but her arm was getting cold. She decided against it, sacrificing her arm to the cold, at least until the car warmed up.

Rowan said, "That wasn't so bad."

"It definitely wasn't what I expected. When she said a tattoo or a piercing, I thought she meant a real tattoo."

"Do you have any real tattoos?"

She glanced at him. "No. I almost got one when I was younger, but I'm so glad I didn't."

"Why?"

Putting on the blinker, she turned at the light. "Because my plan was to get a very emo quote from a Nirvana song. It was deeply profound when I was young. Not so much anymore."

"What was the quote?"

"Nope, not even going there. What about you? Any tattoos?"

"A few."

"Really? Where?"

"I have one on my left upper arm, one on my right shoulder, and one on my chest."

"What are they of?"

He was quiet for a long moment. "I was in the Army. So I have a flag on my arm, an eagle on my shoulder, and dog tags on my chest."

"Wow, so they're really meaningful."

"Yeah. They're for three… um, my… men I used to know. Damn good men." He cleared his throat. "You hungry? I didn't get much of a lunch today."

"Sure." She let the abrupt subject change go, even though she was dying to ask him about his time in the service. "What are you hungry for?"

"How about the diner? I could eat a good club sandwich."

"Sounds good." She made another left and drove to the diner, wanting to ask questions, but not wanting to overstep the boundaries of their fragile new friendship.

At the diner, Rowan held the door open for her. She walked ahead of him to a corner booth – no, not the Ladies' Society's booth – and slid in. "Tomorrow night we have to go all the way out to the mall. I'm really curious about what that challenge might be."

"It could be anything."

"I wonder how we'll know. It just says to go to the fountain. Do you think there'll be somebody there? Or a sign?"

"I'm guessing someone will be there, but who knows." His voice was a little subdued.

"You okay?"

He looked up, surprised. "Yeah, fine, why?"

"You've been quiet."

"Hungry." He gave her a half-smile and turned his attention back to the menu.

Sarah watched him for a moment longer, then looked at her own menu. They ordered their food and the waitress brought their drinks. She picked at her napkin, then her straw wrapper, waiting for Rowan to say something. Anything.

The silence stretched until the waitress brought their plates of food.

"Looks good."

Sarah nodded. "Yeah." It looked average. A fish sandwich and french fries wasn't exactly exotic or exciting.

A group of teenagers came in and sat at the far side of the restaurant. They were laughing and talking and loud. One of them got up and dumped a bunch of quarters into the jukebox, so music added another layer of noise.

It helped her feel like silence wasn't quite so loud.

After they ate, Rowan paid the check and dropped a generous tip on the table before she had a chance to pull her wallet out.

"Thanks."

"You've been doing all the driving. It's the least I can do."

"It's not like we've been going that far."

"Still, I appreciate it." His voice was more subdued than usual.

The entire drive back to his place, Sarah discarded a dozen topics of conversation. Rowan stared out the window, lost in his own thoughts. She didn't want to pry or intrude, but she was desperately curious.

She pulled into his driveway and put her hand on his arm. "Rowan? You sure everything's okay?"

He put his other hand over hers and squeezed. "I, um…" he trailed off and cleared his throat. "The whole tattoo thing. It just got me thinking about things I haven't thought about in a while."

"From when you were in the Army?" she asked softly.

"Yeah."

She turned her hand and laced her fingers with his. "I know it's nothing that I could ever understand, but if you want to talk, I want to listen."

One side of his mouth curved up in a half-smile. "I appreciate it, but it's not something I want to talk about. I'm not mad or upset or anything. Just sometimes a lot of stuff comes up to the surface and I need a minute to put it all back where it belongs."

"Okay." She wished there was something she could say to help, but she understood those internal demons all too well.

"I'll see you tomorrow night."

Sarah nodded. "Tomorrow night."

He let go of her hand and opened the car door. He got out, but instead of closing the door, he leaned down and looked in at her. "Thanks for the toy for Blue." He looked like he was going to say something else, but instead, just nodded once and closed the car door.

She watched him go in. What was he going to say?

Chapter Fourteen

Rowan closed the front door and ran a hand over his face, then reached down to scratch Blue's head. "How was your evening?"

Blue wagged his tail, then trotted through the kitchen to the back door and rang the bells that meant he had to go outside.

"You got it, buddy." Rowan slid the glass door open. Blue ran out to the middle of the yard, sniffed and turned around in circles, locating the exact perfect place to poop. Rowan shook his head and left the door open, ignoring the cold air rushing into the kitchen. He got a glass of water and sipped until Blue came back in.

"I'm going to have to teach you how to close the door."

Blue wagged his tail and looked expectantly at the box of treats.

Tossing a treat, Rowan sighed. "How come I don't get a treat for going to the bathroom? Huh?"

Instead of answering, Blue ran into the living room.

A telltale thump let Rowan know Blue was on his back,

rubbing against the carpet, kicking his feet into the air. His dog was nothing if not predictable.

Rowan flopped on the couch and flipped the television on. He turned it to a Wheel of Fortune marathon and tried not to think about his tattoos or what they meant, or the three men who were ageless memories, frozen in time.

It should have been four.

He pushed away the little voice in his head that never quite went away. Sometimes it lay dormant, but it always came back to fill his ear with hateful words about how he should have died alongside them, how he was a coward and shouldn't have taken his honorable discharge.

He'd finished his time and chosen not to reenlist. All three of them had signed back up, and it ultimately cost them their lives. Meanwhile he was back stateside, sitting on his couch in the air conditioning.

Blue whined, pulling Rowan back to himself. Blue's nose was inches away from his. He stared into Rowan's face as if he could see the darkness pulling at him.

Maybe he could. Blue surely had demons of his own. He was a retired military dog, decorated and discharged from service after he'd been injured in the field. He'd lost part of his back leg, but saved nine lives that day. Rowan scooted back on the couch and Blue climbed up beside him and licked his face. Rowan wrapped his arm around the dog and pushed his face into his fur.

The whining stopped and Blue lay his head down.

"You're such a good boy. I don't know what I'd do without you."

Blue's tail thumped against his leg.

The darkness receded, at least for a while.

"What do you think about Sarah?"

Blue's tail thumped again.

"Yeah, I like her, too."

The wee hours of Friday found Rowan still on the couch. At some point, Blue had jumped down and relocated to the recliner, where he was curled up, snoring.

Rowan got up and headed for the bathroom. It was too late to go back to bed, too early to get up for the day. He pulled on sweats and went to the makeshift gym in the basement. A treadmill and a heavy bag were all he needed. He put his headphones in, cranked the music, and punched the bag until his arms shook, then ran until his legs threatened to give out.

It helped.

He let Blue out, showered, and packed his lunchbox for work. He "accidentally" dropped a slice of cheese, much to Blue's delight.

Scratching Blue's head, he left for work, the demons in his mind hushed for a change, quieted by the anticipation of seeing Sarah in eleven short hours.

As Fridays are wont to do, the day passed with that communal buzz of anticipation of the last bell of the work day. When it came, Rowan was first in line to punch out, and first to pull out of the parking lot and drive home, using the posted speed limits as a sort of helpful suggestion.

When Sarah pulled into his driveway, he couldn't help but smile.

The smile didn't last after they got into the mall. The place was unusually packed, and he had a bad feeling about whatever challenge they were about to be assigned.

The Ladies' Society had a table set up beside the fountain at the center of the mall. The teams congregated close to the table until everyone had arrived. The ladies handed out clipboards and pens to each team and explained the challenge.

Rowan's mouth went dry as Sarah's eyes lit up. Their task was to have ten strangers – strangers! – draw a picture on their clipboard.

"This is so much fun." She bounced on her heels.

He couldn't envision anything *less* fun. Swallowing hard, he already knew he was going to disappoint her. He was okay in crowds, as long as he didn't have to interact with them. He was great in small groups. Even better one on one. But going up to complete strangers? Nope, not something he wanted to do. At all. Ever.

Not even for Sarah.

He pulled on her arm, turning her attention from the clipboard.

"We have to get ten people to draw stick people," she said. "This is awesome."

"Sarah, I can't do this." His tongue felt too big for his dry mouth.

"Of course you can. It's fun."

Being outgoing, bubbly, and talking to strangers was definitely in Sarah's wheelhouse, but it was so far outside his comfort zone it wasn't even in the same zip code. "I'll let you take the lead."

"No problem." She went up to a family and chatted excitedly. The man and woman looked at each other, skeptical, until Sarah pointed to the Ladies' Society table, then the woman took the pen from Sarah and scribbled something on the clipboard. "Awesome! Thank you so much!"

She was giddy as she scurried back to him. "Check it out." The woman had drawn a smiling stick figure on the page.

He forced a smile. "Good job." All he wanted to do was melt into the background.

"Your turn." The clipboard she held out might as well have been poison.

He swallowed hard. "I'm not doing this."

"Come on, don't be a party pooper."

"I can't do this."

She tilted her head and pushed the clipboard at him again. "You're just being silly."

"Sarah!" His voice was way sharper, way louder than he'd intended. Several people turned to look at him. He hated the wounded look on her face, but it wasn't enough to overcome his reservations. He stepped closer, hating the way she pulled back, and lowered his voice to try to explain. "I'm serious. I can't just go up to people I don't know. You don't understand."

Agnes scurried over. "Is there a problem?"

"No," they answered in unison.

Tut-tutting, Agnes lingered for a moment, then finally walked away.

"What is your problem?" Sarah hissed.

"All these freaking people. I hate crowds." He knew he had to do better than that. "I'm sorry, I know it sounds lame, but walking up to strangers for something like this literally makes me want to puke."

Annoyance and sympathy warred across her features. She shook her head, then plastered a bright smile on her face and spun away from him. "Hi! Excuse me, we're doing a—okay, have a great evening. Sir? Hi, excuse me. We're doing a challenge and we need people to draw a stick figure. That's it. Would you please draw one for me?"

Rowan hung back, his hands shoved in his pockets, watching Sarah bounce out and around, charming the streams of shoppers, easily convincing strangers to draw pictures for her.

"Letting her do all the work, huh?" Chad smirked.

"Piss off." Any patience he had was reserved for Sarah, not this jackass.

"Looks like that guy's doing more than filling out her form." Chad laughed like he'd said something greatly amusing, then added, "Guess you've got some competition, huh?" Thankfully, he wandered off to annoy someone else.

Rowan scanned the crowd and found Sarah, smiling up at some gym rat douchebag with a crew cut. For crying out loud, the guy was wearing shorts. In February. And it looked like he'd skipped leg day a time or ten.

A pang of annoyance, coupled with maybe just a hint of jealousy, made him more annoyed and anxious than he already was. He couldn't wait to get out of here, away from the screamingly bright fluorescent lights, sharp chatter, and the mishmash of music clashing from the main mall sound system and the nearby stores.

The guy took Sarah's clipboard and scribbled something, then took the pen and tapped the tip of her nose. He grabbed her hand and wrote on it. She kept a smile on her face, but Rowan knew her well enough by now to read her expression. Just as he took a step forward, ready to go rescue her, Sarah pulled her hand back, grabbed the pen and clipboard, thanked the moron jerk loser and turned away.

She came over to Rowan and rolled her eyes. Shoving the clipboard at him, she grumbled, "What a creep. Hang onto this while I go to the restroom and scrub my hands, okay?"

He didn't have a chance to respond before she whirled away and strode down the hallway to the restrooms. Glancing down at the clipboard, there was only one block left to fill. He scowled at what The Jerk had drawn. Two stick people. One had a penis. A disproportionately large one at that. The other had gigantic boobs. What an idiot. He looked too old to still be in a fraternity. Or middle school.

Looking around the mall, Rowan spied an old couple sitting on a bench. Maybe they'd be approachable. Before he could walk over, Chad and Stephanie cornered them. Deflated, Rowan tapped the clipboard against his fist. If he didn't do anything, he'd be letting Sarah down. All week, she'd been harping about being a team. That meant stepping outside his comfort zone.

He was about to give up when he spied a woman in a hoodie with ARMY emblazoned across the front. Her straight posture and her hair tied in a tight bun at the base of her skull suggested she might be military, and not just wearing a random hoodie. She walked with a muscular man in a plain t-shirt who carried himself like he might also be a soldier.

Before he could lose his nerve, he walked over. "Ma'am. Hi, um, your Army shirt…"

The couple regarded him with curiosity.

"Uh. I was in the Army, too. Six tours in the desert."

"Oh." Immediately their wary looks gave way to cama-raderie. The woman spoke. "I just got home. Chris has been back for a few months. I'm Marcy."

They all shook hands and introduced themselves.

"Look, this is really silly, but I'm doing this competition thing with my girlfriend." The little white lie slipped out. "We have to ask strangers to draw a picture. She's washing her hand after some douchebag wrote his phone number on it and I hate going up to people but I was hoping you might be willing to help a brother out."

Chris looked down at Marcy and grinned. "The things you do for love, huh?" He took the clipboard and they drew in the last empty block. Two stick figures with the caption, "GO ARMY!"

"Thanks. I really appreciate you helping me out."

"Hi," Sarah appeared at his elbow.

Marcy smiled at her. "You must be the girlfriend."

Rowan froze, but Sarah smiled back without batting an

eyelash. They shook hands and talked for a few minutes, then the couple went on their way.

As soon as they were alone, he hurried to explain. "Sorry about that, it was just easier." He hoped his little white lie hadn't offended her. They were in a pretty good place, and he didn't want anything to rock the boat.

"It's fine. It makes sense." She gestured to the Ladies' Society table. "Let's go turn in our clipboard."

As they walked toward the fountain where the ladies were stationed, Sarah grabbed his hand and gave it a squeeze. "Thanks for wrapping it up." Apparently stepping out of his comfort zone and getting that last drawing was the exact right thing to do.

Millie took the clipboard and patted his cheek. "Good job, guys. We'll do the drawing at eight, so be sure to come back."

Sarah looked up at him. "Food court? I'm starving."

"Sure." They were a few yards away from the fountain when he said, "What drawing?"

She gave him a look. "Weren't you paying attention when we got our instructions? All the teams who complete the challenge this evening are entered into a drawing for some gift cards."

"Oh. I missed that." He'd been inside his head, worrying about talking to strangers instead of focusing on the challenge. Or the instructions, apparently.

They picked a Mexican restaurant and ordered a tray full of tacos. Rowan carried the tray to the table Sarah pointed to and set it down. Before he could pull his chair out, she grabbed his arm, then put her hands on the sides of his face.

"I know that wasn't easy. I'm proud of you." She went up on her tiptoes and planted a kiss on his lips.

Before he could respond, she was at the other side of the

table, sitting down and unwrapping a taco like the world hadn't just tipped on its axis.

Heart pounding, he pulled out his chair and sat down. His stomach flip-flopped. It was a simple kiss. A peck, really. It didn't mean anything.

Just a quick kiss.

No big deal.

Except his lips still tingled and his heart wouldn't settle.

Chapter Fifteen

Sarah unwrapped her fourth taco and squeezed a packet of hot sauce inside it, followed by a packet of sour cream. "These are the best tacos ever."

"They're really good."

He seemed subdued. Sarah felt bad that he'd had a rough time with the challenge. As an extrovert herself, sometimes it was hard to remember that not everyone was a people person. Like Rowan. This challenge was perfect for her, but it must have been a nightmare for him. She let go of any lingering annoyance about his reluctance to participate. He'd been honest with her and told her right up front that this wasn't his thing, but he'd sucked it up and gotten the last drawing anyway. "Tonight was kind of a lot, huh?"

One shoulder lifted in a shrug. "It was okay."

"I didn't realize crowds were an issue for you."

He finished the last bite of a taco. "It's not crowds, really. It's the whole going up to strange people that I hate. I mean, I don't like crowds, but as long as I can keep to myself, it's not a big deal. And it's not like I have panic attacks or anything, I just don't like it. It makes me very uncomfortable. I'm not good with talking to people I don't know."

"You do fine. Except for people who aren't properly dressed for the weather," she teased.

He laughed. "I couldn't have a frozen corpse in Millie's front yard. What would her neighbors think?"

"Excellent point. I hadn't considered the neighborhood gossip." She was glad to see his shoulders relax. Even though they were surrounded by people, Rowan wasn't bothered by their presence.

He gave her a serious expression. "You're clearly not ready to join the Ladies' Society, then. You always, *always*, above all, consider the neighbors."

The teasing caught her a little off guard, in a good way. "You've put a lot of thought into the Society."

He wiped a bit of taco sauce from the corner of his mouth. The mouth she had kissed on impulse. And couldn't wait to do it again. *Whoa, Sarah, slow your roll.* Besides, he hadn't reacted, other than his wide eyes. Obviously she'd shocked him, but she had no idea if it was a good thing or a bad thing. Or a nothing thing.

He grinned. "I'm going to be the first man to break into the upper echelon of the Society."

"The *Ladies'* Society."

"For now."

She couldn't help but laugh. "And why would you do such a thing?"

"They have cookies."

"Just like the dark side, huh?"

"Have you been around all four of them at the same time?" He shuddered. "It *is* the dark side."

"So you're planning to usher in a new era of the Ladies' Society. And here I wasn't sure how ambitious you were."

Unwrapping another taco, he looked up, his bright blue eyes captivating her. "Now you know."

After they finished eating, they walked around the mall, killing time until the drawing. Sarah swallowed hard as they passed a Victoria's Secret store. One of the mannequins wore a red outfit Sarah knew she'd look amazing in – what was it about the color red all of a sudden? And she tried not to think about whether or not Rowan would agree.

She fought to rationalize her thoughts. Okay, so it had been a while since she'd been in a relationship. Like, a *while*. She'd only been on a handful of dead end first dates since her divorce from her horrible ex almost five years ago. And lousy attitude or not, Rowan was hot. Those blue eyes, that grin, that unshaven face and those few top buttons of his shirt undone to give a view of just a few chest hairs. Dang.

She shook her head and made a beeline for the kitchen gadget store. That was a much safer mental space. Nothing sexy in the kitchen store. Good. Until she thought about her own kitchen. Kitchen counter. Rowan backing her up against the counter, picking her up to sit on the counter, making out on the counter—

"You okay?"

Startled, she nearly jumped out of her skin. Heat burned its way up her neck and into her cheeks. "Yup, yes, great, fine. I, um, I need one of these." The bin closest to her was full of vegetable peelers. She grabbed one and carried it to the register. She paid for it and spent an obnoxious amount of time wrapping the bag around it tightly and sticking it in her jacket pocket until her face stopped burning.

It didn't help when Rowan put his hand on her back to steer her out of oncoming traffic and it felt like his hand was burning a hole right through her shirt. Relieved when it was finally time to convene back at the fountain, Sarah wondered where she was going to put another vegetable peeler. She already had at least six.

The other teams had all finished their challenges, and the Ladies' Society put slips of paper with the teams into a plastic bowl.

"We have a bunch of gift cards to give away," Agnes began. "Our first prize is a two hundred and fifty dollar gift card for the mall. It can be used in any store or restaurant accessible through the mall." She reached into the bowl and pulled out a slip of paper. "Congratulations, Stephanie and Chad."

Standing behind her with his hands on her hips, Rowan snorted next to her ear. "Figures."

Sarah stifled a laugh and lightly elbowed backward. "Behave." She totally didn't mean to lean back against him.

Agnes pulled more slips and gave away more gift cards, until Sarah and Rowan were the only team left. "That leaves you two with the fifty dollar gift card for the day spa."

"Thanks." Sarah took the card from Millie.

"It's all yours," Rowan said as they walked through the mall toward the exit.

"What, you don't want to get a pedicure?"

"First of all, not ever, and second of all, you did all the heavy lifting for this challenge. You deserve it."

"Easy to say when it's something you'd never use."

"Shhh, let's not ruin the moment." He hesitated. "You didn't get your selfie."

"Oh." She was surprised and pleased he'd reminded her. She thought they annoyed him, even though he'd never complained. She pulled out her phone and snapped a picture. When she was done, Rowan opened the door for her to go through.

"Brrr, it got really cold." The bitter air went down the back of her coat.

They hurried to her car. Rowan opened the driver's door for her before dashing around to get in the passenger seat.

"Thanks. You didn't have to freeze to open my door, though."

He blew into his hands and arched an eyebrow. "Are you crazy? What if Millie had seen me not open your door? I'd never get into the Society."

"You're goofy." She liked this playful side of Rowan. She'd bet good money it was a side that not many people got to see.

Rowan put their token into the envelope with the others and pulled out the itinerary sheet. "Tomorrow's going to be a long day."

"What all are we doing?"

"Grocery store, paintball course, bookstore, pet store, and the junkyard."

Sarah's nose scrunched as she considered the list. "They're all so different. I wonder what we're going to do at all of them? A junkyard? What on earth can we do at a junkyard?"

"Beats me, but I'd wear warm clothes and sturdy shoes."

She pulled out of the parking lot and onto the main road. "How cold is it supposed to be tomorrow?"

"I don't think it's supposed to be bad. Let me check." The light from Rowan's phone reflected off the windshield. "Mostly sunny, high of forty-one, so it shouldn't be too cold."

"That's not too bad." She rolled to a stop at a red light.

They speculated about the challenges during the twenty minute ride back home. Sarah said, "Hopefully we can fit a lunch break in there somewhere."

"We could get breakfast first."

"Cracker Barrel?"

"You read my mind."

She was infinitely glad he couldn't read hers, because the image of making out with him on the kitchen counter hadn't strayed far. A few minutes later, she turned down his street and pulled into his driveway.

He asked, "What time should I pick you up?"

"I can drive tomorrow, I don't mind."

"You've been driving all week. Besides, if I drive, you can sleep an extra ten minutes."

How did he know exactly what would convince her? "Sold. Pick me up at seven?"

"See you then." He gave her a smile and got out of the car, holding his coat tight against the wind until he pushed through the front door.

The entire drive home, she obsessed about the kiss. On the one hand, he didn't seem bothered. On the other hand, he didn't seem affected at all. Was it a huge mistake? Did he think she was ridiculous? Was he glad she kissed him? Was he completely indifferent?

In her own garage, she smacked her hands against the steering wheel. "Why? Why did I do that," she shouted into the car.

With one last grunt of frustration, she turned the car off and went inside.

"Harvey, you aren't going to believe this."

Harvey's neck craned forward.

"You're going to have to eavesdrop, sorry." She fished her phone out of her pocket and called Corinne.

"So I was really annoyed but then I could see how much it was bothering him, then when I came back from washing that idiot's number off my hands – I mean, who does that? – he was talking to this military couple, and I was just so impressed that he'd stepped up and we went to the food court and I kissed him."

Corinne's shriek nearly split her eardrum. "You what? I thought you didn't even like him!"

"I don't. I didn't. But I do. I think." At this point, she didn't know *what* to think about Rowan.

"Wow."

"Yeah, I know. But he didn't react. Like, at all." She kept playing it over in her head. Had she made a massive mistake?

"He didn't kiss you back?"

"Well, I mean, he didn't *not* kiss me back, it was just a peck on the lips, really, so it wasn't like I stuck my tongue in his mouth and he bit me or something." She let out a long groan of frustration. "Did I screw this up?"

"How did he act afterwards?"

"Right afterwards, he was quiet, then he was pretty much his normal self the rest of the night."

"I'm sure if he didn't like it, you'd have known it for sure. Rowan doesn't seem like the kind of guy who'd let you think he was okay with it if he wasn't. He probably would have mushed your face and asked you what you thought you were doing."

Sarah snorted a laugh. "Okay, that's accurate."

"My guess is that you caught him completely off guard, on the heels of crowd anxiety, and he didn't have any idea how to react, so he didn't do anything at all."

She was probably right. "What do I do now?"

"Nothing. Let him make the next move."

Her head dropped back against the couch. "Your advice is to be patient. Me. You expect me to wait and see what he does."

"Yes."

She heaved a dramatic sigh. "I suppose I can probably do that."

"It's just for one day, right? And who knows? Maybe his position will be obvious early in the day and you won't have to exercise any self-control or patience at all."

"We can hope."

Corinne told her, "Relax. It'll be fine."

"Easy for you to say. You don't have to deal with this nonsense anymore. I didn't even *like* him forty-eight hours ago, and now I'm having all these dirty thoughts. What the heck."

"Apparently he's growing on you. Like some sort of blue-eyed fungus."

"Funny. I'm hanging up on you."

"Love you, too. Tomorrow night I want to hear every detail."

As if the reminder was necessary. Sarah always told her everything. "Unless I die from pure mortification."

"Unlikely."

They hung up. Harvey was still watching her.

"What do you think?"

He stared for another long moment, then turned away.

"Not helpful."

An hour later, Sarah climbed into bed and pulled the covers up to her chin. She assumed she would have trouble falling asleep, but the next thing she knew, her alarm was chirping. The anxiety, cleverly disguised as curiosity about what Rowan was thinking, rolled back into her belly.

She went through her morning routine without much thought, looked over their itinerary without actually seeing it, and nearly screamed when Rowan knocked on the door, since she hadn't heard him pull in.

"Hey, come on in." She pulled the door open and stepped back. "I was just looking over today's kiss and – uh. List. *List.* I was looking over the list." Mortified, she turned her back to Rowan and busied herself with her coat, reaching into the pockets for something she wasn't looking for, not that it mattered since the pockets were empty anyway.

"About that."

Sarah waited for him to finish his sentence, but he didn't. She couldn't decipher his tone. So she forced herself to turn around and face him. Might as well get it over with. "It" probably being a lecture on how he didn't even want to be friends.

Instead, he stepped closer to her, so close she could see the individual threads of his sweater, and that there was a tiny crack in one of the buttons. A black button. On a gray sweater. Stretched over a rather lovely chest.

Crap. She was losing her train of thought again.

An instant later, her attention was laser-focused as Rowan's fingertips lightly touched her cheek and his thumb traced the bottom of her lip.

Her fingers curled at her sides, and her gaze slid up to his face.

Yeah, probably no lecture was forthcoming, if the intensity of his eyes was any indication.

He leaned a little closer, and her hands went to his sides, clutching his sweater. His breath reached her mouth, and time lost all meaning as his lips touched hers.

It started off slow, hesitant, each of them waiting for the other's reaction, then, in an instant, the universe shifted and they were making out like teenagers, tongues and hands exploring and touching.

Breathless, Sarah nearly lost her balance as he pulled back. The world flooded back in and Sarah's head filled with a million random things. Harvey was watching. They were going to miss breakfast. Holy *shit* could Rowan kiss. Her sock was twisted and the seam rubbed her toe. Corinne was going to flip. Rowan seemed as breathless as she was. Her coat was on the floor. Apparently he wasn't mad that she'd kissed him.

His hands were still on her hips, hers still clutching fistfuls of the chest of his sweater.

"Wow. That was..." She couldn't think of a word.

"Yeah. It was." He cleared his throat and took a step back. "If we're getting breakfast, we should probably get going."

Sarah nodded vigorously. "Yup." She picked her coat off the floor and directed all of her focus on putting it on and zipping it up.

Rowan waved. "See ya, Harvey."

Why was it so sexy when he talked to her turtle?

They finally got in his Jeep and headed to Cracker Barrel. When they were seated and had placed their orders, Sarah took a deep breath. "Soooo, is this something we should talk about?"

"Breakfast?" There was a twinkle in his eye.

"Ha, ha, very funny. I don't just go around casually making out with random people." She tried to remember the last time she'd kissed a man – or been kissed – and came up blank.

"Now I'm random?"

"You know what I mean."

The waiter interrupted by bringing their drinks. He took a really long time setting down two cups of coffee and two glasses of orange juice. Sarah was ready to grab them off his tray herself.

"Do you need anything else right now?"

Privacy! She wanted to scream. "No, thanks."

He finally ambled away.

Rowan looked amused. He reached across the table and turned his hand up for her to give him hers. "I'm not big on talking. I don't think a bunch of conversation does a lot of good."

"Not talking doesn't do much good, either, if nobody knows where they stand. Look, I'm not trying to make a big deal—"

The waiter reappeared, balancing his tray and putting

down each plate as slowly as he had the drinks, driving Sarah nuts. Harvey moved faster.

When the plates were all down, the waiter carefully noted that everything was there before handing over the little bottles of warmed syrup. One at a time. "Can I bring you anything else?"

Rowan answered, "No, thanks."

Sarah shook her head after the waiter had turned away. "Anyway. I'm not making a big deal out of anything, and it's not like you even suggested such a thing, but just so you know, we will not be having sex."

The waiter's eyes went wide as he tried to nonchalantly set down a plate with biscuits and cornbread. "Uh, forgot to leave these."

Instead of leaving, he carefully set down a small bowl full of packets of butter.

When had he come back?

Sarah's face burned. Even worse, Rowan stabbed at his eggs, trying valiantly not to laugh.

The waiter finally, *finally*, left for real, and Sarah covered her face with her hands. "This is not going like I thought it would."

Chapter Sixteen

Rowan enjoyed her embarrassment quite a bit more than he should. She was gorgeous with her face all red and huge brown eyes, trying to backpedal and explain. The waiter hearing her pronouncement was just icing on the cake. Not that he wanted her to feel humiliated in any real sort of way, but it was cute that she was flustered and laying down her ground rules.

He liked that. He respected it. He'd encountered far too many women who went along, never saying what they expected, wanted, or demanded, but somehow expecting him to magically know and change to suit their vision.

He waited until she straightened herself and took a bite of her French toast. When her cheeks no longer blazed, he said, "How about this? We don't need to have some big, heavy discussion over breakfast. We'll do the challenges, have a great day with zero sex, probably have dinner tonight, where we'll probably be really tired after today, then I'll take you home, you can kiss me again, and I'll go home and we'll have whatever discussion you want to have later."

"Wait, you kissed me." Her eyes blazed with indignation.

"That's not how I remember it." He was having too much fun teasing her.

"Oh, so we're rewriting history again."

He grinned and stabbed a forkful of pancake. "Not at all."

"You're impossible."

Pointing, he said, "And you're getting syrup on your sweater."

"Shoot." She wiped at the spot.

Rowan watched her blot at her sweater until she was satisfied the syrup was gone. He liked her. A lot. He was having more fun than he'd ever imagined he would. But that didn't mean he was signing up for a relationship. Those never seemed to work out in his favor. He switched gears back to the challenge. "What's our first stop?"

"Prescott's. Followed by the paintball place. Ugh. I hope we're not going to be covered in paint for the whole rest of the day."

They finished their breakfast and headed for the small grocery store on the outskirts of town. Inside, they went to the customer service desk.

"Glad you're here. Your task is to deliver a load of groceries to the Hickory Hollow Food Bank." Grant Prescott, third generation owner of the small grocery chain, motioned for them to follow him to a long row of carts already filled with bags of groceries. One for each team. "Each cart already has the bags sorted and ready to go, you'll just deliver them. Once you deliver the groceries, a volunteer will give you your token."

They paused at the back of the Jeep for a selfie with the full cart, then Rowan loaded the groceries into the vehicle. Ten bags of groceries in all, plus a case of canned dog food and a case of canned cat food.

"What?" he wondered why she was grinning.

She motioned to the bags in the back of his Jeep. "This is

such an awesome idea. I feel like such a pampered jerk because I never think about getting stuff for the food bank. From now on, every time I get groceries, I'll also buy something to donate."

While Rowan returned the cart to the corral, Sarah got in the vehicle. When he got in, she was typing on her phone.

"Corinne?"

She laughed. "No, I'm emailing myself a reminder. I'm going to get a box and put it somewhere in the kitchen so I can just keep filling it up."

"That's a great idea." He thought maybe he should do something similar.

"It is, but I'll surely forget it by tonight if I don't write it down."

They pulled into the parking lot of the busy food bank and carried the bags inside, where a volunteer greeted them.

She said, "We have to weigh the items in, then we'll get your token."

Sarah looked down at the bag in her hand, full of paper towels. "I thought you guys only accepted food."

The volunteer took the bags and pulled the items out, grouping them on the counter. "Nope, we try to provide all the necessities we can. Our grants and funding come with strict guidelines. We can only use those funds for food. But people need toilet paper, tissues, cleaning supplies, and things like that. I never realized how expensive toilet paper and paper towels are until I started volunteering here and started paying attention."

Rowan hung back while Sarah talked with the volunteer.

"Yeah, I've never given it much thought. Can I ask what you're doing?"

"We separate donations by food and non-food. Donations are tracked by weight instead of item. I'll weigh all the food, then log it here, and then log the non-food here." She weighed all their items, wrote the numbers down, then gave them a big smile. "All set. I'll get your token."

She opened a drawer and pulled out their token.

Something kept his feet from moving to the door. "Do you accept donations? Like cash, I mean?"

She beamed at him. "Of course. Cash is the best donation. We can buy food for pennies on the dollar, stretching it farther than most shoppers can, but we have a list of our most requested items here." She produced a paper.

Sarah took the list as Rowan pulled out his wallet. "I'd like to make a donation, if that's alright."

"Of course! How wonderful. Let me find the receipt book. I'll be right back." She was back in a flash.

Handing her some cash, Rowan collected his receipt, thanked the volunteer, and they went back out to the car.

Sarah put the token in its envelope, then buckled her seatbelt. "I'm really glad we did this. I get too comfortable in my own life and don't do enough for other people."

"Yeah, me, too." His voice caught.

She must have noticed. "What?"

Starting the Jeep, he said, "I'm going to start sending regular donations here." Being inside had reminded him of something he'd long since forgotten.

"Good."

Instead of putting the car in gear, he blurted out, "When I was a kid, after my dad died, my mom had to use the food bank. It's kind of embarrassing to admit."

"Why? It's not like it was your fault."

"It wasn't my mother's fault, either." He immediately regretted sharing that part of his past and dreaded the questions that were sure to follow.

Sarah sucked in a surprised breath. "I'm so sorry. I didn't

mean to imply it was. I meant that it wasn't anybody's fault. If it sounded like I was blaming anyone, I promise I wasn't."

He knew she was sincere. Maybe his mind had gone there because so many other people *had* blamed his mother. For not having a job that paid enough. For not making sure his dad had life insurance. For not putting enough money in savings, and whatever other judgmental crap they could come up with.

Reaching over and squeezing her hand, he said, "I know you weren't." He let go and put the car in gear. "I hadn't thought about it in years, so it's not something I've ever told anybody."

He could feel the wheels turning in Sarah's mind, like she wanted to say something, but didn't want to say the wrong thing. There was no need to get into a heavy discussion, so he put on his turn signal and said, "Where to?"

"Um." She rifled through the envelope and pulled out the itinerary. "Next stop, For Pet's Sake."

"That should be fun."

"I was in there the other day – the day I got Blue's tire and crickets for Harvey – and they wouldn't even give me a hint about the challenge."

"Maybe they'll have us deliver dog food somewhere."

"Or stock shelves."

After Rowan parked the car, they got out and walked down the sidewalk to the pet store. A cheerful set of bells jingled when Rowan opened the door.

At the counter, one of the owners, Midge Foster, an older woman who looked like she could join the Ladies' Society, greeted them. "Hello, hello, follow me. We have the challenge set up in the back."

They followed her through tight aisles packed with all manner of pet accessories to a large open space in the back with a table set up with two huge tanks. The tanks were covered, so they couldn't see what lurked inside.

"I don't like the look of this," Rowan said quietly.

The sweet cookie-baking-grandma type gave them an innocent smile. "Your challenge is this: One of you will hold a rat for two minutes. The other will hold a snake for two minutes. You can choose who does what, but you can't both do the same thing."

Rowan swallowed hard. He didn't like rats, and he for sure didn't like snakes.

Sarah looked up at him. "What's your preference?"

Rowan made a face. "Don't you have a puppy we can hold instead?"

Midge laughed. "Surely you're not afraid of a little snake."

"Little?"

Her smirk suggested otherwise. He nudged Sarah. "You have a turtle, that's almost the same thing."

She rolled her eyes. "Fine, I'll take the snake. You take the rat."

The woman who definitely didn't seem so sweet anymore motioned for Rowan to come behind the table with her. "Okay, now don't drop her."

"Okay."

She opened one of the cages and took out a white rat the size of a cat.

"Holy crap."

"Hold her like this." She demonstrated. "Once you have a good hold of her, I'll start the timer. This is Babs."

Rowan looked at Sarah, who was looking a little smug. "Okay."

A second later he was holding a rat. With beady red eyes and a long hairless tail. He was pretty sure it didn't like him. It squirmed around and he tried to keep a firm hold without squishing it... or pissing it off.

"One minute to go. You're doing great." Sarah cheered him on, even as she took a picture of his discomfort.

He stayed still, holding the rat as it glared at him like it wanted to eat his soul.

"Thirty seconds."

The next longest thirty seconds of his life ticked by. The rat squeaked and twitched its whiskers. Rowan didn't speak rat, but he was pretty sure it was a threat.

"Time!"

He shoved the rat back toward the grinning woman, who gave it a kiss on its evil head before putting it back in the cage.

Shuddering, he pointed at Sarah. "Your turn. And do *not* send me that picture."

"Bawl baby."

She traded places with him.

"I'll put the snake over your shoulders, and once she's in place, I'll start the timer."

"Okay."

She opened the top of the tank and pulled out a long yellow and white snake. Huge. At least six feet long. Rowan was glad he'd had the rat.

"Say hello to Ginger." The woman put the snake around Sarah's shoulders. "Two minutes, starting now."

Rowan watched as the snake undulated its head, its tongue flicking out. It turned as if looking at Sarah. He caught a picture of them eyeing each other. He had to admit, she was a total badass. No way could he have managed two minutes with the snake.

"Hey, Ginger. Don't get any ideas. I'm not that appetizing."

Two minutes passed and the woman took the snake back.

Sarah shuddered dramatically and hurried back to Rowan's side.

"Good job, you two. Here's your token." Midge handed it to Rowan.

"I can't believe you made me take the snake."

"You did great. Practically a natural."

She pulled her coat back on. "You better hope there aren't any snakes in the junkyard, because there's no freaking way I'm touching another one."

"I wouldn't think there'd be any snakes in February."

"Let's get a move on. It's already after ten and we have to be at the junkyard by ten thirty."

"Then stop holding me up."

She gave him an open-mouthed glare. "Brat."

Outside, Rowan jumped into the Jeep and started it. "Next stop, junkyard."

"Yes."

He drove to the junkyard and parked in front of a massive garage that had been a landmark for at least five decades.

Chapter Seventeen

Sarah jumped out of the car before Rowan could come around to open her door. There were already four teams waiting in the parking lot.

"Hey, guys." She waved to the crowd.

Everyone returned her greeting, except Chad and Stephanie, who were off to the side, arguing.

Rowan leaned down and whispered, "Team Chucks."

She giggled and fist-bumped with him.

"You two seem to be getting along pretty well. Nobody expected that," one of the other women said, casting a pointed look at Rowan.

"It's been great. We're having a lot of fun." Sarah refused to take the bait. It wasn't exactly a secret that Rowan kept to himself and didn't make a lot of friends.

Another car pulled in and a sixth team got out.

At ten twenty-eight, Young Ernie Goyer, the grizzled old man who owned the place and hadn't been young since well prior to the forty years since Old Ernie passed on, came out of the garage, chewing on the end of an unlit cigar. His eyes narrowed as he pointed at them. "Ain't responsible for accidents." He glowered for a moment, then cleared his throat. "This here's how it's gonna work. Each team collects five flags. Flags have numbers. You get one one, one two, one three, and so on. After you get your flags, bring them in the garage and you'll get your token. First team to collect five flags –"

Chad interrupted. "I can see different colored flags. Is there some significance we should be aware of?"

Young Ernie's nose scrunched like he'd smelled skunk. His sharp blue eyes traveled over Chad and obviously found him lacking. "As I was saying, first team to collect their flags and get them to the garage gets something extra."

"What is it?" Chad asked.

Sarah and Rowan exchanged a glance. Peppering Young Ernie with questions just seemed like a bad idea.

Young Ernie ignored Chad. "Alright, go!"

The teams took off running along the side of the garage, down the hill into the junkyard. It was surprisingly neat, with rows of car corpses lined up. Sarah tromped through some brush and grabbed a flag off a windshield. "I got a two."

Rowan pointed. "There's a flag up there." He climbed onto the hood of a junk car and reached up to the top of a bus shell. "Three."

"Perfect."

The rest of the crowd spread out, but mostly to the right. Sarah grabbed Rowan's hand and pulled him to the left. "One."

"There's one. Crap, it's another three." He put the flag back.

A few rows over, they found a five, then a string of six twos.

Looping around, they met up with some other players.

"What do you think you're doing?" The voice caught Sarah's attention. One of the other men pointed in Chad's face. "You're cheating."

She grabbed Rowan's arm. "What's going on?"

"I'll find out." He walked over. "Problem?"

"Yeah." The other man, Greg or Craig, Sarah wasn't sure, was ticked. "He was taking flags. Cheater."

"Oh, grow up," Chad sneered. "It's just a stupid game."

Rowan stood shoulder to shoulder with Greg/Craig. "Then there's no point to cheating."

"Screw you." Chad turned and jerked his chin at Stephanie. "Let's go."

She looked embarrassed.

"Now!"

Jumping, she took a step, then stopped. "This isn't fair." She pulled a handful of flags out of her jacket and put them on the hood of one of the junk cars, then pulled another handful out of her other pocket.

"Idiot." Chad looked disgusted, then walked away, leaving her behind.

"Sorry," she mumbled and went after him.

"Well, that kind of sucked the fun out of it." Amber poked through the pile of flags.

They were all kind of looking at each other when Chad reappeared, snatched one of the flags and held up his middle finger before leaving again.

"What an idiot."

Sarah didn't know who said it, but she was pretty sure they were all thinking it. After a few minutes of everyone standing around muttering about Chad's stunt, she said, "We're missing a four."

Amber sifted through the pile and handed her a flag. "Anybody else?"

A few minutes later, all the teams had all five flags and they headed up the hill as a group. As they climbed, Rowan grabbed Sarah's hand to help her up the incline.

Amber and her partner, Ty, were directly in front of Rowan

and Sarah. Amber said, "I can't believe he was such a jerk and ruined everyone's fun. Who does that?"

Sarah shook her head. "He's been ridiculous the whole time."

The group poured into the garage, where Chad stood, red-faced and sneering. Stephanie looked embarrassed, her hands shoved deep into her pockets, staring at the floor.

"We were here first, it's ours."

Young Ernie sat in a rocking chair, watching Chad's meltdown with a minimal amount of interest.

Lina, Young Ernie's adult granddaughter, crossed her arms. "Not happening."

Amber asked, "What's going on?"

Lina shrugged. "Pap was watching out the window. This guy was cheating, so he doesn't get the prize."

"No token, either," Young Ernie added.

"You can't do that! You better watch your back, old man." Chad stormed from the garage, knocking a set of wrenches to the ground as he went past.

Stephanie picked up the wrenches and apologized, then started for the door.

One of the women asked, "Why are you going after him? Let him go."

Sarah agreed with the woman who'd spoken. "No kidding. He's not worth it."

Stephanie hesitated, but went out the door and got into Chad's car.

A murmur of "What is she thinking" went through the crowd.

Young Ernie got everyone's attention by hefting himself up out of the chair. "Only got one prize, decide among your-selves." He tossed an envelope onto the workbench the wrenches had been knocked from. Lina handed out the tokens.

"Drawing?" someone asked.

One of the guys said, "I think Craig and Erin should get it. They're the ones Chad really screwed."

Agreement rippled around the room, and Craig/Greg and Erin gracefully accepted the envelope containing a fifty dollar gift certificate to a local winery. Craig held it up. "We'll buy everyone except Chad a drink."

Someone cheered with a loud whistle, everyone clapped, and headed for the parking lot.

"Where are you headed next?" Amber asked.

Sarah answered, "Paintball course."

"We're off to the pet store."

Sarah grinned at her. "We were there earlier."

"What did you have to do?"

"Oh, no, I'm not spoiling anything. Have fun!" She ducked into the Jeep before Amber could ask more questions.

Back on the road, Rowan asked, "Have you played paintball before?"

"Never. My brother used to play. He'd come home with all these little round bruises."

"I didn't know you had a brother."

She got that reaction a lot. "Trent. He lives in Colorado. He went to college out there and met his wife Cindy. Her family is out there, so they stayed. They did come in for Christmas, so that was nice."

"What did her family think of that?"

"They're super nice. It's usually an every-other-year thing. Trent and Cindy will come in here one year for either Thanksgiving or Christmas, then the next year we go out there for one or the other. If we do Thanksgiving, we kind of mash our family Christmas into it."

"Sounds fun. Do they have kids?"

"No. I think they'd like to, but it's none of my business so I don't ask. I'd love to have nieces or nephews to spoil, but it's their call. They've only been married four years, so it's not like they need to be in any rush."

"He's younger?"

"By a lot. He's twenty-eight. I got to be an only child for eight years before he came along and ruined everything." She grinned with the last words. Trent was one of the people she most adored in the whole world. "What about you? Any siblings?"

"My father – if you can call him that – had a whole bunch of kids all over the place. I only met one half-sister, but I've heard there's at least five other kids. I don't even know if they're brothers or sisters."

"Wow. Busy guy." No wonder Rowan had such a hard time getting close to people. It sounded like he'd never had a very firm foundation of people to count on.

"Yeah, too bad he wasn't busy with a job so he could support any of us before he died."

The hurt and frustration in his voice was no surprise. The fact he'd shared this with her was. "Where's your mom now?"

"Dead." He glanced over. "I know that sounds harsh, but I hate the phrase 'passed away.' Like it sounds nicer than dead or something, but it is what it is. Using prettier words doesn't make her any less gone."

"I'm so sorry." Sarah couldn't imagine losing her mom. Or her dad.

He lifted one shoulder in a shrug. "I have Millie."

After several turns taking them out of town, they pulled into the parking lot at the paintball course. As he pulled into a space, he said, "Looks like an old warehouse or something. I've never been back here."

Sarah grinned. "I was here a few times when Trent played.

Of course that was just because I got to be his chauffer when Mom was busy."

"What did you do while he played?"

Thinking back, she said, "I sat in the lobby and did homework or read a book or some other such geeky endeavor."

"That doesn't sound like you," he said.

"I was pretty shy in high school."

He raised a disbelieving eyebrow. "You? Really?"

"Yes, me." She hopped out of the vehicle and waited for Rowan to meet her.

"I'm having trouble imagining it."

"College brought me out of my shell. That's where I discovered my extroversion and got comfortable in my own skin."

"I didn't think anybody got comfortable in their own skin in college."

"I guess I was one of the lucky few." She cracked her knuckles. "Now let's get this butt kicking started."

"You're awfully eager to get your butt kicked."

She guffawed and pulled the door open. "Oh, no, sweetheart, I'll be doing the kicking."

One of the other teams was standing near a counter.

"There's Greg and Erin." Sarah waved.

Rowan looked confused. "I thought it was Craig."

"It's one or the other, but I can't remember."

They walked over.

"Hey guys," Erin said. "There's supposed to be three teams."

Sarah cocked her head. "Ew, are they going to make us paintball each other?"

"I hope not. I just got my hair done and can't wash it for a couple more days. I don't want to get paint all through it."

"Oh, no. Maybe the helmet will protect it?"

The guys wisely let the conversation go on without joining.

"You've got to be kidding me." Craig/Greg groaned.

Erin gave a heavily annoyed sigh.

Sarah and Rowan turned to see what they were looking at. Chad and Stephanie had just come through the door.

Rowan put his arm around Sarah and squeezed. "Hey, this could be fun."

She snickered. "You're not suggesting something naughty, are you?"

Greg/Craig and Rowan fist bumped while Erin said, "Yeah, this might be worth getting paint in my hair."

Chad and Stephanie came over and stood off to the side.

"Hey, Steph, come on over," Sarah said. "*Chad.*"

Chad grabbed Stephanie's arm to keep her from walking over. "We're here to win, not make friends."

"At least you're succeeding at something," Sarah quipped.

Chad muttered under his breath, "Whatever, bitch."

Rowan took a step toward him. "You got something to say?"

"Yeah. Keep your bitch on a leash."

Sarah grabbed Rowan's arm and stood in front of him as he moved toward Chad. "He's so not worth it." Besides, if anyone was going to deck Chad, she wanted it to be her.

Sneering, Chad slung an arm over Stephanie's shoulders. She didn't look happy about it, but she didn't move. "Let's get this over with."

Craig/Greg motioned for an employee to come over.

"You're all here? Great. Follow me." He went through a doorway and down a stairwell, lined with white concrete walls, then through an industrial-looking steel door, into a shooting range.

"This is cool," Sarah said to Rowan.

The employee handed them each a set of goggles. "These are required. Since we know the contest teams are short on time, the challenge we have for you is simple. Target shooting. Each person will take five shots, so that's ten shots total for each team. Each circle on the target has a points value, starting with one. The closer to the center, the more points you get. Bullseye is worth ten. Team with the most points wins bragging rights and a t-shirt."

He spent the next few minutes demonstrating how to operate the paintball gun and having everyone take a test shot.

"Okay, take your stations." He clipped fresh paper targets to lines, then pressed a button and the targets spun backwards until they were far away. "Goggles on. Ready, Aim, Fire."

The paintball guns popped as everyone fired.

Sarah squealed. "Holy crap, Rowan, look!" Her paintball landed just left of the bullseye.

"Good job. Keep it up." His was several inches below the bull's-eye.

On the instructor's go, they fired four more times. Each time, Sarah's paintball landed close to the bulls eye.

The instructor hit the button that brought the paper targets flapping back toward them, then tallied up the points.

"Team one, you guys have a total score of fifty-nine." Craig/Greg and Erin high fived.

"Team two, nice job. Your total score is eighty-one."

Rowan held up his hand for a high five, then caught Sarah's. "Great job. That was all you."

"Yeah, it kind of was." She laughed and put her arm around his waist, then took a quick selfie with their painted targets while they waited to hear Chad and Stephanie's score.

"Team three, you ended up with a total score of seventy-eight."

"This is bullshit. You cheated." Chad pointed at Sarah, his finger about ten inches from her face.

The instructor held up a hand. "Whoa. Chill, man. Nobody cheated."

Rowan raised an eyebrow. "You better move that finger, son."

"Oh, now you're threatening me? You and your cheater ho can back off." He did, however, stop pointing.

Sarah looked up at Rowan and slightly shook her head, hoping he understood the "let it go" message she was giving him.

The instructor looked back and forth between Chad and Rowan, then gave a nod. "Let's head back upstairs and I'll get your tokens. Nice work, everybody."

"Except you," Chad muttered to Stephanie. "Your shots sucked."

Stephanie sighed, but didn't say anything.

Sarah wanted to grab her and shake her. Why on earth was she even still hanging around with Chad? The prizes weren't worth that kind of nonsense. And if they won the grand prize? Why would Stephanie even entertain the idea of taking a trip with this idiot?

Back upstairs, the instructor handed out tokens and coupons for a free paintball game. Rowan and Sarah each got to pick a t-shirt. He picked blue, she picked purple. They got their coats out of their lockers and all headed back toward the door.

Erin tugged on Sarah's arm. "Do you think we should say anything to Stephanie?"

"Would it do any good? We've run into them a few times, and he's always a jerk and she always goes with him."

Erin nodded. "I noticed that. I wonder why. It's so weird. Like she's in an abusive relationship when they've just been matched up for this silly challenge. It's not right."

"I know. At least it's almost over."

"I think I'll talk to her when we get back to the community center."

Sarah reached over and squeezed her arm. "Good idea. I'll go with you when you do."

She speed-walked to catch up with Rowan, who waited by the door with Greg/Craig. Chad and Stephanie were already crossing the parking lot and getting into Chad's crappy Nissan before they reached their respective vehicles.

Rowan opened the door for Sarah. When he got in the driver's seat, she sighed. "I really hope Chad isn't headed to the bookstore. I'm sick of seeing his stupid face."

He agreed. "No kidding. That guy's got an attitude problem that I'd love to fix for him."

Chad turned right out of the parking lot, and Rowan turned left.

Sarah breathed a sigh of relief. "Hopefully that means they're going somewhere else."

"Maybe he'll get lost in the woods out here and run out of gas and get eaten by a bear or something."

Sarah laughed and held up her crossed fingers. "We can dream."

"I can't figure out why she's putting up with him. That's messed up."

"I don't know, either. That's what Erin and I were talking about."

Rowan gave his head a shake. "Enough talking about them. Did you get the token?"

"Yes. I better put it in the envelope before I lose it." She pulled the token out of her pocket and slipped it in the large manila envelope that held all their tokens so far. "Only one left."

At the bookstore, they were given a clipboard with a paper

clipped to it. On the paper were five things they had to find or solve.

The bookstore owner handed Sarah a pen and admonished them. "No looking things up with your phone. When you're done, I'll check your answers and when you get all five correct, I'll give you your token. Good luck."

They moved to one of the aisles of books. Rowan asked, "Where to?"

Sarah read the first item. "How many chapters are in Stephen King's book *'Salem's Lot*? Okay, we need the horror section."

They hurried through the aisles of the used bookstore and by pure luck came across the horror section. "Stephen King, Stephen King… here it is." Rowan flipped to the back of the book. "There's an epilogue. Does that count as a chapter?"

"I have no idea."

He flipped back a few pages. "There are fifteen chapters, then an epilogue. So, is that sixteen?"

She considered. "I don't think so. It's not numbered. I'll just write down fifteen, plus epilogue. Hopefully that counts."

"Okay. What's next?"

"Number two. A trilogy is a set of three books. In Nora Roberts's *The Inn Boonsboro* trilogy, what are the first three words of each book?"

"Nora Roberts. Doesn't she write thrillers?" Rowan asked.

"As J.D. Robb. I think most of the books under her name would be under romance."

"Are you sure?"

"No." Sarah shrugged.

"Let's try there first." They walked up and down the aisles until they came to an aisle with paper hearts hanging from the ceiling. "Guessing this is romance."

"Looks like it." Sarah scanned the shelves. "There she is. Nora Roberts. Now we have to find *The Inn Boonsboro* trilogy."

"How the heck do you know which ones they are?"

"Check the cover. They usually list if they're part of a series."

"Here's one, *The Perfect Hope*. It says it's third in the series."

Sarah clicked the pen open. "What are the first words?"

"'With a few.'"

"Crap, what's that title? I'll mark that in case they have to be in order."

He showed her the cover and she wrote the title with a number three beside it. "Geez, how many books has this woman written?"

She answered, "Over two hundred, last I heard."

"I can't even write a grocery list without screwing it up," he muttered.

Sarah laughed. "Me, either."

"Here's the first one. *The Next Always*." He flipped the pages. "First three words are 'The stone walls.'"

Sarah scribbled on the paper. "One to go."

He pulled out several more books and replaced them. "Got it. *The Last Boyfriend*. The first three words are 'A fat winter.'"

"A fat winter what?"

"Moon. But we don't need that. Okay. What's next?"

Sarah read from the paper. "Some twenty years after being published, the Left Behind series is still a popular post-apocalyptic story. Who are the authors?"

"I remember seeing the movie. Wasn't Mike Seaver in it?"

"Mike Seaver was the character on Family Ties. The actor is Curt something?"

Rowan snapped his fingers. "Growing Pains."

"That's right. The guy that played Mike Seaver is a preacher or something now, isn't he?"

"Not sure, but wasn't that a religious series? Let's try the religious fiction section."

They walked the aisles again until they found the section labeled "Christian Fiction."

"Here it is. There's a whole shelf of them."

Sarah shrugged. "Guess it was a bigger series than I thought."

He pulled a book off the shelf so she could write down the authors, Tim LaHaye and Jerry B. Jenkins. She thrust the pen into the air and practically shouted, "Kirk Cameron!"

"What? No." Rowan pointed to the book.

"No, Mike Seaver. He was played by Kirk Cameron. He did that movie Fireproof a few years back. It wasn't bad."

"Haven't seen it. Did you get the authors?"

Sarah turned her attention back to the list. "Yeah, sorry. Number Four. Jane Austen wrote six major novels. What are they?"

"Classics. We passed them over there." Rowan led the way to the shelves of classic novels.

"*Pride and Prejudice*, obviously. Oh, crap. There's a second part. We have to put them in order."

"What kind of order?"

She checked the instructions. "Publication date."

"Okay. Let's just list them first, then we'll put them in order." He pulled *Pride and Prejudice* off the shelf. "1813." He selected the novels one at a time. "1817, *Northanger Abbey*. Also 1817, *Persuasion. Sense and Sensibility*, 1811. *Mansfield Park*, 1814. *Emma*, 1815."

"Let's see." Sarah made notes on her paper. "*Sense and Sensibility* is first in 1811. Then *Pride and Prejudice* in 1813. *Mansfield Park*, 1814, *Emma* 1815, *Northanger Abbey* 1817, *Persuasion* 1817. I wonder if it matters which one is first for those two?"

"I hope not, it just has the year."

"Okay, we'll just go with what we have. And now the last item. Number five. In the Little Golden Book, *Cookie Monster and the Cookie Tree*, what does Cookie Monster have to do in order to get a cookie?"

Rowan laughed. "I think the children's books were over there."

They found the children's section, and were faced with several shelves of gold bound books.

Sarah ran her fingers over the spines. "I remember these from when I was a kid. I think they had a mail order service or something, so you'd get a new book every month."

"I had some of these, too. My mom was big on books," he said.

"Mine, too."

They rifled through the books until they found the Sesame Street book.

"I don't remember there being any witches on Sesame Street."

"Or cookie trees." She laughed as Rowan read the book out loud.

Rowan snapped the book shut. "Obviously we need a picture with the Cookie Monster book for this challenge."

"Obviously." She took pictures of Rowan holding the book between them.

Rowan put it back in its proper place. "Share."

"Huh?"

He tapped the clipboard. "The answer. Cookie Monster has to share to get a cookie from the tree."

"Yes, right." She scribbled on the paper. "That's it, we got them all."

"Awesome." He held up his hand for a high five.

Sarah returned the gesture, then stood on her tiptoes and lightly kissed him. "We did the whole challenge."

"We didn't get our token yet."

"True."

They went to the front counter, where the owner checked their answers and handed over their token.

Sarah took the token and tucked it into her pocket. "Thanks. I never knew you guys were here. I'll definitely be back to do some shopping."

"We'd love to see you." The owner took a bookmark and handed it to her. "This has our hours."

"Perfect. Thank you."

"Thanks," Rowan added as he followed Sarah out the door.

"I haven't sat down to read a whole book in forever. I need to do that. Usually when I have free time, I work on my quilts."

"I had no idea we had a used bookstore this close." He opened Sarah's door. "If nothing else, we're seeing what's around here."

When he got back in the car, Sarah checked the time. "We're not supposed to be back to the community center until six, and I'm getting hungry. You?"

"Starving. We can double check our tokens and make sure we have everything we need."

"Excellent plan."

"I'm guessing the diner is mostly empty at this time, does that work for you?"

"Of course." She put the token in its proper envelope and shivered. "They should do this around July Fourth when it's warm."

"What, you don't like being cold?" he teased.

"No. Unless there's a darn good reason for it."

Chapter Eighteen

As he'd expected, the diner's parking lot was nearly empty.

They pushed through the heavy doors and a bell jingled. The sound brought Corinne from the kitchen area, wiping her hands on her apron.

"Sit any—hey, guys! I thought you were doing your challenge thing today?"

Sarah pulled her coat off and slid into a booth. "We are. We just finished our last challenge and needed to fuel up."

"When's the drawing?"

"We have to be back to the community center at six. Have there been other teams coming in?"

Rowan watched the conversation like a tennis match. He envied the easy way Sarah talked with Corinne. She was still guarded with him, even though things were better than they had been.

"Nah, there hasn't been much of anyone coming in today."

A frown creased Sarah's brow. "I didn't think you were working this weekend?"

"One of the girls is off sick. I'm covering her shifts today and tomorrow. We don't need to be spreading germs around."

"'Tis the season."

"Fa la la la la. What are you having?"

"No idea."

"Sorry, I'll grab menus. What are you drinking?"

"Coffee for me," Sarah said.

"Hot tea, please."

Corinne ducked behind the counter and reappeared a few minutes later with two menus, a cup of coffee and a cup of hot water and a tea bag.

"You're the best." Sarah blew her a kiss and laughed.

"Remember that when you're leaving the tip," Corinne joked.

Rowan closed his menu. "Can I get a bacon cheeseburger and fries, please?"

"How would you like that done?"

"Medium well."

"Ma'am?" Corinne tapped her pen against her order pad. "Ma'am? What'll you have, ma'am? I don't have all day, ma'am."

Sarah laughed as she scanned the menu. "I've seen the parking lot. You most certainly do have all day."

"Got me there."

"How about the chicken and waffles."

"You got it." Corinne gave them a wink and left to put their order in.

Rowan picked up the large envelope and carefully pulled the smaller envelopes out of it. "This was fun. We got a lot of extra prizes, too."

"I can't wait to see you get the pedicure."

He made a face and bounced his tea bag in the water. "You'll be waiting a while."

"You're right, this was a lot of fun." She hesitated. "More fun than I expected, if I'm being completely honest."

"Me, too, if I'm being completely honest," he echoed. He'd fully expected this to be a disaster. He never thought they'd end up in a good place. Too bad it couldn't last.

"I'm glad you were my partner. Despite the rocky start."

He couldn't deny the warm fuzzy feeling her words inspired. "I'm glad, too." He pretended to pay serious attention to making sure he scooped the correct amount of sugar into his tea. "Hopefully we win."

"At this point, I don't care if we win, as long as Chad doesn't. He's such a jerk."

At the sound of Chad's name, irritation grew in Rowan. "He should have been disqualified after that stunt he pulled at the junkyard."

"Agreed. He completely ruined that entire challenge for everyone."

Corinne brought their food and set it down. "Anything else?"

Glancing over the table, Rowan said, "Ketchup, please?"

"You got it." She left and came back with a bottle of ketchup.

As Rowan took it, he said, "Derek said something about helping him put up some drywall in the garage."

Corinne nodded. "Yeah, I'm pretty sure he's not planning to mess with it until it gets warm, though."

"I have a big heater I use in my garage I can bring over if he wants to do it sooner. It works great." He'd never make a big deal about it, but he was so glad Derek – and Corinne – had moved in next door. It had been a long time since he'd had an actual friend.

"Aw, thanks. I'm sure he'll give you a call."

"Did you guys get everything unpacked?"

Corinne groaned. "Pretty much, except for the mystery boxes in the spare room upstairs. I haven't looked at them, and we haven't been missing anything. I told Derek that we'll just leave them alone, and if we haven't opened them in six months, we'll get rid of them since it's obviously junk we don't need."

Sarah piped in. "What if it's priceless family heirlooms?"

"Good point. Might be my Picasso." She laughed as she left them to their meal.

"How'd you two meet?" Rowan was curious. Sarah and Corinne seemed like they'd known each other forever.

"High school. We didn't really know each other then, though. We connected after I got home from college and we've been inseparable ever since. What about you? Who's your BFF?"

He came up blank. "I don't have one. I have a bunch of acquaintances, but nobody I really hang out with."

"Why not?"

"Why? I've always kept more to myself." He dipped a fry into ketchup and tossed it in his mouth.

"By choice or by circumstance?"

"Probably both." He shrugged, trying to keep it light.

"Care to elaborate?"

Not really. Might as well give her the unvarnished truth. "The last time I had a best friend, he helped himself to my wife. Who, I might add, was also supposed to have my back." Seeing it coming from a mile away hadn't made it any easier when it became reality. The betrayal was bad. The feeling of being unworthy of love at all was worse.

Sarah sucked in a breath. "That's horrible."

"Horrible was walking in on them." The scene replayed in his mind, every detail crisp and pristine. Most memories faded, why wouldn't this one?

"Oh no."

He downed another fry. "Immediately after a therapy

appointment, wherein my therapist had told me I was projecting my paranoia onto my wife, who was most likely an innocent victim of my deluded suspicions."

Her eyebrows scrunched. "Why would he say that?"

"Well, I'm just projecting my suspicious paranoid delusions here, but I'm pretty sure she was screwing him, too."

"For real?"

In fact, she was probably banging every willing man in the tri-state area. "But she gets a pass because I was deployed so often and she was lonely. And if that excuse doesn't work, she had some childhood trauma that manifested itself in destructive behaviors in adulthood that created a loop of negative self-fulfilling prophesies." He made air quotes around the last bit.

"Why would he tell you any of that if it was all just a delusion on your part?"

Rowan pointed his fork at her and winked. "Bingo. But I was imagining things."

"Was it a marriage counselor?"

"No." He set his fork down. In for a penny, in for a pound, right? Might as well tell her everything. It's not like they were going to be hanging out after tonight anyway. "I had some issues when I got home from overseas."

"When you lost the men on your tattoos?"

"Partly. I mean, when I was over there, I saw things. The stuff of nightmares. It wasn't long after I got home that I caught my wife, and it was only a few days after that when... *it* happened." He poked at his fries. "They were supposed to go on a patrol. Routine. No big deal. No reason to think anything was up." Keeping his eyes on his plate, he figured he might as well finish the story. "They didn't come back. IED took out the Jeep. All three of them were killed instantly."

He stared at the glob of ketchup, thick and red. Nothing

like blood, really, but of course his imagination played a thousand split-second clips of his brothers, clips of their smiles and laughter, clips of blood-soaked boots and empty scraps of fatigues with deep red stains drying to a crusty brown. He waited for her to say one of the phrases he'd come to hate: "It wasn't your fault." "You couldn't have known." "It was a blessing you were back home." Or his least favorite, "You were so lucky."

His fingers drummed on the table while he waited. He couldn't look up. He didn't want to see the pity in her eyes.

Her hands crossed the table and grasped his tapping fingers, then pulled his hand to her side of the table, where she lifted it to her lips and pressed a soft kiss against his knuckles. Finally looking up to meet her gaze, he still waited.

She didn't say anything he expected. Instead, she kissed his knuckles again and whispered, "I don't know what to say."

The raw honesty went through him like a knife. That's what it always was with her, wasn't it? Something real and honest. And scary. Less than a week, and she was the first thing he thought of when he got up, and the last thing he thought of when he went to sleep.

Just a few more hours, then they could get back to their regular lives and he could get back to doing what he did best – doing his own thing, his own way, in his own time, without answering to anyone about anything.

So if he wanted to go back to being by himself, why did he just unload all his stuff on her? Maybe he was hoping it would chase her away. Just like everyone else in his life – she'd eventually leave, one way or another.

Yeah, that was it.

But it didn't look like she was going anywhere.

A loud clang from the kitchen pulled him from his

thoughts. "Sorry. I don't know why I put that all out there. I'm not looking for sympathy or anything."

She stroked the back of his hand with her thumbs. "I'm glad you trust me enough to share those things with me."

He pulled his hand back like she'd burned him and pushed the wall back up. "I don't trust anybody, Sarah. It's not like those were big secrets. You could probably find it all if you googled me. Like I said, I don't even know why I puked it all out, it's not a big deal, so don't think it's more than it is."

"Okay." Her brown eyes were wide, stunned.

He felt like an ass. Her brow furrowed, obviously confused by his Jekyll/Hyde shitshow, but he didn't know how else to handle it. He couldn't unsay the words.

Turning, Rowan lifted his hand to get Corinne's attention. She abandoned the far counter she was scrubbing and came over with a smile. "Dessert?"

"Just the check, please."

"Sure." She pulled the pad out of her apron and tore a sheet off. "I'll take it when you're done."

He noticed a look pass between Corinne and Sarah, some best friend sixth sense telepathy. Great. He peeled a few bills out of his wallet and put them with the check. "No change. Thanks."

"Thank you," she said as she picked up the money and check. "I'll be sure to let Derek know about your heater."

He nodded and slid out of the booth. While Sarah put on her coat, he picked up their envelope. "Do you mind if we stop at my place so I can let Blue out?"

"Not at all."

They drove to his place without talking. The radio station broadcast live from a high school basketball tournament, so Rowan turned it up. Hickory Hollow High School was being soundly beaten. No surprise. They'd been on a losing streak since Tanner's injury.

At his house, Rowan unlocked the front door and pushed it open for Sarah to walk through. Blue greeted them with the tire toy and a wagging tail.

"Hi, sweetie, do you like that toy? Do you? I'm so glad. What a good boy you are."

Blue ate up the attention, rubbing against Sarah's legs and gazing adoringly up at her.

Rowan sighed at the traitorous beast. "Do you have to pee?"

Blue glanced over at the kitchen, then scrooched his side against Sarah. Which meant he did have to pee, but he wanted to rub up on her more.

"Let's go, dog."

Sarah scratched his head. "You better go pee."

Rowan went through the kitchen and opened the sliding door. Blue reluctantly went through, casting a look back at Sarah before trotting off to do his business.

"How old is he?"

"Twelve."

"How long have you had him?" She slipped her coat off and hung it on the back of a kitchen chair, then sat down.

"Five years. I got him about a year after I left the military."

"He's a good dog. Did you have to train him?"

Rowan gave a little laugh and slid into the chair across from her. "No, he's military, too. Highly trained. Although there aren't too many bombs in Hickory Hollow."

"He was in the Army?" She sounded impressed.

"Yup. He was even awarded a K-9 Medal of Courage for his work sniffing out bombs. He was discharged when he was injured after an explosion. He lost a chunk of his left back leg, but you can hardly tell." He sat up straighter. "He saved nine lives that day," he added proudly.

"I had no idea. Sounds like you're good for each other."

He had to smile. "He's saved my hide a time or two. Kept me from doing stupid stuff because he depends on me."

"I believe it. I've left some questionable parties – and dates – to get home to Harvey."

Now he was curious. "Tell me about a questionable date."

She laughed. "How many would you like to hear about?"

"Pick the first one that comes to mind."

"Okay, here's one. About nine months ago. Steven. I met him online. He said – well, typed – all the right things, and went on and on about how enlightened he was and equality and feminism, blah blah blah. We met at a restaurant, an expensive one, of course, and when the check came, he gave the whole thing to me. Okay, whatever, I paid for dinner. It was annoying because he'd gotten the most expensive stuff on the menu and left half of it on his plate."

Rowan got up and poured two glasses of iced tea while she talked.

"When we got to the parking lot, he walked me to my car, then he tried to put his hand up my skirt. He insisted that since I'd bought dinner, he 'owed' me and wanted to get me off."

He nearly dropped a glass. "What?!" Steven better hope he never crossed his path.

"I know, right? I told him to pound sand, and he asked for my address so he could come to my house and give me what I'd paid for." She shuddered. "I'm glad I met him there instead of letting him pick me up. He was a weirdo. Your turn. Worst date."

He crossed the room and closed the door when Blue came back in. "Most of them are bad in a sort of no connection kind of way rather than scary bad. Well, there was this one woman who had a thing for military vets. She asked all these questions about my time overseas and told me about all these injured vets in her family and friends circle. I thought she was nice, but when we met in person, she flat out told me she was hoping for someone who'd lost a limb or was in a wheelchair. She'd also expected me to show up in uniform."

"Wow. That's some kind of Munchausen's right there."

"Needless to say, we didn't work out."

Sarah reached down to scratch Blue, whose head rested on her leg. "Whatcha doing, Blue?"

His tail thumped against the floor.

"Did you want me to take you home and pick you up later? Or do you just want to hang out here? We have like an hour and a half to kill."

"There's not a lot of point to me going home, if you don't mind me staying here."

No, he didn't mind at all. "We can watch tv."

"Sounds good. Can I use your bathroom?"

"Second door on the right. Which will be obvious, since it's open." He shook his head at how stupid that sounded.

She laughed. "Obvious is good."

While she was in the bathroom, he grabbed the remote and turned the television on. He scrolled through a few channels, settling on Family Feud.

Sarah came down the hallway. "Ooh, I love Family Feud. Steve Harvey is so funny."

"I can't believe some of the answers these people come up with."

"Or the obvious ones they miss." She sat beside him on the couch.

He decided not to think about why he'd sat on the couch instead of the comfortable chair he usually sat in. Keeping his focus on the television screen, he tried not to notice the dark curls that bounced across the top of her shoulder every time she moved her head. Or the floral scent of her shampoo, or was it perfume? Or the warmth of her legs so close to his. Or the fact that his arm rested mere inches above her shoulders, and if he lowered it ever so slightly, she might lean back into him.

In the end, Blue solved the dilemma by jumping up on the far end of the couch and leaning heavily on Sarah, so she was nearly forced to lean back against him. He'd have to give his wingman an extra treat. He put his arm down around her shoulders and made a real, conscious, tortured effort not to peek down the neckline of her sweater. Now his mind whirled with a whole host of new thoughts. What color was her bra? Was it lacy or plain? Practical or sexy?

He ran his other hand down his face and pinched the bridge of his nose. *Get it together.*

Sarah laughed at something on the show.

Then, she turned her head to look at him. "Did you see that?"

The only thing he saw was how close her lips were to his.

Don't kiss her. Don't kiss her. Don't ki- shit, she's going to kiss me.

Sarah moved her head, ever so slightly, and that was it. Rowan's mouth clung to hers, his hand cupped her face, and she shifted her body toward him and wrapped her arms around his neck.

I thought we weren't gonna do this.

We need to stop.

This is a bad idea.

Shut up.

She made a noise, a soft sigh against his mouth when his tongue touched hers, and the voices in his head quit arguing.

Chapter Nineteen

Wow, this man could kiss. If she'd been standing, she probably would have fallen over. Her knees weren't just weak, they were useless as jelly. Her fingers tangled in his hair, keeping his mouth tight to hers. His hands splayed across her back, his arms were strong and pulled her against him.

At some point, her jelly knee with the mind of its own bent over his leg and he grabbed it, hauling her across his lap until she straddled him. All without breaking the kiss.

On his lap, Sarah clung to him, delighting in the feel of him everywhere around her. She didn't want this kiss to ever end. It was perfect.

Unfortunately, Blue agreed and took that exact opportunity to join them. He snuffled his nose against their cheeks, then slurped his tongue across both their faces.

Laughing and breathless, Sarah sat back and wiped her cheek.

Rowan tapped Blue's nose. "Bad dog," he said with a laugh. "Awful, rotten dog."

Blue's tail thumped against the couch and he licked Rowan's face again.

Rowan's hands rested on her thighs, his gaze leaving the dog and locking on her. He reached up and tucked her hair behind her ear. The gesture sent a shiver up her spine.

Her lashes fluttered as she quickly blinked a few times. "I guess I should move."

"Why?" His voice was hoarse.

She couldn't think of a good reason. Or a mediocre one. Or a bad one. Nope, no reason at all why she should climb off his lap and away from those warm hands.

Maybe one reason. This wasn't going anywhere. Okay, there was a really good chance it could go back the hallway and into Rowan's bed, drawing be damned. But that would be a mistake. He'd been clear. This was a temporary partnership, and nothing more. They'd agreed to get along and make the best of being stuck together, and the end of the drawing was the end of this... unrelationship.

They'd done that. They'd worked together and made the best of it and had a good time.

Nothing more.

A few more hours and this would be nothing more than a fond memory. She didn't want to muddy the waters in her own head by adding sex to the mix and then building up expectations in her head that she knew wouldn't come close to fruition in reality, because that just wasn't her.

Yeah, it'd be great.

It would be really, really great.

But.

She sighed heavily.

"What's going on in your head?" Rowan's voice was soft.

Running her hands through his hair, she leaned forward and pressed a kiss to his lips. "All kinds of stuff."

"Like?"

She'd already told him where she stood on the issue, but it seemed like a new conversation was in order. "Sex."

His eyes widened. "Sex?"

"Oh, like it hadn't crossed your mind at all."

"Sarah, we—"

Oh, great. That tone. She pushed against his chest and stood. "No, Rowan, don't you dare 'Sarah' me like you're trying to let me down gently, because I wasn't... It's not... Wow... Just no." Embarrassment heated her face. She never should have kissed him. Again. *Again!* Would she never learn?

"Okay?" He was still leaning back against the couch, looking a lot confused and a little like he was dealing with a crazy person. He even put his hands up, showing his palms like he was approaching a rabid raccoon. The front of his jeans kind of belied the idea he'd been trying to put the brakes on.

"Whatever. I'm going to the bathroom." She spun and went down the hallway. In the bathroom, she patted cold water on her burning face. After she wiped her face on a towel, she glared into the mirror and quietly gave herself a harsh pep talk. "Seriously? Get it together. No more kissing. No more deep conversations. Just get through tonight and be done with it. Think you can handle that?"

Nodding at her reflection, she agreed with herself. "We got this."

She straightened her shoulders and went back to the living room.

Rowan had moved into the kitchen. "Coffee?"

"Sure. Thanks." She slid onto a stool at the island counter.

He filled a mug and set it in front of her, then filled one for himself. "Think we'll win?"

The subject was closed. Excellent. "One in nineteen chance we'll win something, right?"

"Three in nineteen, technically."

"Hmm. I suppose if we're being really nitpicky, we don't actually know our odds. It's three in nineteen if all the other teams have completed their tasks. Might be three in eighteen, since Young Ernie didn't give Chad a token." She really hoped Chad would be disqualified.

"Good point."

"Although he probably went back and threatened to beat Young Ernie with a lead pipe unless he got it."

"I could see him making the threat, but I could see Young Ernie beating the crap out of him." He gave her a tentative smile.

"For sure." Sarah sipped her coffee. "I guess if we win one of the cash prizes, we just split it, right?"

"Sure. What if we win the trip?"

"How about we cross that bridge if we come to it?"

Rowan got up and rinsed out his mug. "We should get going."

She hopped up and rinsed out her mug, too. Blue followed behind her, staring up intently until she reached down and scratched his head. "You're a good boy."

He sprinted off and raced back a second later, holding his tire toy.

"Sorry, Blue, I can't play now, we're leaving."

He dropped the toy and looked up at her, looked down at the toy, looked up at her, looked down at the toy…

"I know what you want, but we have to leave." She put her hand on her hip and cocked her head, mirroring Blue's stance.

He lifted his front paw and touched the tire, then looked back up at her.

With a sigh, she picked up the tire.

Blue danced back and forth, waiting for her to toss it.

Instead, she handed it to him. "Next time." Even though he

probably couldn't understand her, she felt bad for lying to the dog. There wouldn't be a next time.

He took the tire and wagged his tail.

Sarah looked up at Rowan. "I better get my coat on before I feel too guilty to leave."

Rowan laughed. "He does it to me all the time. Hurry before the puppy dog eyes trap you."

Slipping her coat on, she hurried through the living room toward the front door before Blue could convince her to blow off the drawing and play with him instead.

Rowan gave the dog a treat, then closed the door. In the Jeep, Sarah shivered. "Hopefully the heater warms up fast."

"No kidding." He touched the steering wheel, then pulled gloves out of his pocket and put them on before touching it again. "We weren't even out of the car that long."

"I wonder how long the drawing will take." She couldn't care less how long the drawing would take, but she wanted to keep the pointless conversation going so her mind didn't have a chance to focus on Rowan. Funny, sexy, impossible, infuriating Rowan, who would be out of her life in a matter of hours.

"Probably forever. Millie made it sound like it's a mini-ball with food and music."

"I think they're having a local band at this one, aren't they?"

Rowan nodded. "I think so."

"Gotta hand it to the Ladies' Society. They know how to throw an event. I don't think they've overlooked a single detail."

"Too bad they're not detectives. They could probably have all the crime in Hickory Hollow wrapped up in a matter of weeks."

"But then the police would be out of work."

"Eh, there's always traffic violations and teenagers doing stupid stuff."

"Good point," she agreed. And it wasn't just teenagers. She'd just about done something stupid herself, hadn't she? What if Rowan had encouraged her instead of giving her that obnoxious tone? Nope, nope, nope, not going to go down that rabbit hole.

At the community center, Rowan drove around the lot twice, trying to find a parking space that wasn't in a different zip code. "Guess we should have gotten here earlier."

"Looks that way." Sarah pointed. "There's one."

Rowan pulled in and turned the Jeep off. "Here's to Team Chucks." He held out his fist.

Sarah fist bumped him. "Go Team Chucks." The silly words felt so final.

Inside, a festive atmosphere filled the community center, even though there were no decorations this time, and no one was dressed in fancy clothes. This was more like an after-party, where everyone threw their jeans on and came back to the dance because they were too wired to sleep.

A local band played an eclectic mix of oldies, country, and rock.

Sarah found herself tapping her foot and drumming her fingers against her leg. "They're really good," she said to Rowan.

"They play at The Rusty Nail a lot. We should go see them sometime. Let's hang up our coats."

Sarah slid her coat off and followed Rowan to the racks, staring into the back of his head, mentally poking him in the brain. *Seriously? Make up your mind. This is over tonight. No, wait, let's go see this band sometime. "Let's." You know what that means, right? Let us. Us. And you think women give mixed signals? Good grief.*

She was so busy willing him to get a clue that she ran into his back with a decidedly unladylike "Oof!"

"You okay?" he asked over his shoulder.

"Yep. Didn't realize you stopped. Sorry."

Agnes's voice came over the loudspeaker. "Teams, please come to the stage with your tokens."

Sarah and Rowan went over and the ladies counted their tokens. Once they'd been counted, a ping pong ball with their names was dropped into a basket.

Sarah watched with a side-eye as Agnes counted Chad and Stephanie's tokens, then quietly informed them they would not be in the grand prize drawing, but their names would be added for the smaller prizes.

Surprisingly, neither of them made a scene. Stephanie pulled Chad away. Sarah heard her say, "Don't worry about it. I'm sure we'll end up with a great prize anyway." After a week of dealing with Chad, Sarah hoped Stephanie ended up getting something worthwhile out of the experience.

Once all the teams had checked in, Agnes took over the stage and shushed the band. "Welcome, everyone. If we could have our couples, excuse me, *teams* come gather near the stage, we'll get started with the drawing."

There was a rustling and quiet rumble of voices as the teams made their way to the stage. Sarah smiled at Erin and Craig/Greg as they met along the side of the stage. "Hey, guys. Good luck."

Erin returned her smile. "You, too."

Rowan's hands settled on her shoulders. She shoved her hands into her pockets, not wanting to reach up and hold his hands. Okay, she wanted to, but she wasn't going to. The mixed messages weren't going to be coming from her.

"For the main drawing, we will announce the top three prize winners. Afterwards, we will be drawing from the remaining teams for some nice consolation prizes. Without further ado, please welcome Mayor Clifton Riggle to the stage to announce the winners."

The portly man who had been mayor for more than a few decades waved to the applauding crowd and took the mic from Agnes. "Thank you, everyone, for coming out to support this wonderful community event. Let's give a big hand to the Ladies' Society, who put this whole event together." He paused while enthusiastic applause thundered and the ladies acknowledged it with demure nods.

"Everyone should have gotten a booklet listing this year's sponsors. If you didn't, there are extras on the refreshment table. Please, please support these local establishments so we can continue to have wonderful community events. such as this and the Fourth of July festival. I see a few of our esteemed business owners in the crowd. If your business is one of the sponsors, please give a little wave."

Several hands went in the air, while several more barely wiggled their fingers, not wanting the attention. The crowd applauded again.

"Wonderful, wonderful. And now, it is my great honor to draw the winners for this year's team challenge."

Gertie and Ruth stirred the balls, then shook the basket for good measure. Millie lifted the lid and Mayor Riggle reached in to pull out a ball. "For our third place drawing, thanks again to Bert and Dolly Myers of Myers Insurance Agency for this generous prize of *One! Thousand! Dollars!* The winner is…" he looked around the room, enjoying giving a dramatic performance. "Mike and Juanita!"

Sarah clapped enthusiastically and grinned as they kissed before heading to the stage to claim their prize. When they were back on the floor, Mayor Riggle made a show of pulling out a second ball and holding it high. "Sponsored by Stewart and Jody Caretti of Caretti's Coffee Shop, the second place prize is *Two! Thousand! Dollars!* And our winner is…" After a long pause, he announced, "Amber and Ty!"

Amber squealed and threw her arms around Ty before they ran onstage and collected their prize.

"Isn't this great, folks?" Mayor Riggle lowered his voice like a game show host. "And now, the moment we've all been waiting for. Special thanks to Toby and Phyllis Warner of Hickory Hollow Travel for sponsoring the biggest prize we've ever given away. This prize is an all-inclusive trip for two. You'll meet with the agency and select your trip from four *international* destinations. Your airfare, food, and lodging is all included. There's even some cash for spending money. This prize is valued at a whopping *Seven! Thousand! Dollars!*"

Spontaneous applause erupted while the mayor reached into the basket and made a show of swirling his hand around to select a ball.

Rowan's fingers tightened on her shoulders. "Team Chucks," he said into her ear.

Sarah leaned back against him, her mind whirring with possible scenarios. If they won, would he be more likely to start thinking of them as couple material? If they lost, was she ever going to see him again? Did she *want* to see him again?

Mayor Riggle lifted the ball high over his head and put the mic to his mouth. "I have in my hand the winner of the amazing grand prize. Could I get a drum roll, please?"

The drummer for the band hopped back on stage and sat at his drums, then played a long drum roll.

"And now. The winner is… Congratulations to… Here we go, folks. The! Winner! Is! Gregory and Erin!"

Rowan's hands left her shoulders as he applauded, then his hands came to rest on her waist. He leaned close to her ear. "Guess it's not Craig."

"Now we know."

"Well, if we didn't win, I'm glad it was them, and definitely not you-know-who."

Sarah held her fist over her shoulder for a bump. "Team Chucks."

He tapped her fist with his. "Team Chucks."

Mayor Riggle held the mic under his arm as he shook their hands and clapped. Greg and Erin looked shell-shocked as they took the stage. Toby and Phyllis joined them on stage to congratulate them and present them with their winners' certificate.

After a few long minutes, Mayor Riggle turned back to the audience and lifted a hand to quiet them. "What a wonderful group of participants we've had this year. We've heard great things from all the business owners about the conduct and performance of the teams. We'll be giving each team a survey to fill out so we can continue to grow and improve the event. Thank you all so much, and I'll turn it back over to Agnes to wrap up the prizes."

As the mayor handed Agnes the mic, a lone voice called out above the crowd. "This is BULLSHIT."

Sarah leaned back into Rowan. "That's gotta be Chad."

"Yup." He tensed, like he'd intervene if he had to.

"It's all rigged. I can't believe you assholes didn't get the grand prize." He pointed at Sarah and Rowan.

Agnes's voice boomed through the speakers. "Enough!"

Chad turned and opened his mouth to speak.

"Don't you dare disrespect her." The warning came from Ty.

"Piss off." Chad glared around the circle that was tightening around him. "You're all a bunch of idiots. Being run around by a bunch of old hags who think they run this town."

Motion from the back of the room caught Sarah's attention.

She nudged Rowan. Sheriff Grady made his way toward the stage. "Let's go for a walk, son."

"Screw you. I know my rights."

Stephanie took a step back toward the stage.

Sarah watched Stephanie's face. Oddly, it seemed like she was trying not to laugh. Maybe Chad had finally pushed her off the deep end. Then, Stephanie's gaze flitted away from Chad and landed on Amber. In a flash, Stephanie slipped the prize envelope from Amber's back pocket and shoved it into her own.

Sarah couldn't believe what she'd just seen when Stephanie relieved Juanita of her envelope as well. She grabbed Rowan's hand and squeezed. "I'll be right back." She tried to be as inconspicuous as possible as she slipped away from the crowd watching Chad's tirade.

She found Deputy Branson watching the Sheriff, ready to assist, and touched his arm. "Excuse me."

He looked down at her with an unreadable expression. "Yes?"

She kept her voice low. "I just witnessed a crime."

With one more glance at the sheriff, he took Sarah by the elbow and led her to an unoccupied corner at the back of the room.

"Stephanie. Chad's partner. She just pickpocketed the prize envelopes from Juanita and Amber."

"Are you absolutely sure?"

"Yes."

He pointed sternly in her face. "Don't leave." He hurried through the crowd and disappeared from her line of sight.

She made her way back to Rowan.

"What was that all about?"

"I'll tell you later." She scanned the crowd for Stephanie and saw Deputy Branson approach her from the side.

A second later, Stephanie screamed bloody murder.

Chad's tantrum stopped, and all eyes went to Stephanie. It seemed everyone was holding their breath.

"No! You have no right. You're judging me because of that idiot. I haven't done anything!"

"Then you won't mind turning out your pockets."

"I have rights!"

"Ma'am."

"My envelope is gone!" Amber cried.

Juanita reached to her own pocket. "So is mine!"

All eyes went back to Stephanie.

"What, you think I took them? Chad's right. You're all a pack of wolves. I'm out of here." She spun to walk away.

"Not so fast," Deputy Branson stepped into her path.

"You can't keep me here." She whirled away and an envelope fell to the ground.

"Arrest her," Sheriff Grady said.

"What?" She shrieked. "You can't do this!"

Deputy Branson snapped a handcuff to her wrist and spun her to clip the second one. "You have the right to remain silent."

"He made me do it! It was all his idea! I want a lawyer!" She burst into fairly believable tears. "Please, I'm so sorry. I was desperate, it's not my fault."

Chad looked shocked. If he was faking, it was convincing. "Wait, what did you do?"

Stephanie glared. "Shut up, Chad. Keep your stupid mouth shut!"

Genuine confusion crossed his face. "What did you do?"

Deputy Branson looked up at Agnes. "What was the amount of cash?"

"Three thousand dollars between both prizes."

He clucked his tongue. "Anything over two thousand dollars is a felony."

"What? Felony?" Chad deflated. He looked at the sheriff and back to Stephanie. "You stole the money?"

"I'm not saying anything without my lawyer."

Sheriff Grady sighed. "Let's go down to the station, Chad."

"I didn't… I know this looks bad, but I didn't steal anything."

"We'll talk about it downtown."

"But…" Chad squeaked.

"Am I going to have to cuff you?" Sheriff Grady reached for his handcuffs.

The wind completely left his sails. "No, sir."

Agnes stared after them for a moment, no doubt shocked that they had dared disrupt her event as much as shocked that a crime was happening under her nose.

Clearing her throat, her first words were shaky, but she quickly regained control of the situation. "Well. I'm sorry we had such an unpleasant moment, but let's get back to the drawings, shall we? We do have some wonderful gifts for our remaining coup- er, teams. First, we have a lovely bouquet done by Marsha's Florals over on the square. She specializes in wedding and event flowers. With the bouquet is a gift card for dinner at Rousseau's." She gestured to Ruth, who held the basket aloft. Millie pulled out a ball and handed it to Gertie.

Agnes held the mic for Gertie to announce the winner. "Jessica and Jeremy!"

Everyone clapped politely.

The ladies kept drawing prizes and announcing winners. At one point, Millie tossed a ping pong ball over her shoulder, disgusted. Must have been Chad and Stephanie's ball.

"What happened?" Rowan asked in her ear.

Sarah turned and stood on her tiptoes so she could tell him

without being overheard. "I saw Stephanie take the envelopes. So I slipped out to find Deputy Branson before Stephanie got suspicious."

"Geez."

"I know."

"Sarah and Rowan!"

Sarah turned and gave the ladies a big smile as she and Rowan went to the stage to collect a large gift basket and an envelope. They thanked everyone, then went back to their spot along the edge of the crowd.

"What did we win?"

Rowan peered down through the red cellophane into the basket. "Looks like a bottle of wine and some other stuff. Glasses, maybe? I can't see much through the plastic. What's in the envelope?"

Sarah flipped it over and popped the seal on the flap. She pulled out a card. "Oh my gosh, how awesome. It's a 'VIP Snow Day' package up at Mountain Peak Ski Resort. Snow tubing, skiing, snowboarding, any activities we want, all equipment rentals and basic lessons included. It even includes lunch in the lodge. I'm excited. I've never been there, but it's one of those places I've always meant to go someday."

"I was there years ago. Couldn't tell you much about it, but I remember it was fun." He shifted the basket to his other hand. "Let's get a table. This basket is heavy."

They made their way to a table in the back and got a selfie with the basket and certificate. They were just getting settled in their chairs when Corinne and Derek appeared.

"What the heck happened? We got here late and saw somebody being put in the back of the cop car. What's in the basket? Is the drawing over? Did you guys win?"

"Take your coat off and breathe," Sarah laughed.

Corinne slipped her coat off and hung it on the back of her chair. "I'll breathe while you talk."

Sarah filled her and Derek in on the evening's excitement, while Rowan added details here and there.

"We didn't win any of the big prizes, but we got a VIP Snow Day at the ski resort, and this basket."

"Oooh, what's in it?" Corinne asked.

Rowan shrugged. "Let's find out." He untied the ribbon holding the cellophane bunched together at the top of the basket's handle.

Helping push the red cellophane down, Sarah grinned. "Oooh, this is so great."

"What is it? Lemme see."

Derek shook his head. "Geez, Rin, let them see their own stuff first."

"Fine." Corinne pulled her hands back with a laugh.

Rowan turned the basket so it was facing Sarah and Corinne could see.

Sarah poked at the items. "There's so much. A bottle of wine from Redneck Vineyards, two wineglasses. Here's a card. What's it say?"

Rowan pulled the card out and opened it. "'We hope you've enjoyed being teammates so much that you've decided to add a little romance to the mix. Let us help with this date night in a basket. Just add pizza.'"

They all laughed.

Sarah touched more of the items. "Crackers, smoked cheese, a candle – oooh, it's wine scented. What's this? I don't want to pull anything out because we'll never get it back in."

Rowan peered at the square box. "Couples Table Topics? What's that?"

Corinne flapped her hands excitedly. "Oh my gosh, it's so fun. It's a card game. I mean, it's not really a game, it's a deck of cards with all kinds of questions to start conversations and get to know each other better. Someone got it for us as a wedding gift."

Derek shrugged. "It's fun. I actually like it. It's not all deep feelings crap, although you can go there if you want."

Rowan muttered, "I don't want," then snickered.

Sarah shook her head at him. "Men."

She still couldn't figure him out. He flat out said he wasn't interested, but his actions sure didn't match up with his words. Oh, well. No use worrying about it now. She'd just enjoy the rest of the evening, do a Scarlett O'Hara and think about it tomorrow.

Chapter Twenty

Rowan got up to get drinks for himself and Sarah. Derek jumped up to join him. They filled cups at the punchbowl, Gertie's watchful eye making sure they weren't spiking it.

"You and Sarah seem to be getting along really well."

"Yeah."

"You could do a lot worse."

Rowan carefully picked up the plastic cups he'd filled a little too full. "I'm not sure she could, though." Before Derek could answer, he went back to the table to dodge the conversation.

"Thanks." Sarah smiled up at him and for a second he entertained the idea of being with her for real. He could do nice things for her and she'd look at him like that, and life would be good. Until he hurt her. Because he would. And at some point, he'd get tired of feeling like she was better than him, and he'd hurt her on purpose to prove the point. Then she'd leave him, just like everyone else he ever cared about.

With a sigh, he sat and sipped at his punch while Sarah and Corinne talked and laughed and she occasionally reached over to touch him. He could tell she wasn't even really thinking about it. She'd set her drink down and put her hand on his leg and pluck her fingernails under the seam beside his knee for a few moments, then she'd take her hand back.

He put his arm around the back of her chair, half-listening to her fill Corinne in on every detail of the day's challenges.

"Aww, I'm sorry you guys didn't win." Corinne patted Sarah's hand.

Sarah shrugged. "I'd say we did pretty good. We got some great prizes. At least I think they're great. Rowan's not so keen on the spa gift certificate."

"Yeah, that one's not quite my cup of tea."

Sarah laughed. "I told him he should use it and get a pedicure."

Corinne groaned. "Pedicures are the *best*."

"I'll pass, thanks."

Derek made a face. "Yeah, me, too. I wouldn't put anybody through that."

"They deal with nasty feet all the time. I'm telling you, you'd enjoy it." Corinne said.

"Thanks, but no. Never." Derek shook his head.

Rowan held his plastic cup up. "Hear, hear."

Sarah slung an arm over Corinne's shoulders. "We'll go. It's only a fifty dollar gift certificate, but we can split the difference."

Corinne shook her head. "Pedicures, yes. But we should wait until sandal weather, and we're not splitting the difference. It's your prize."

"Fine. I'll cover mine and whatever's left will go towards yours. That's my final offer."

"Deal."

Derek said, "If only world peace could be so easily attained."

"It could be, but you men don't want pedicures," Sarah said.

Rowan and Derek exchanged a look. "Nope, not even for world peace."

Corinne shook her head. "You guys are ridiculous."

Rowan said, "I might do a manicure for world peace, but only if no one ever found out."

"I could do that," Derek agreed.

Corinne rolled her eyes.

Agnes's voice came over the loudspeaker. "One final thing. If any of our coup- er, teams continue dating, and are still dating at the Independence Day festival in July, the Ladies' Society will buy you a romantic lakefront dinner. But we'll just have to wait and see for that one, won't we?" She chuckled into the microphone. "I have a feeling, though, we're going to be buying a lot of dinners this year."

The other ladies nodded in agreement.

Rowan looked around the room. It certainly seemed like most of the pairs were getting along really well. That little insistent bubble of hope appeared in his gut again. He *could* be with Sarah. All he had to do was ask, and he knew she'd be willing to try with him.

The problem was, he liked her too much to let her go down that road.

"Rowan?" Sarah put her hand on his arm.

He jerked his head up. "Huh?"

"Where'd you go?"

"It's just been a long day."

"It has. We should probably get you home or Blue's going to send out a search party."

"He would."

They stood and Corinne reached over to hug Sarah. "Call me when you get home."

Rowan stifled a groan. He knew what they'd be talking about, and he wasn't sure how he felt about his every word and action being dissected and examined for motive and meaning.

Oh, well. He pulled the cellophane back up over the basket and retied the bow. Not nearly as neatly as it had originally been, but it would get the basket to the car and to the house. Which house, he had no idea. Probably hers. She'd have more use for a basket. And he didn't need it sitting on his kitchen table, reminding him of what he couldn't have.

"Get used to it," Derek said quietly. "I've saved myself from saying and/or doing a lot of stupid things just because I know they're going to be talking about it later."

"So if I piss Sarah off, it's a guarantee Corinne will be mad, too."

"Let's just say, if you're fighting with Sarah, stay out of the diner until you patch it up."

They laughed and followed the women out of the community building.

Rowan opened Sarah's door, then put the basket on the backseat. Hopping in the driver's seat, he started the Jeep and rubbed his hands together to warm them. "You can take the basket to your place so you can see what all's in it."

"We should go through it together, don't you think?"

He avoided her big brown eyes. "It doesn't matter if we do or not." He tried to lighten the mood. "I trust you not to steal the cheese."

It worked. She relaxed back into her seat. "But do you trust me with the crackers?"

"Hmm. That changes things a bit, doesn't it?" He gave her a smile and pulled out of the parking space.

"I'm happy to keep the basket if you don't want it. It'd be

perfect beside my chair to keep my work-in-progress quilt squares in."

"It's all yours." He took his eyes off the road long enough to glance down and flick the heater on. "Hopefully that heats up soon."

"Yeah, my feet are freezing. I even wore two pair of socks since I knew we'd be outside part of the day. When I get home, I'm putting on my bear feet."

"If you're freezing, why would you run around with bare feet?" Sometimes she made no sense.

She giggled. "No. Bear. Like raaaawwrrr bear. Black bear, grizzly bear, the big fuzzy animals that hibernate, which is so smart and I wish I could do that."

"Bear feet."

"They're ridiculous. My parents got them for me for Christmas one year as a joke. They're huge thick slippers made of brown fur and they have bear toes with claws on them. They're the most obnoxious things you've ever seen, but they're reeeeally warm."

"I bet." He could easily imagine her wearing big fuzzy slippers around the house.

"And they're quirky and they make me think of my parents, so they make me happy."

"You can't ask for any more than that."

"Nope. You sure can't."

He pulled into her driveway. "I'll grab the basket. Do you have the ski certificate?"

"Yes. I hope." She patted her coat pockets. "Yes. It's in this one. Whew."

"Good."

"Did you want me to hang onto it?"

"Yeah. Keep it with the other stuff. We can go through it some other time." His plan was to keep making sure 'some other time' never actually came around, then she'd have all the prizes and she could use them. Maybe that'd help ease his guilty conscience.

Guilty? For what? It was better for her all around if he made a clean break.

He balanced the basket while she unlocked the door. "Would you set it on the kitchen table, please? I'll be right back."

"Sure. Hey, Harvey, what's up?"

He paused by the tank to see where the turtle was hiding, then went to the kitchen and set the basket down.

"These are bear feet," Sarah said from the doorway.

He turned and started laughing. She held up two huge slippers, one in each hand. "How do you even walk in those?"

"Carefully, so I don't trip. They're great for sitting still, though."

"Good thing you don't have stairs to go up and down."

"Right? Because I'd be too lazy to take them off first and then I'd fall and crack my head open and end up in a coma and probably die before anybody missed me."

"You've really thought this out."

"It's only common sense."

"You don't have a basement, do you?"

"I do, but I don't go down there. It's only ever occupied by repairmen and the souls of the undead."

"I didn't know you had roommates."

"Aren't you clever." She tossed the bear feet in the general direction of the couch. "Any idea when you'd want to do the ski day? I'm really excited about it. It'll give me an excuse to bust out my old snowsuit. I knew there was a good reason to hang onto it."

"Whenever you want." Oops, he was supposed to be ending things, not making plans to spend more time with her.

He reasoned that it was their prize, they should share it, and besides, if they went in the next week or so, it still counted as part of the team thing and was therefore acceptable. "Maybe next weekend?"

"I have to work Saturday. How about the next? Unless you wanted to do it Sunday, but I'm guessing I'll need a day to recover afterwards."

He checked the calendar on his phone. "Good call. March 7 works for me."

"Perfect. Let me write it down. Not that I'll forget, but I'm terrible with dates, so if someone asks me to do something on the whateverth, I won't know." She hummed while she tapped into her phone, a happy, tuneless noise. "Done. We're official."

He startled, then covered by standing straight and gesturing toward the living room. "I should get going."

"Yeah, I'm beat. This was a great day. Long, though." She smiled up at him.

He had to look away before he kissed her. "Go put your pajamas and bear feet on and call it a night."

"That's the plan."

"Me, too. Except the bear feet."

"You should get—"

"No." He cut her off and she laughed. "No fuzzy slippers."

"Okay, no pedicures, no bear feet."

"No." He moved past her. She followed him to the front door. "I'll talk to you sometime before the ski thing." There. Noncommittal and vague. Nothing to give her any expectations.

"Sounds good." She stood up on her tiptoes to kiss him on the cheek.

At the last second, he turned so her lips met his, and kissed her like he didn't want to leave. So much for not setting up expectations. It'd probably be a lot easier to end things if he'd quit putting his tongue in her mouth. Which he wasn't too keen on doing, not when her hands were tangling in his hair and she was leaning into him as he put his arms around her.

He'd chalk it up to physical attraction and nothing more. Yeah. That was it. He wasn't pulling away because of pure physical attraction. Instinct. Primal urges.

Nothing more.

In the end, she was the one who pulled away.

She smiled up at him, those big brown eyes with the long lashes and those pink lips... Lips that were saying something that he hadn't caught. "...like tomorrow or the next day."

"Um." Crap. What did she say?

"I'll let you know."

"Okay." He had no flipping idea what he'd just agreed to.

Another smile and a quick kiss on the lips, then she said, "I should probably stop kissing you so you can leave."

At that, he smiled. "You're definitely making it hard."

Her eyes widened, and he realized his double entendre.

"To leave. Hard to leave." Okay, so either way it was accurate, but still.

Her cheeks blushed bright pink. "On that note, good night, Rowan."

"Good night, Sarah."

He left before another stupid thing came out of his mouth.

Chapter Twenty-One

Sarah watched out the window until Rowan's car left the driveway.

"Harvey? What do you think?"

Harvey stared at her through the tank.

"I don't know, either. He says he's not interested in a relationship, but then… well, you saw it. I guess we'll have to talk about what we're thinking as far as anything from here on out. Maybe after the ski day. I think I'll just give him some space between now and then. Wait for him to reach out to me. Sound like a plan?"

Harvey agreed, she could tell.

"I have to call Corinne."

Corinne answered on the first ring. "Start from when you got up this morning and don't let a single detail out."

"First, before I even got up, I picked the crust out of the corner of my right eye. I must not have gotten all my mascara off, because there was a big lump and it left a little red mark on my eye. Then, I pulled the cover off and sat on the edge of the bed and yawned."

"Ha, ha, ha, you're a freaking comedian."

Sarah laughed. "Okay, let me grab the itinerary so I have all the stops in order. I don't want to get mixed up." She grabbed the paper and filled her glass. She flopped onto the couch and covered her legs and *bear* feet with her favorite quilt. "You ready?"

"I'm filling my cup, hang on, okay, walking into the living rooooooooooooooommmmmmm, sitting dowwwwwn, and go."

Sarah waited until the rustling in the background stopped, then she started her tale, pausing only to take sips of water and check to make sure she was going in the right order. The only place she skimmed was the part Corinne saw in person. "We're planning to do the ski resort thing not this coming Saturday but the next one. Then he kissed me and went home."

"Wow. I'm telling you, the guy's into you."

Sarah let out a frustrated growl. "I'm trying not to think so. He says he doesn't want anything. He hasn't even said he wants to be friends. I'm trying to respect what he's saying and not read too much into what he's doing."

"What he's doing is sending mixed signals."

"Ugh. They're not just mixed, they're criss-crossed and tangled and tied in knots. He's a hot mess. I'm doing my best to say what I mean, but he's making it difficult. Why would he tell me all his deep dark stuff one minute and then be all 'hey this isn't going anywhere' the next? Ugh. UGH! Men!"

"I wish I had some advice. It was so easy with Derek. Our first date he said he was going to marry me, I laughed and said he was crazy, and now here we are. I would guess Rowan *likes* you, but maybe he's got so many issues he just doesn't want to put himself out there. I don't know. He's so standoffish. No, that's not quite it. Private. He's really private, so I can't guess what's going on in his head."

"Neither can I."

"Then I guess you have to decide how much indecision

you're willing to put up with before you stop trying to figure him out."

"You're right." She was probably willing to put up with more indecision than she should be, just because of those kisses. They made up for a lot.

"Of course I am. Keep me posted. Let me know what happens between now and the ski trip."

"Harvey and I decided I'm not going to contact him. I'm going to wait for him to get in touch with me."

"There you go. Listen to Harvey."

"Maybe one text a few days before if I haven't heard from him."

"Sarah."

She groaned. "Okay. Fine. No contact unless I haven't heard from him on Friday night. If he wants to bail, I'll sleep in."

"I suppose that's acceptable."

"As long as you approve."

"I do."

True to her word, Sarah didn't contact Rowan the whole next week. At work, she endured the sympathetic glances and comments that were meant to be supportive.

"Maybe he's in a coma," Julie offered.

"I probably would have heard. Besides, Corinne has seen him going in and out of his house." Sarah turned back to her computer and typed in some notes.

"Maybe it's not really him. Maybe he's been body snatched by aliens or something. Or maybe his phone broke."

Sarah rolled her eyes. "Or maybe he's not interested."

Julie leaned down and gave her a one-armed hug from the side. "If that's the case, he's an idiot."

"Thanks."

"Last patient just left. Time to lock up."

"Halleluiah."

Julie locked up while Sarah finished on the computer. Half an hour later, they had cleaned up, closed the office, and gotten in their respective cars.

Pulling her collar up and rubbing her gloved hands together, Sarah wondered if winter was going to last forever. At least it was the last day of February, so the calendar was rolling toward spring. Winter wasn't good for anything.

Well, maybe one thing, the ski resort, but she didn't even know if they were going. If she had to guess, she'd guess he was going to contact her at the last minute and make good on his promise to go on the ski trip with her.

She pulled onto the main road and tried to imagine how that was going to go. Would it be awkward since they hadn't talked? Would it be like no time had passed at all? Would she still think about climbing him the second she saw him?

Probably.

Her flesh was weak.

Chapter Twenty-Two

Saturday found Rowan doing chores for Millie.

"No, I haven't talked to her." Yes, he'd wanted to. Rowan braced himself for a whap to the back of the head. Instead, he got the stern disappointed expression.

"She's a wonderful girl." Millie's tone matched her expression. Definitely disappointed, with a side of 'you're an idiot' mixed in.

"Yes." He held the picture frame against the wall. "Is this where you want it?"

"It needs to go to the left a couple of inches."

He shifted the frame. "Here?"

"You should call her. Aren't you going skiing next weekend?"

"This is heavy."

"Fine. Yes, put it there."

He balanced the frame and marked the wall with a pencil.

"She's probably wondering why she hasn't heard from you."

He stepped off the stool and leaned the frame against the wall. "She hasn't called me, either." Wrong thing to say. Millie's face lit up and apparently Sarah's stock just jumped even higher.

"I told you she was perfect for you."

"Because she hasn't called?"

"Yes."

That made no sense, but he didn't argue. He turned back to the wall and busied himself with hanging the picture frame.

"She's trying to give you space, Rowan. Problem is that one of these days she'll start believing your silence and she'll move on."

"Good. I don't want to talk about this."

"Of course you don't. You're wrong."

He hung the frame and jumped off the stool and stood back to check his work.

Millie crossed her arms. "That's why you don't want to talk about it. You don't like admitting when you're wrong."

"I'm not wrong, you are. Not everybody needs to be in a relationship, Auntie. Some people are perfectly happy being alone."

There. That shut her up.

"Oh, Rowan." Sympathy filled her eyes and she reached out to grasp his arm.

Or not.

"Some people *are* happy on their own. But sweetheart, you're not one of those people."

He obviously wasn't going to win this argument. "I'll go look at that washer hose."

In the laundry room, he pulled the washer out and tightened the drain hose that had come loose. Thankfully, she hadn't followed him. He pushed the washer back into place and for good measure, pulled the dryer out and used a long handled brush he'd teased her about buying to clean out the vents. So she'd been right about the goofy looking brush. Didn't mean she was right about him and Sarah.

Securing the dryer vent, he pushed it back into place and went to the kitchen where she sat, sipping at a cup of coffee and reading her newspaper. "Coffee?"

"I'll get it, thanks." He poured himself a cup of coffee. "Did you need me to look at anything else?"

"No, you've done plenty. Thank you."

"Any time." He sat down and picked up a section of the newspaper she'd already read. "Hey, the old mansion is being turned into a winery."

"I saw that. It's a great location. I think they're going to do music events and whatnot." She side-eyed him. "Be a nice place to go on a date."

Rowan didn't bother disguising his sigh. "Yep."

"I don't know why you're being so contrary."

"Didn't we just go over this?" He pinched the bridge of his nose.

"Not really," Millie sniffed in annoyance. "You're just making up silly excuses and not addressing the issue."

He leaned over and kissed the top of her head. "Because it's none of your business. Let's go get some lunch and talk about something else."

Millie pulled her coat out of the closet. Rowan took it and held it so she could put it on. "You're such a gentleman. You'd make a good husband."

"Auntie." He tried to be stern.

"Rowan." Aaaaaand she won that round, too.

He waited until she was settled in the passenger seat, then shut the door and went around to his side. Pulling onto the road, he said, "Where did you want to get lunch?"

"How about Sonny's? I could eat a good club sandwich."

He relaxed a fraction. Maybe the topic had run its course,

for the day at least. They got to the diner and went inside. Millie immediately steered toward the left, toward the booth the Ladies' Society had claimed long ago. Fortunately, it was empty.

The counter was not. She was beautiful, and clearly doing her best to not look directly at him.

"Sarah! What a lovely surprise." Millie put her hand on Sarah's shoulder and gave it a squeeze. "How are you today?"

"Great, thanks." Sarah gestured to her scrubs. "I just left work."

"How about that. Look, Rowan, Sarah's here."

"I see. Hey, Sarah."

"Rowan."

He couldn't quite decipher the expression on her face. Guarded, maybe. Like if he'd stop being ridiculous, she'd smile and let him know she was glad to see him.

"When are you going skiing?" Millie did a great job of sounding innocent.

"Next Saturday, as far as I know." She glanced at him.

Yep, she was sending out feelers. Because he was an idiot and left her hanging. "Next Saturday." He caught a glimpse of Corinne out of the corner of his eye, maintaining a conspicuous distance.

"Oh, I hope the weather holds. I used to ski all the time, but now I'd probably break a hip. Enjoy these things while you're young."

Sarah gave her a genuine smile. "You used to ski?"

"Oh, yes. I was really good, too. What time will you be leaving?"

She glanced to Rowan again. "I'm not sure."

"Early," he offered. "It takes an hour to get there, so if we leave by seven thirty or eight, we should be in good shape."

Now he was the recipient of her smile.

"I'm going to sit down, dear, my knee's bothering me something awful. I'm glad to see you." She patted Sarah's shoulder again and walked to the booth. Looked like her knee was fine.

"So, um, I've been busy." He ran a hand through his hair.

"Sure."

Too lame. She didn't buy it for a second.

"Do you want to get dinner tonight?" Where did that come from?

Didn't matter. That smile was worth it. "Yeah, great."

"I'll pick you up around six?"

"Perfect."

He shifted his weight. "I should get over to Millie."

"Sure."

"See you later."

"Yup."

"Six." He shoved his hands into his pockets.

"Six."

"Okay." He gave a nod and fled to Millie's booth, where his aunt looked precisely like the cat that swallowed the canary. Rowan glared. "Knock it off."

Millie broke into an all-out grin. "Why, whatever do you mean?"

"I wouldn't be the least bit surprised if you orchestrated this whole scenario."

"Don't be silly."

Chapter Twenty-Three

Corinne slowly refilled Sarah's coffee cup. "What just happened?"

"We're having dinner tonight."

"That seems kind of random. Think he was planning to ask you out or he just thought of it?"

Sarah lifted the cup to her lips and blew across the hot liquid. "I think he panicked and said the first thing that came to mind."

"Are you going to give him an out?"

"Heck, no. I'm going to make him wallow in his awkwardness."

"One of the many, many reasons I love you."

Sarah snickered and glanced over at Rowan. "It'd be easier to blow him off if he wasn't so darn good looking. Or such a good kisser."

Corinne snapped her fingers in front of Sarah's face. "Focus. Mr. Hot Lips doesn't get a pass to ghost."

"I know." She sighed and took another sip of coffee. "Why does everything have to be so complicated?"

"Pffft. It's not."

"Easy for you to say." Sarah pushed her mug away. "I'm going to go. I'll keep you posted."

Corinne gave her a wink and dropped the dirty dishes into a bin behind the counter. "Every detail."

"Always."

Sarah waved to Rowan and Millie and left. When she got home, she put her hands on her hips and stood in front of Harvey's tank. "I feel like I should be mad. I mean, he blew me off for a whole week and only said something because he panicked. I know that's what it was. Panic. I should be insulted."

Harvey munched on a cricket. It might look like he wasn't paying attention, but he was.

"But I'm kind of excited. I missed talking to him this week, and to be fair, I didn't call or text him either, so I shouldn't be all judgy, right?"

She changed into jeans and a sweatshirt and made a half-hearted attempt to tame her unruly curls.

Back in the living room, she ran the vacuum and wiped a dustcloth over the television. "Good enough."

Harvey agreed.

"I have to run a few errands. I'll be back in a bit." She grabbed her coat and her purse and made her weekly trek to Target.

She had just put her bags in the back seat and pushed the cart to the corral when her phone vibrated with an incoming call from her mom. "Good timing. I'm just leaving Target."

Debbie clucked her tongue. "Oh, shoot. I wish I'd known. We're almost out of cat food."

"Want me to run back in?"

"No, we'll get some at the grocery store tomorrow. I called because your dad and I are going to the movies and wanted to see if you want to go along. It'd be good for you to go out and not grouse over that guy not calling."

"I am out. Target is out. And I'm not grousing. We're going to dinner tonight."

There was a long pause. "Really?"

"Why are you so shocked?" Probably because Sarah hadn't gone on more than a disastrous first date with anyone since the whole Thomas thing.

"I'm just surprised. From what I've heard, he's pretty anti-social, so I was surprised he went through with the challenge thing in the first place."

"You may have heard things, but I've actually spent time with him. He's not antisocial. Selectively social." She wasn't sure why she felt so compelled to defend him.

"If you say so."

"Mom. We're friends. We had a good time and we're going to have dinner. Probably to iron out the details about next week's ski trip. It's not a big deal."

"Just be careful."

"Mom."

"I'm sure he's a nice guy."

"He is."

Her mother let out a long sigh. "I don't want you to get hurt. It wasn't easy seeing you go through that mess with... *him*." She spit the word. Thomas's name hadn't crossed her lips since the day he left.

"I know. But I was completely blindsided there." And Rowan had his faults, but he wasn't anything like her crazy ex.

"We all were." Her voice still carried guilt because she hadn't been able to shield Sarah from Thomas's awfulness.

"Exactly. I can't live my life waiting for the next bogeyman to jump out from behind a tree. And I don't think Rowan's deceptive at all, he's just closed off and private."

Her mom sighed. "Honey. Don't take on a fixer upper."

Sarah matched her tone. "Mother. We're friends. I'm not looking for anything else."

"I just worry."

"And I love you for it. Thanks for the invite."

"Maybe next time."

"Yes." Honestly, she had half a notion to cancel on Rowan at the last minute and go to the movies with her parents, just for some small measure of petty revenge for his week-long silence.

"Love you."

"I love you too, Mom."

"Wear the blue sweater."

Sarah laughed. "I will."

They disconnected the call and Sarah pulled out of the Target parking lot and headed home.

When she got there, she managed to get all the bags into the house in one trip, even though she nearly broke her arms.

"Two trips are for sissies," she explained to Harvey, who seemed a little concerned about her load. "Although I suppose I'd be able to log more steps on my FitBit if I brought in one bag at a time."

She heaved the bags onto the kitchen table, sorted everything to be put away, and put the items for the food bank into the box she'd put in the corner. Carrying a package of toilet paper to the bathroom, she paused to look in on Harvey. "I got some carrots. I'll chop the tops off for you in a minute, okay?"

Harvey was something of a pig, so she knew he'd be happier once the food was in front of his face.

The afternoon passed more quickly than she expected, and soon she was fluffing her curls and smoothing down the front of her sapphire blue sweater. For the final touch, she fastened her silver necklace and the tiny diamond pendant settled itself in the v-neck.

Dark jeans and knee-high black boots finished the outfit. She figured it would be appropriate wherever they went. Which would probably be someplace generic, since it wasn't a date. Because he didn't want to date.

"Whatever," she muttered to the mirror.

A rap on the front door pulled her attention. It was a quarter til six. One last glance in the mirror, and she went to open the door.

"You're ear –" The words died on her lips.

"I need your help." Her ex-husband Thomas stood, holding the screen door open, Lucifer in the flesh.

"No." Sarah slammed the door shut and turned the lock. Her heart pounded.

He rapped on the door again. "Sarah," he said. "This will only take a minute. Please."

Her hands pushed against the door, trying to make sure it stayed shut and helping her maintain her balance. He sounded so reasonable. Not crazy at all.

She knew better than that. "You need to leave!" It probably wasn't necessary to yell it through the door, but she wanted to be clear.

"Sarah, I just need a signature. Some old business my attorney needs me to take care of. I'm sorry to bother you."

"Put it between the doors."

She heard shuffling and the click of the screen door closing. Carefully, she unlocked the door and opened it a crack, keeping her foot braced behind it. She flicked the lock on the screen door before bending to pick up the paper. "What is it?"

"An affidavit. Saying our divorce was final before I married Lucy."

"It wasn't. And I don't see a notary around to make this legit."

Thomas was in full schmooze mode. Charisma oozed from

him, like a modern day Jim Jones, and he was just as crazy. And dangerous.

"You don't need me for this." She crumpled the paper into a ball. "Go away, and don't ever come back."

His eyes flashed danger. "If anyone asks, Sarah, we were divorced before I married Lucy."

"Believe me, I'm not talking to anyone about our marriage. It's not a pleasant topic. Now leave before I call the police. There's a permanent restraining order, remember?" She didn't give a flying fart about him or his wife – no, *wives*. She had no idea who would be asking, and she didn't owe them any kind of answer. If anyone came sniffing around, she'd tell them to check the public records and leave her alone.

Thomas regarded her for a long moment, probably searching for a weak spot, then nodded once and went back to his car, a little red sporty number. Hardly practical for a man who had a stable full of wives and children he was deeply devoted to. Charlatan.

He slid into his car as Rowan pulled into the driveway. The men looked at each other curiously but thankfully didn't exchange any words.

Rowan came up the porch with an eyebrow raised. "You okay?"

She unlocked the screen door and pushed it open. As soon as he was inside, she slammed the door shut and locked it again, then peered out through the blinds to make sure Thomas was actually leaving.

"Sarah?"

"Huh?"

"Are you all right?"

She glanced down, realizing what he was seeing. Her arms were crossed across her chest, her hands gripping fistfuls of her sweater. She shivered, suddenly freezing, and probably pale. More pale than usual.

"Who was that? Did he scare you?"

"Um." She glanced over to Harvey, who was standing on his rock, his head stretched as far out of his shell as it could go. "Carrot."

"What?"

"I never gave Harvey his carrot. He needs his carrot. Excuse me." She fled to the kitchen and opened the fridge. "I don't see the carrots. Where are the carrots?" Her voice rose an octave.

Rowan came into the kitchen. His voice was low, calm. "Sarah, there are carrots on the counter."

She whipped around and grabbed the bag, clutching it in her hands like a lifeline. "Okay. Okay. Okay. Harvey needs his carrot top. I have to get him his carrot top."

"You're shaking like a leaf." He came to stand next to her, his hand extended, but he seemed almost afraid to touch her.

Her hands fumbled with the plastic bag, and she eventually ripped a hole in the side and pulled out a fat carrot with long leaves at the top. She reached out toward the knife block and Rowan grabbed her hand. "No."

"Harvey needs his carrot." She felt slivers of carrot sinking under her nails. Her hands felt disconnected from her body.

"Sarah." Then, he did touch her, putting his hands gently on her shoulders. "Look at me."

She couldn't.

He pulled the carrot from her hand.

"No, Harvey needs a carrot." She barely recognized her own voice.

"Okay. I'll cut it. How much?"

Laser focused on the carrot, she pointed to a spot near the top. "There."

"Right here?"

"Yes." Rowan took a knife from the block and chopped the top off the carrot, then slid the knife as far away from her as he could reach. "Let's give Harvey his carrot, okay?"

Sarah felt herself nodding. "He needs his carrot."

"Okay." He slid an arm around her waist and steered her back to the living room.

Her hands were still shaking, so he opened the lid and put the carrot into the tank. "Harvey has his carrot, okay?"

"Okay." She stared into the tank, watching Harvey open his pointy-lipped mouth to claim his prize.

"Sarah."

She pulled in a deep breath and turned to face him. "I…" She didn't know where to begin. The protective layer of numbness that held the shock of seeing Thomas was wearing off, and a fresh spike of terror-driven adrenaline coursed through her, causing her to shake. "I…"

Rowan timidly reached toward her and she launched herself into his arms and clung to him. Half a second later, she was wracked with sobs. Rowan held her tight, murmuring soothing words until she calmed.

When she finally pulled back, she wiped her face and ran a hand through her hair, a tinge of embarrassment undoubtedly coloring her warm cheeks. "I'm sorry," she whispered.

"No. Stop."

"I have to wash my face." She practically ran into her bathroom and closed the door. So much for not having a lot of drama in her life. He'd probably be gone by the time she was done, so she took her time pressing a cold washcloth to her face, using the bathroom, and washing her hands. She cleaned away the smeared eyeliner, and took a second to be impressed that her mascara was mostly intact. Yay, CoverGirl.

There were no sounds from the living room, so she figured

he'd gone. It was just as well. There was no good way to explain *that* hot mess.

The light switch felt cold as she turned the light off and left the bathroom. Her conversation with her mother must have been some sort of cosmic omen she should have paid more attention to.

Her stomach rumbled, reminding her that she was going to miss dinner.

"Oh!"

Rowan sat on the couch, waiting.

"I figured you would have made your escape," she said with a little laugh that held not much humor.

He shook his head. "You okay?"

"I'm fine."

His expression made it clear he didn't believe her answer.

"Look. Maybe you should go. I know how you feel about drama, and I know you only asked me to dinner because you felt cornered running into me, so I hereby absolve you of any sort of interaction, you can go and be done with all this. I'm not feeling up to going out anyway, and… so… yeah."

He stood, slipped off his jacket, neatly folded it over the back of the chair, then went back to sit on the couch. "Let's order a pizza. Maybe one of those brownie dessert pizzas, too?"

Confusion furrowed her brow. "What?"

He pulled his phone out of his back pocket. "Pepperoni and mushroom okay with you?"

"What is happening right now?"

"I'm ordering pizza. We can watch a movie or something. We can talk. We can *not* talk. Whatever. But I'm not leaving you alone until you're okay."

She considered the situation for a moment and settled on, "Pepperoni and mushroom is fine."

He nodded and spent a few minutes messing with his phone. "It'll be here in thirty minutes."

"You have a pizza app?"

"You don't?"

Hovering in her own doorway was starting to feel weird, so she picked the remote up from the chair and went to sit beside him on the couch. "That was my ex-husband."

"Did he hurt you?"

"Now? No." No, he'd just startled the crap out of her, appearing like a demon from an old nightmare. It wasn't even so much that she was afraid of him anymore, but seeing him was a shock to her system that she needed to process.

His jaw clenched, but he said nothing.

Sarah unzipped her boots and tossed them under the coffee table, then tucked one leg under her as she shifted to face him. "I haven't seen or heard from him in almost five years. It shocked me to see him standing there. I... I wasn't prepared. The last I'd heard, he was in California. He wanted me to sign some form. It was like opening the door to the devil himself."

Rowan put his hand on her knee. She put her hand over his, comforted by the warmth.

"It wasn't a good ending." That was an understatement.

"Did he hurt you?"

"Yes." She took a deep breath, trying to figure out how to give him the ultra-condensed version. "Um, well, he never actually *hit* me or anything, but he and his new wife and some other people held me hostage for three days trying to 'train' me."

Chapter Twenty-Four

Rowan struggled to keep his face neutral. "Hostage. For three *days*?" He'd never felt so useless. He wanted to rage and scream and beat Thomas's face in to protect her, but the damage had been done long ago. There was no going back to keep it from happening.

She nodded, setting her curls in motion. "It was probably a year and a half before that when he joined a new 'church' and wanted me to go with him. At first it was okay, way more conservative than I care to be, all the women wore long skirts and stayed pretty quiet. I felt pretty weird about it, but I went along every now and then to keep him happy, and then he became a deacon and wanted me to get more involved and be 'more appropriate.'" She shuddered.

"Long story short, as he got higher up, he wanted me to join the church officially. We even met with the elders several times to address my concerns, where they patiently reiterated verse after verse after verse about a woman's place." She thought back. "Then he dropped the bomb. He wanted me to start these 'study sessions' where I would learn to be a properly submissive wife. The elders of the church would be the ones to 'teach' me how to submit to my superiors. And yes, it's exactly what you're thinking."

Rowan's stomach clenched.

"Obviously I refused, and then he told me he was deserving of a proper wife, and he'd found a candidate. Because of my insubordination, I would be demoted to second wife, but he would graciously allow me to stay so my immortal soul wouldn't be condemned to hell."

"How generous."

"I declined, and as a last ditch attempt to convince me to go along with this nonsense, he drugged me and they took me to this compound and spent three days trying to brainwash me. Finally the cops showed up with my parents and they let me go." She gave a little laugh. "I guess I was more trouble than I was worth. We got divorced, he married Lucy, not necessarily in that order, then he married some barely legal girl. I don't even know her name. Last I heard he had four or five wives and was keeping them all 'blessed' and perpetually pregnant."

"Holy shit, Sarah." If he'd known this before he'd encountered Thomas, he might not have just walked past the man.

She took a long breath. "I'm lucky. He was never able to come between me and my parents, so they noticed immediately when I wasn't answering my phone."

The doorbell chimed and Sarah nearly jumped out of her skin. Rowan patted her leg. "Pizza."

"Yeah."

He got up and looked out the window before opening the door to the pizza delivery kid. Peeling bills out of his wallet, he handed the kid money and took the boxes before closing the door. "You want this locked?"

"Yes, please." She let out a breathy, humorless laugh. "Boy, that restraining order really means a lot, doesn't it?"

He set the boxes on the coffee table. "Do you want to call the cops?"

"If he comes around again, I will." She gave her head a shake and straightened her shoulders. "I'll grab plates and napkins. I have iced tea, water, and Pepsi."

Hard as it was, he followed her lead and let her change the subject. As much as he hated it, handling this was her call. "Pepsi's fine."

She came back into the living room with paper plates, a handful of napkins, and two cans of Pepsi.

Rowan pulled two slices of pizza out of the box, put them on a plate, and handed it to her, then took three for himself. "Looks good."

"The cheese is nice and melty. It's always hit or miss with delivery."

They ate in silence for a few minutes. He watched her intently, glad to see that little by little, she relaxed. "What's on tonight?"

"I have no idea." She pointed the remote at the TV and it came to life. "Let's check the guide." She scrolled through the show guide on the screen. "There's a Seinfeld marathon."

"Sounds good."

When the pizza was gone, Rowan flipped open the box for the brownie pizza, a warm round brownie cut into wedges.

Sarah peered into the box. "That looks so good."

As the antics of Jerry and the gang played out on the screen, Rowan only half-noticed. His mind played this new information over and over, imagining all kinds of scenarios that Sarah might have endured. In the end, cults and terrorists were cut from the same cloth, so he could understand a little bit, although from a much different perspective.

The show cut to commercial and the brownie was gone.

Sarah stretched. "Bottle of water?"

"Yeah, thanks. I can get it."

"Good. You grab the water while I run to the bathroom."

Rowan grabbed the bottles out of the fridge and carried them back to the couch.

When Sarah came back into the room, she settled onto the couch and leaned back into him, pulling his arm around her. "Thanks for tonight."

"I didn't do anything."

She turned her face up to look at him. "Oh, but you did. You gave me an evening of normal and let me get myself off the ledge. I appreciate it."

His brow furrowed. "Don't give me credit I don't deserve. You would have been fine without me here."

"You're right, I would have been fine eventually, but it was nice having you here. Relax, Rowan, I haven't put you up on some pedestal."

He shifted uncomfortably as Sarah sat up and turned to face him directly. He probably wasn't going to like this.

"Look. I like you. I like spending time with you. But I can't figure out if you're so narcissistic you think I'm madly in love with you because you're impossible to resist, or if your self-esteem is so low you think I couldn't care about you unless I was also hopelessly messed up. Either way, you've got some stuff to work on, and you need to decide what you want. If you don't want to spend time with me, lose my number. And if you do, then stop acting like you're only here because you're doing me some kind of favor. I assure you, I'm not desperate."

Aaaand, he was right. He didn't like it at all. "Okay."

She turned back to watch television, not leaning on him this time. He didn't like that, either. "Poor Elaine. That's why I don't dance in public."

Rowan managed a little laugh, more than happy to let the topic go. She was wrong about one thing, though. He'd already worked on his issues, and they were about as fixed as they were going to get. Which is why his ping-ponging emotions were driving him crazy. Just because he didn't deserve Sarah and couldn't be with her didn't mean he didn't *want* it more than anything.

They sat through two more episodes. When the credits rolled, Rowan stretched and leaned forward. "I should probably head home."

"Okay." She stood and straightened the hem of her shirt. "What time do you want to leave next Saturday? And who's driving?"

"How about I pick you up around eight?"

"Sounds good." She waited until he put his shoes and coat on, then opened the door. "Have a good week."

Obviously she wasn't expecting to talk to him until the next weekend.

"Sarah…" He didn't know what to say. "See you Saturday, I guess."

"Good night."

"Night." He stepped outside and turned to look at her. "If you need anything or whatever, you can call me."

"Okay."

He knew she wasn't calling. "So, um, I'll see you Saturday."

She smiled and tilted her head. "I'm not paying to heat the outside."

"Right. Sorry. See you." He took a step backward.

"Night. Drive safely." She closed the door with a gentle click.

No goodnight kiss. Not even a hug. He didn't realize how much he'd gotten used to kissing her, or at least feeling her arms around him as she hugged him tight. With a sigh, he drove home, feeling like he was missing something that should probably be obvious. Or maybe it was just wishful thinking.

Back home, Blue greeted him at the door.

"Women are impossible."

Blue cocked his head and snapped his mouth shut.

"Don't you dare take her side."

His tongue lolled out again, but his ears stayed perked, probably waiting for Rowan's next brilliant gem.

"She insulted me. Told me she wasn't sure if I was a narcissist or if I have low self-esteem. What the heck, right?"

Blue's butt dropped to the floor, his tail swishing.

Rowan scratched his head. "You have to pee?"

At the magic word, Blue jumped up and trotted to the back door. Rowan let him out and hung up his coat while the dog was outside. After Blue came back in, Rowan locked the doors and turned off the lights. "Bedtime."

Another magic word. Blue headed straight for the bedroom, jumped up on the bed, turned around in a few circles, then plopped down. In the middle of the bed.

"Huh uh. Move over."

Blue yawned, looked rather put upon, gauged Rowan's seriousness, then moved.

By the time Rowan was done in the bathroom, Blue was asleep. In the middle of the bed. Grumbling, Rowan scooted under the covers, trying to shove Blue with his hip. He might as well have been trying to move an elephant.

Blue let out a snore and Rowan gave up, turning on his side and making do with the sliver of bed Blue had left him.

Sleep eluded him for most of the night, and when he did drift off, his mind filled with twisted images from the desert, snakes, cults, torture chambers, and Sarah tied to a chair behind a thick glass wall where he couldn't reach her.

Sometime during the night, Blue must have sensed his

discontent, because he woke up to Blue's head on his shoulder, softly whining and staring intently at him.

"Hey, a little personal space, huh?" he croaked out.

Blue's tail thumped, but he didn't move.

"It's okay, buddy, I'm good. Crazy dreams, that's all." He scratched Blue's head and earned a big slurp on the cheek, but at least the beast moved then.

Rowan checked the time. On cue, his phone vibrated.

Millie. He'd promised to take her to church.

He sighed and answered the phone. "On my way."

"Are you sick? You sound terrible."

"No, just a long night. Overslept. I'll be there in twenty minutes."

"Don't drive if you're tired."

"I'm fine, I'm up."

"Okay. Love you."

They disconnected the call. Rowan flopped back onto the pillow and groaned up at the ceiling. With a deep breath and a burst of fake energy, he whipped the cover back and sat up.

Blue grumbled and rolled onto his back.

"Tell me about it." Rowan scratched the dog's belly and got up. Seven minutes later, he gulped a cup of coffee while Blue did his business outside. Once the dog was back in, Rowan gave him a biscuit and headed out the door.

Millie came out her front door as he pulled into the driveway.

"Sorry I'm late." He helped her into the Jeep.

She fastened her seatbelt. "How was your date with Sarah?"

He paused for a long moment. "Do you know anything about her ex-husband?"

Millie made an angry, very unladylike snorting noise. "Disgusting, foul beast, that one. Fancied himself some sort of religious man. He's somewhere out west now. Good riddance."

Rowan wasn't sure how much he should tell Millie, so he didn't say anything about Thomas being back in town. "He didn't treat her well?"

"I should say not. Took up with some young girl and eventually left Sarah alone, thank goodness." She let out a heavy breath. "He *kidnapped* her. Took her to some compound up the country. Thankfully her parents were able to track them down and the police had to go in and rescue her. Horrible ordeal."

"Sounds like it." He should have known she'd already know the whole story.

"The cult up and left everything behind and moved in the middle of the night. He should have rotted in jail but I'm not sure it ever even went to trial."

Rowan parked the Jeep and went around to open Millie's door.

After the service, when they were back in the car, Millie put her hand on his arm. "I know you don't want me to meddle, and I'm trying not to."

He laughed.

With a sheepish smile, she said, "I really am trying. What I want to tell you is that I know you have your issues, and I think if you let her in, she could help you and you could help her. She understands you."

True enough, she did. That didn't mean they should be together.

<h1 style="text-align:center">Chapter Twenty-Five</h1>

All week, Sarah checked her phone constantly, hoping to hear from Rowan, but knowing she wouldn't. Even sitting in a booth across from Corinne and Derek, she kept glancing down at it.

"Do you think he'll show up tomorrow?" Corinne asked.

Sarah shrugged. "I think so."

"You haven't been texting him, have you?"

"No." She'd wanted to, but didn't want to justify it to Corinne. Or Harvey.

"Good. If he's not reaching out, neither should you."

"Yep."

Derek popped a french fry in his mouth. "Why's it have to be so complicated? If you want to talk to him, call him."

Sarah and Corinne both gaped at him.

"What?"

Corinne rolled her eyes. "Why would she put herself out there?"

"Maybe he's just nervous about making the first move. Maybe he's waiting to hear from her."

Sarah shook her head. "I highly doubt it. I'm one hundred

percent sure that we'll go tomorrow and have a wonderful day, and that'll be the last of it."

"Why would he even bother going if he didn't want to see you?" Derek asked.

"I think he likes seeing me when he sees me, but he doesn't want anything more complicated." That was the conclusion she'd come to. It made the most sense.

"Or anything requiring any effort on his part," Corinne added.

"So what's your plan?" Derek asked.

"My plan is to go skiing tomorrow and have a great time, and then go home, give my wounded pride a little bit to get over it and then maybe I'll sign up for online dating or something."

"Solid plan." Derek turned his attention back to his food.

Corinne looked unconvinced.

Sarah picked up a wedge of her quesadilla.

Corinne said, "Is he worth all this angst?"

"No angst here. I told you, I'm going to go skiing tomorrow and have a good time and then it's all on him. If he wants to keep seeing me, that's fine, but I'm not chasing him."

"Good. No man is worth chasing after," Corinne agreed.

"Hey, now," Derek said with a smirk.

Corinne leaned over and kissed his cheek. "Sorry, babe, not even you."

Sarah pushed her empty plate away and pulled her napkin off her lap and wiped her mouth. "Okay, my favorite people ever, I'm going home so I can dig out my snowsuit." She got up, then leaned over to hug Corinne. "I know, every detail."

"All of them. And if you need us to come get you, just call. I don't think we're doing anything tomorrow."

"He wouldn't strand me. I do know that much."

"Okay."

Sarah grabbed her coat and made her way through the crowded sports bar. Out in the parking lot, she hurried through the darkness and got in her car. Only after she was safely locked inside did she realize her hands were clenched around her keys and she was breathing hard. Waiting for the bogeyman to jump out. Or Thomas. She wasn't sure which was worse. Or if they were different at all.

Once she got home, she told the whole story to Harvey, who stood at the edge of his rock and listened intently.

"I have to find my snowsuit. I'm pretty sure it's in the back of the closet, at least I hope it is because I wouldn't know where else to look."

Harvey offered no alternate location.

In the bedroom, she kicked off her shoes and pulled open the closet door. Her walk-in closet was one of her favorite things about the house when she'd bought it. The previous owners had remodeled and converted a small bedroom into the closet and added custom shelves and drawers. It was closet perfection as far as Sarah was concerned.

She went to the back corner where she stored off-season items and found a bin labeled "Snow Suit" – a happy discovery left over from an organizing fit she'd had a couple of New Years ago.

She pulled the hot pink snowsuit out and shook the folds loose. Trying it on, she was glad to see it still fit. Good thing, since it was a little late to find an alternative.

Laying out the day's clothes, she briefly considered texting Rowan, but she didn't. In spite of their issues, she was looking forward to the trip and hoped he was, too.

Chapter Twenty-Six

Rowan stared at his phone, willing a message from Sarah to appear, but none did. He typed out four different messages, then deleted them. Finally, he typed a simple,

Is 8 still good?

and hit send before he changed his mind.

A few minutes later, his phone dinged with a reply.

Still good. See you then.

No smiley face. Sarah loved her emoticons, nearly every message had some sort of little cartoon image in it. Not this one, though. He shoved his phone in his back pocket and decided not to give it any more thought. Yeah, right.

"Do you think she's mad?" he asked Blue.

Blue looked up from his chew toy, the tire Sarah had gotten him, and perked up his ears.

"Stop being so judgmental."

Eventually, he went to sleep and in the morning, he was up

with the sun, rooting through the closet until he found his coveralls and boots.

Blue followed him around, watching with great interest.

"Sorry, buddy, you're on your own today. Derek will be over to let you out to pee."

Blue heard the word "pee" and trotted to the kitchen where he waited at the back door.

"Yeah, yeah." He opened the door and let Blue out to run in the back yard.

He checked the time every two minutes until it was time to leave. He gave Blue a treat, scratched his head, then said, "Wish me luck."

In the car, he tried to imagine how the day would go. If nothing else, they'd have some fun.

He pulled into Sarah's driveway at eight on the dot and went to knock on the door. She opened it and nearly took his breath away. Why was he keeping her at arm's length? He couldn't quite remember. He waited inside the door while she bustled around.

"Can you take this, please?" She thrust a tote bag containing a hot pink wad of fabric at him.

"This your snowsuit?" Duh. What else would it be? He was off to a great start.

"Yeah."

"It's really… pink."

She rolled her eyes. "Yes, it is. This is probably overkill, but I have an extra outfit in case I need to change."

Seeing her made him want to make promises he wouldn't be able to keep. "I did, too. We can leave those in the Jeep."

"I'm excited." Her curls bounced as she talked. "I was looking at their website and I think I want to try tubing first. If that's okay with you."

"Yeah. Of course." He'd give her the best day he could.

"I mean, I'm not ruling out the possibility of changing my mind once we get there."

Rowan nodded. "Tickets?"

"Side pocket of my tote bag." She double checked. "Okay, Harvey, we're leaving. You be a good boy."

"See ya, Harvey," Rowan added, then went out the door. He waited while Sarah locked the door and dropped her key into her purse.

"I wonder how crowded it'll be. It's kind of on the warm side for March, so I'm betting there'll be a crowd."

He opened her door, then put her bag in the back of the Jeep. "Probably."

"You going to be okay with that?"

Backing out of the driveway, he said, "Yeah, as long as they don't want me to give a speech or anything."

"No speech. Got it."

They made small talk on the way to the ski resort. She seemed so relaxed and he couldn't control the anxious knots in his gut. This was it. The last time he'd spend any real time with her, and it sucked.

"The parking lot doesn't look too bad." Rowan found a spot straight back from the entrance.

"Should we put our snowsuits on before we go in?"

"Makes sense."

They stood beside the car and pulled their snow gear on over their clothes. Sarah got the passes out of her bag and they went up to the ticket window.

"Oooh, VIPs," the man at the window said. "You get these badges." He slid two bright red badges through the ticket slot. "Pin them over your heart. Whatever activity you're doing, follow the VIP signs and you'll go right to the front of the line."

Sarah grinned. "Awesome. Thanks."

"Thanks for visiting Mountain Peak. Have a great day."

They stepped through the turnstile and off to the side, where they pinned their badges to their chests and took their first selfie of the day.

Rowan wanted today to be fun for Sarah. Maybe it'd give her a few more good memories of him to replace the jerky ones. Colorfully marked trails lay in several directions. "Do you still want to go tubing first?"

"Yes." Sarah studied the signs, then pointed. "Thataway."

They walked along a packed snow path until they reached the line for snow tubing. They followed the other people who were selecting big black inner tubes and carrying them to the line. The line was relatively short, so they didn't bother veering off into the unmanned VIP line. When it was their turn, an employee in a snowsuit clipped Sarah's tube to a moving cable and had her sit on it before the cable took it too far.

Sarah sat on the tube. Rowan's tube was clipped next. The cable pulled them up the side of the mountain. After a lengthy ride, they had to jump off their tube while an employee unclipped it from the cable, then hurry out of the way of the next person in line. A third employee stood at the top of a set of snow-carved stairs overlooking four tracks, where she kept track of the spacing between tubers. As soon as the people sliding reached a marker, she'd let the next one go.

She motioned Sarah to the farthest lane and told her to go. Sarah sat on her tube and screeched as she sped down the mountain.

Rowan was in the lane beside her. He bounced and slid until he was backwards, seeing where he'd come instead of where he was going. He did manage not to scream as the freezing wind tickled his neck. His tube hit a bump and went airborne for a second, then shot back and forth between the ice bumpers on the track.

Finally he hit the flat finish line and was slowed by the straw covering the packed snow. He slid easily into the bales of straw that served as bumpers.

"Oh my gosh, that was so awesome. I want to go again!" Sarah jumped up and down, beaming. Her cheeks were bright pink.

"Let's go." Rowan grabbed his tube and they went back to the line.

She pointed up the hill. "Oh, look at those people. They're going together. Let's try that."

"They're facing forward, that's a good thing."

"I know, right! I was freaking out a little bit when my tube spun around. I thought maybe I was doing something wrong, but I couldn't get turned around again. When I got down here, I saw everyone else was backwards, too, so that must be how it goes."

He had to grin at her enthusiasm. They reached the front of the line and once again rode the cable to the top. The employee at the top showed them how to clip their tubes together. Rowan held the back while Sarah climbed on the front, then he sat in the back tube. When the employee gave the ok, he used his heels to pull them forward and as soon as they were moving, he put his feet up and Sarah grabbed his knees.

Their tubes swayed and bumped and went airborne a few times while they laughed and held on and sailed to the bottom.

"Again! Again!"

Rowan laughed. "We're going to do this all day, aren't we?"

She pushed a curl out of her face. "I could totally do this all day. Did you want to ski? Or snowboard? I'm up for anything."

"How about we do this until lunchtime, then we'll eat and decide from there."

"Great plan. Love it."

They ended up using the VIP line when the resort started getting crowded.

"I almost feel guilty about this," Sarah said quietly as they were motioned past thirty or forty other people to take their place at the front of the line.

"I don't. Not even a little bit."

She gave a guilty laugh and moved to have her tube clipped to the cable. At the top, she waited for Rowan and they clipped their tubes together for the ride down.

The air stung his face, but he laughed anyway. Riding the tube down the mountain felt like flying. Several hours later, they turned their tubes back in.

"My stomach is growling so loud I'm afraid it'll set off an avalanche," Sarah grumbled.

They went into the lodge's cafeteria and got soup and sandwiches, then sat at a table near a roaring fireplace to thaw out.

"This is so pretty. I bet they hold a lot of weddings in here. The view out those big windows would be gorgeous."

"I bet," Rowan said around bites of food.

After they finished eating, they went to the lobby and looked at the brochures for skiing lessons.

"Hmm, what do you think?"

Rowan hated to say anything if she wanted to take a lesson, but he shrugged and bit the bullet. "Two hours until the next public lesson, then the lesson is an hour and half long, I don't think we'll have much time to ski afterwards. What do you think?"

"We could get on the list, then go back to the tubes. I'm sure the lesson will be fun, even if we don't get to ski much later."

"Okay." He followed her to the counter, where they signed up for the next lesson, then made their way back to the tubes.

Chapter Twenty-Seven

Sarah loved the feeling of flying down the hill, the freezing wind scraping her face as tiny bits of ice shavings blew back and stuck to her cheeks. Rowan rode in front of her this time, his hair blown back and messed up by the time they slid into the straw bales at the bottom.

The tube jumped and sent them into the air. Sarah clutched the handles on the tube and screeched in delight.

A few more runs, and they turned in their tubes and went to find the ski lessons.

"That was awesome. I'm thinking I should have worn something over my face, though. I'm pretty sure I'm windburned."

Rowan touched her cheek. "You are a little red."

She wanted to slap his hand away and tell him to stop touching her if this was over today, but she also wanted to feel his touch and burn it into her memory. "You are, too. We should probably both put a little Vaseline on before bed. Help it heal up."

He cleared his throat and took a step back. "I, um, think the lessons are over there."

In the ski shop, they were outfitted with skis and poles.

"Oh, geez," Rowan groaned.

She looked in the direction he was staring. "What? Oh. Oh, boy." The other people there for lessons looked to be about ten years old. At the oldest. "We're about to be shown up by some little kids, aren't we?"

"Looks that way."

They lined up beside the kids, some of whom chuckled, but most of them ignored the two "old" people.

"Welcome, everyone. We're going to get some basics down and then get you on the slopes to practice what you've learned."

The lesson was fun. Sarah enjoyed learning how to shift her weight back and forth to move forward on the skis. She had a little trouble keeping both skis going in the same direction.

Rowan wasn't faring as well. She glanced over and he tried to stand up, brushing snow off the side of his leg. He looked over and gave her a thumbs up and a smile.

The kids, of course, took to skiing like ducks to water, gliding back and forth and getting antsy to do some real skiing.

Finally, they rode the lift to the top of the bunny slope, jumped off the lift, and coasted to the trail.

"I'm so nervous," she said, clutching her poles.

"You'll be fine. I, on the other hand, am thinking I should have updated my will."

"You're not going down the black diamond slope, are you?"

He snorted. "This is as much of a death wish as I care to have."

"Me, too."

One of the kids zipped past them. Then another. And another.

"Shall we?"

Rowan took a deep breath. "We shall."

Sarah stabbed her poles into the ice and shoved forward. She slid for half a foot, then came to a stop. "Oh, no, this isn't going to be easy, is it?"

Rowan also poked at the ground and didn't get very far. A couple more of the kids from the lesson whizzed past.

Finally, Sarah got her skis pointed in the right direction and moved forward. The hill sloped and she surged forward, picking up speed.

Halfway down, she panicked and slid sideways to stop, afraid she was going to hit the tree that was probably actually a hundred feet away and posed no danger at all. Rowan slid past, hunkered and holding his poles in a death grip.

Sarah laughed. "We're quite the pair."

"Gah," he answered, poking at the ground with his poles to keep moving.

They eventually found themselves at the bottom of the hill and looked at each other.

Rowan wore a pained expression. "Are we doing that again?"

"Um, we could, but I'd kind of rather not."

"Thank you."

"You don't want to?" Sarah walked awkwardly to a spot they could remove their skis.

"Not even a little bit." He was clearly relieved to get his skis off. "We could go tubing some more if you want."

As fun as tubing was, she was beat. "You don't sound too enthusiastic. And to be completely honest, I'm wiped. I probably won't be able to move my legs tomorrow."

"You and me both."

"Are you okay if we tap out right now and go home?"

"Yes. Absolutely." His face relaxed, clearly relieved that she was ready to leave.

"Let's go."

They turned their ski equipment back in and headed for the parking lot. She suggested, "You could start the Jeep while we take off our snowsuits, maybe it'll warm up a little bit."

"Good idea."

They reached the vehicle and Rowan started it and opened the back gate. They both stood behind the car and stripped off their boots and snowsuits. Sarah balanced on one foot at a time to get her leg out of the snowsuit and get her regular shoe back on, so she didn't get her socks wet. Tossing her snowsuit and boots in the back, she stretched, putting her palms on her lower back. "I'm definitely going to feel this tomorrow."

"You're getting old," Rowan joked.

"Hey! I can still kick your butt."

"Pffft, you think?"

"I *know*." She laughed. "And if I can't, I know where I can hire some ten-year-olds to do it for me."

"Okay, okay, you're probably right."

"I'm always right."

He finished the gymnastics required to get his shoes back on without stepping on the wet ground, then grinned up at her. "I'll remember that."

"You'd better." She flounced around the side of the Jeep and got in.

Rowan got in the driver's seat and fiddled with the buttons on the heater. "It usually doesn't take long to heat up."

"Good." She rubbed her hands together. "The numbness is wearing off and my flesh is slowly realizing I'm a popsicle."

Rowan eased out of the parking space and headed for the highway. "Did you have fun?"

She nodded. "I had a great time. I probably took a hundred pictures. You?"

"Yup. Make sure you send them to me when we get home.

The skiing part wasn't so great, but the tubing was a lot of fun."

She brushed her hair back from her face. "Agreed. I might have done better skiing if I wasn't being intimidated by a crowd of nine-year-olds."

"Bunch of showoffs."

"I know, right? 'Oh, look at me all upright and moving.' Pffft, brats. And where were their parents? Probably whizzing down the diamond slope like a freaking professional."

"Whizzing? I don't think that's allowed." Rowan snickered.

She groaned, loud. "Oh, har. Very funny."

"It was bad, but I couldn't help myself."

"I'll be more careful about my phrasing from now on."

He changed the subject. "Are you hungry? I'm hungry."

"I could eat." Who was she kidding? She was always up for food.

"There's a good Chinese place up here. I hardly ever go since it's so far away, but since we're here, we could go there. If you're good with that."

She loved the suggestion. "Absolutely. I haven't had Chinese in ages."

"It's a buffet."

Even better. "Sold."

A few minutes later, they were shown to their seat in the Panda Lounge, which sounded much fancier than it was. The hostess directed them to the buffet.

Sarah piled her plate full with a little bit of everything, then added liberal dashes of soy sauce in a few strategic locations.

Back at the table, they ate in silence for a few minutes.

Rowan pointed to his food. "This is good. We should come here again."

Sarah's head jerked up from her plate, a noodle slapping against her chin and leaving a trail of soy sauce. She grabbed her napkin and wiped the sauce off while she slurped the noodle into her mouth. "Are you kidding me? Seriously, Rowan, that's the kind of stuff you can't say." She leaned back in the booth and crossed her arms. "You're jerking me around and it's not okay."

"I'm not trying to jerk you around."

"I'd hate to see it if you were."

"I guess I don't see the big deal, but if I said something wrong, I'm sorry."

"Wow." Her appetite faded fast as her stomach knotted up.

"Wow what?"

"That's the lamest, shittiest, most pathetic apology I've ever heard in my entire life."

"Well, I don't really have anything to apologize for, soooo…" He put his palms up.

She stared at him, unable to formulate a response. Finally, she simply shook her head and turned her attention back to her plate, poking at her food and pushing it around with her chopsticks.

After a long, uncomfortable silence, Rowan said, "That's impressive. I'm not coordinated enough to use chopsticks."

"Huh."

"I tried it one time with rice and it flew everywhere." He chuckled. "Probably should have tried something bigger."

She didn't answer.

"Will you show me how to work the chopsticks?"

"It's easy," she snapped. "Unwrap them, bend over, and shove them up your ass."

His jaw dropped. "You're mad."

It was clearly a shocking concept.

All she could do was blink at his stupidity. The man was a rocket scientist.

"Why are you so mad?"

Sighing, she poked at a piece of chicken. "Forget it, it doesn't matter."

He stared at her for a long moment. "I don't like it when you're mad." His voice was tentative. "I don't want to fight with you."

"We're not fighting, Rowan." She blinked. "We're not anything."

Chapter Twenty-Eight

Rowan stood up and went back to the buffet, partly for the sweet and sour pork, and partly to give Sarah some space to cool down.

Apparently he'd stuck his foot in his mouth again. Usually, he didn't care what anybody thought. He hadn't thought his comment warranted her reaction, but as he shoveled some fried rice onto his plate, he thought maybe, just maybe, he could see how she might interpret it as him giving mixed signals. Or, as she'd so eloquently put it, jerking her around.

Okay, she was right. He'd blurted the comment out without thinking about what it meant. Or more importantly, what it might mean to her.

Why had it slipped out at all?

He went back to their table and decided an actual apology was in order.

"I'm sorry."

She looked up from her plate. Hopefully she heard the sincerity.

"I like spending time with you, and when I'm with you, I forget that I'm not really with you."

She rolled her eyes. That wasn't a good sign.

"What? I'm not trying to hurt your feelings."

"Then shut up. Because all I'm hearing is a bunch of bull-shit. You keep blathering about how much you like me, like spending time with me, you're obviously attracted to me, but you'd rather slam your face in a car door a hundred times than be in any kind of relationship with me." She held her hand up. "And you can spare me all the 'It's not you, it's me' rhetoric, because that's bullshit, too. Rowan, I agreed to your terms for today. Go, have fun, no drama, and no looking forward. Don't you dare blame me for getting upset when you can't even stick to your own rules."

"I'm sorry."

She cut off any notion of further discussion. "Are you almost done? I'd like to go home."

He cast a longing look at the last egg roll, debated, then shoved it in his mouth. It was too good to leave behind.

She finished her soda while he chewed.

"Done."

She was out of the booth and halfway to the door by the time he'd gotten up. Outside, he hit the button to unlock the doors since she reached it well before he did. She buckled her seatbelt as he slid into the driver's seat. He wanted to apologize again, but figured it'd come out wrong and piss her off. Again. Instead, he pulled out and once they were on the highway, he turned the radio up a little bit.

They didn't exchange a single word the whole way down the road. At some point, he'd felt Sarah relax a little, but she continued to watch the scenery instead of talking to him. It was just as well. He'd only say the wrong thing.

He pulled into her driveway.

"Crap, I forgot to turn the porch light on."

"I did, too. Didn't think of it until now."

She opened her door. "Open the back?"

"I'll help you carry your stuff."

"You don't have—"

He ignored her protest and jumped out. Letting her grab her snowsuit, he picked up her boots and gloves and hat. "Everything's still wet."

"Yeah, I'll take it straight to the laundry room and hang it up."

"You have your keys?"

She held them up and jingled them.

Rowan followed her into the house and said hello to Harvey on the way past. Standing in the doorway of her laundry room, he waited until she hung up her snowsuit, then handed her the gloves and hat. Finally, she took the boots and tossed them onto a mat next to the dryer.

"Thanks for helping me get my stuff inside."

"Sure. So, uh…" He wasn't sure what to say, but he didn't want it to end like this.

"No." She crossed her arms.

"No what?"

"No whatever you're going to say." She gave him a tired smile. "Let's just leave it right here."

"I just wanted –"

The smile vanished and she raised her voice. "No! Can you just stop? We've done everything the way you wanted, from day one. And now we're done, unless you'd like the art studio gift certificate, which I am more than happy to give you." She pushed past him, grabbed the basket with wine and cheese off the table and shoved it at him. "Here. The value is similar to the gift certificate, I'll keep that, you keep this, we're even, and now we're done."

He glanced at the table.

"Don't you dare put that down."

"Sarah."

"Rowan." She thrust her hand out to shake his.

He shook her hand, wary.

"It's been nice. A few moments notwithstanding, I've had a good time. Thanks."

"Thanks?"

"I have some stuff to do now, soooo…" She gestured toward the front door.

"Got it." He turned and walked to the door. He stepped outside and turned to say something, but he didn't know what. He settled on, "Good night, Sarah."

"Goodbye, Rowan." She closed the door.

The porch light sparkled against the red wine bottle.

He couldn't remember ever feeling shittier.

Chapter Twenty-Nine

The door clicked shut. Sarah let her eyes drift closed and pressed her forehead to the door. It was cold.

She took a moment, then stood, straightened her shirt, then turned around. Harvey pressed his face against the glass.

"What? I'm not going to go back and forth and back and forth until he decides what he wants. I appreciate that he's always tried to be honest, but that's not enough. It's almost like he wants to date until he figures out whether he wants to date. So no. I'm not here for practice."

Harvey didn't weigh in, but she knew he agreed with her.

"Tomorrow I'll be stiff and sore from the tubing and skiing, so I'll indulge and wallow a bit, because I really do like him. But that's it. I'm not wasting a bunch of time." She paused at the tank and reached in to touch Harvey's head. "I know you liked him, too. It's a shame, huh."

Harvey stretched his neck out and let her stroke his rough skin, then apparently had enough and pulled his head most of the way back into his shell.

Sarah laughed. "You're just like a cat. 'Pet me' then 'get away from me.' You're so fickle."

She glanced at her phone. Corinne would be expecting an update. With a sigh, she dialed the number.

"I saw Romeo just got home, I thought it seemed kind of early."

"Not really, we've been going since eight this morning." She yawned.

"Hmm."

"Hmm?"

"Skiing didn't go well?"

The day was like the mountain – up and down, up and down. "Tubing was fantastic, skiing was really hard, and the whole day was pretty great until Rowan ran his mouth."

"Uh oh, he told you again how he doesn't want to be in a relationship?"

"Worse. We were eating at this really good Chinese restaurant and he casually mentions how we should go there again. We."

Corinne groaned as only a best friend can. "Ugh. More mixed signals."

"Exactly."

"What did you say?"

"I told him to quit jerking me around and shove his chopsticks up his butt."

"Simple, direct, I like it."

She sighed again. "It pisses me off. I mean, how dare he act like he assumes we're going to keep seeing each other at the same time he's assuming we won't?"

"He needs to figure his stuff out."

"I may have mentioned that as well."

Corinne laughed. "It's a shame. He's really cute, and he seems to be a nice guy."

"And he talks to Harvey. Do you know how many guys talk to my turtle? None, that's how many."

"But."

"I know." She waited for Corinne's words of encouragement.

"You deserve someone who's all in. Not just deserve it, you *need* it."

"I know." Sarah paced the living room. "I told Harvey I'm going to spend tomorrow wallowing, since I'll be sore and tired and grumpy anyway, and then I'm done."

"Sore?"

"My calves are already killing me. Those freaking skis. And did I tell you about the little brats at our lesson? Afterwards they're just whipping past us like nothing. Unbelievable. Kids are the worst."

Corinne laughed. "Strangers' kids are the worst. My nephews are the best."

"They are pretty great."

"I'll stop by tomorrow after church. I'll bring you some soup and make sure you're not dead."

"You're the best."

"I know. Oh, Derek just pulled in, I'll see you tomorrow. Love you."

"Love you, too." Sarah hung up and couldn't help but grin. Corinne was her rock, she didn't know what she'd do without her.

Harvey was completely inside his shell.

"I guess you're tired of listening to me talk, huh?" She tapped the glass. "I'm going to take a long hot bath. Just in case you wonder where I am. I'll be in the tub."

His shell remained still.

She locked the front door, then went to her bathroom and turned the water on. The deep soaker tub didn't get nearly enough use. Pulling out her favorite plush towels, she decided to go the whole nine yards and lit some candles, poured in some bubbles, turned on some soft music and shut off the lights. In the soft glow, she stripped and got into the tub, sinking deep into the hot water.

Much to her chagrin, her thoughts went directly to Rowan. Apparently her imagination wasn't as done with him as she was. It was too much effort to stop the persistent thoughts, so she let her mind run wild with what could have been. She soaked until the water cooled, then reluctantly climbed out of the tub and wrapped herself in her fuzzy blue towel.

Next she slipped into her plush pajamas and climbed into bed, pulling the comforter up to her chin and went to sleep.

Sunday morning came and she stretched her legs. As she'd expected, her calves were sore, but not sore enough to warrant a day lounging around the house, wallowing in Rowan-inspired misery.

Instead, she went for a walk, theorizing that working the muscles without punishing them would keep them from getting too stiff and sore. Later, she gave Harvey a fresh carrot top and let him roam a blockaded area in the laundry room while she gave his tank a thorough cleaning.

When she was done, she scooped him up. "I rearranged some things. Let me know if you like it." She looked over his shell and legs as she carried him back to the tank. "Here you go, handsome man."

Harvey was clearly impressed with his fresh new digs.

Sarah ran the vacuum, then glanced at her phone. "Crap." She tapped the icon to return the call. "Hey, Mom, I was cleaning Harvey's tank and didn't hear you call."

"Hey. Honey." Her voice was hesitant.

"What are you stalling for?"

"I'm not stalling."

"Mom." What was going on now?

"Oh, all right. Virginia Simmons cornered me after church

this morning. Her son just moved back to town and she thought you might show him around."

"Show him around? If he got from Virginia's house to the church, he saw it all. You didn't give this weirdo my phone number, did you?" She'd just gotten through the Ladies' Society trying to fix her up, she didn't need her mother jumping on the bandwagon.

"Of course not. But he did seem nice, and he's really good looking. *Really* good looking."

"You met him?"

"Briefly."

"What does he do?" Why was she asking? She wasn't interested.

"He's a delivery driver."

"Okay." That didn't help her create a mental image.

"He also models."

Interest piqued. "Models? Like fashion modeling?" She wondered if it was modeling for photos, or the kind of modeling where they wore trash bags and feathers down a runway as some sort of haute couture. This could totally go either way.

"Well, not exactly."

"What? The suspense is killing me."

"He models for romance novel covers."

"No kidding."

"Obviously he had his shirt on at church, but… yeah."

"I assume he told you some of the covers he's been on." Her phone dinged at her ear. She pulled it away and tapped at the photo her mother had just sent. Dang. You could bounce quarters off those abs for days.

"There are more."

"So, uh, he needs someone to show him around town, huh?"

"Yup. You available? I wasn't sure what was going on with you and Rowan."

"Nothing. He made it crystal clear. Nothing, never, so I might as well rebound now and get it over with, right?"

"There you go." Debbie chuckled. "I'm texting you his number."

"What's his name?"

"Trey Simmons."

"Huh." She enlarged the photo of the book cover. Too bad his head wasn't on the cover, but he had a very, very... *very* nice torso.

The phone dinged again.

"Thanks, Mom."

After they hung up, she stared at the number, then called Corinne while sending her the pictures.

"Text him! Now!" Corinne shrieked, nearly bursting her eardrum.

"I can't text him right now, my hair's a mess and I'm wearing grungy clothes."

"You know he can't see you through a text, right?"

"No, but if I look like crap, I'll text like crap."

"You're insane."

"You really think I should text him?" Why not? He had one big item in the plus column – he wasn't Rowan.

"Yes."

She felt a pang of guilt. "What about the whole Rowan thing?"

There was a long sigh. "Sarah."

"Okay, okay. I'll text him. After I change and put on some mascara."

"Go."

She changed into jeans and a cute top, fluffed her hair and swiped on some makeup. For good measure, she put in her favorite pair of silver hoop earrings and picked up her phone.

> Hi, this is Sarah, fulfilling my mother's obligation to pass your number along. If you'd like to get together, great, if not, no worries.

Only a few minutes later, her phone dinged.

> This is Trey. If you're as nice as your mom, let's have dinner.

> Nobody's as nice as my mom.

She laughed and sent the message. He definitely got points for the proper use of your and you're.

> High bar. Half as nice?

> Three quarters.

> Sold. DiMaggio's at 7?

> Tonight?

> Sure. Gotta eat, right?

> Gotta eat. Meet you there at 7.

> Great.

She decided to let his text be the end of the conversation. Okay, so he had a stellar torso, he had a decent sense of humor, great taste in restaurants, and didn't butcher the English language with textspeak. So far, so good.

. . .

DiMaggio's was busy, as it always was, but not uncomfortably so.

"You must be Sarah."

She turned and looked up into one of the most handsome faces she'd ever seen that wasn't on a movie screen. "Trey."

He gave her a charming half-grin and shook her hand. His grip was firm, no limp fish or vice grips. And his hand was warm. Nice.

He was tall, about Rowan's height.

Knock it off. Not going there.

The host greeted them and led them through the dining room to a table along the wall.

Trey put his hand lightly on her back, waiting for her to choose which side she wanted to sit on. He even pulled out her chair. His eyes glanced over her figure, hitting that perfect balance between gentleman and definitely physically attracted.

"What wine would you like?"

"I don't drink much wine," she answered. "So no preference." She sat a little straighter, trying to focus on the menu and ignore the little voices in her head. Voices that clearly preferred Rowan's company.

He ordered them a bottle of wine and a glass of water for her. Thoughtful.

The waiter came, showed Trey the bottle, then poured their wine.

"May I order for you?"

She couldn't decide whether she liked the audacious question or not. "You don't know what I like."

He took a sip of wine, staring at her over the rim of his glass. "I would have ordered the bourbon ribeye with rosemary potatoes and the glazed carrots." He wore a good-natured grin.

Sarah took a long sip of wine. "Okay, you can order for me."

He ordered their meals and as they talked, he maintained solid eye contact, nodding in all the right places, asking all the right follow-up questions.

"Mom says you're a romance novel model."

He blushed a little. "Yeah, that wasn't supposed to get out, but my mom seems to think it's a great selling point."

"She's not wrong."

"Oh, geez, she sent a cover, didn't she?"

"*She* didn't. My mom did. Unless your mom sent it to my mom." It was endearing that he didn't seem vain or conceited, despite his side gig.

"I'd bet money she did. It's more exciting than telling people I drive a soda delivery truck."

"She mentioned you were a delivery driver, but I didn't get any more detail there."

"I'm not surprised."

She kept forcing her attention to their conversation. "Do you want to do modeling? And you're driving truck on the side?"

"No, I like my job a lot. Decent hours, good pay, good benefits. It also helps keep me in shape."

"Obviously." It slipped out before she could stop it.

He shrugged and blushed again. "I kind of fell into modeling. A friend of mine was putting a book out and asked if I'd pose for her cover. I thought it was kind of ridiculous, but I owed her a favor. I did it, and it kind of snowballed from there."

"Sounds like fun."

"It's okay. It can get a little weird, though. I went with her to a book signing and it was kind of uncomfortable how aggressive some of her fans were."

"No more book signings?"

"Never. Not even for a million dollars."

Sarah leaned back as the waiter brought the food and set it on the table. Trey thanked him. *Come on, feel something! He's gorgeous. He's employed. He's intelligent. He's nice. He's single. I think.*

The waiter left.

"Everything looks delicious," she said, inhaling the sweet tang of the bourbon from the steak. They appreciated their food for a moment before she asked, "Why are you single?"

Trey shook his head. "I wasn't, up until a few months ago. Long relationship, bad breakup. This is actually my first sort of date since then."

"Wow. I'm honored." There was no sarcasm in her words.

"I thought it might get my mom to back off a little bit. She thinks I'm going to be miserable and alone forever and ever."

"Moms, huh?"

"Sarah! I thought that was you."

Sarah's head snapped to the direction of the speaker. *Oh, crap.* "Hey, Millie, hi. How are you?"

"Good. I'm good." She was openly curious about this development. "Who's your friend?"

Wow, she wasn't wasting any time. "This is Trey Simmons. Trey, Millie."

He stood and took Millie's hand. "Delighted."

Millie blinked a few times, then slowly pulled her hand from his. "You must be Virginia's son. I heard you were visiting."

Sarah caught movement from the corner of her eye. Agnes and the rest of the Ladies' Society were seated across the room. Great.

"Well, I'll let you get back to your... date?"

Sarah wasn't going to give her an answer to the question she wasn't directly asking. "You ladies enjoy your meal. The bourbon steak is delicious."

Millie was clearly chomping at the bit to say more, but instead, she smiled and went to her table.

Sarah took another bite of steak. "I hope you don't mind everyone knowing you were here with me tonight, along with what you had for dinner and what you're wearing."

"Nah, it's all good. The whole table of them is staring over here, though. Should I be afraid?"

"A little."

They finished their meals and made the requisite small talk.

"Dessert?" Trey asked.

"I couldn't possibly eat another bite." Sarah leaned back in her chair. "I wouldn't have ordered this, but it was incredible. Good choice."

Trey lifted his glass to his lips and said, "The ladies are still staring."

"I went out with Millie's nephew a few times. I'm sure they're over there dissecting my every move."

"Ah. Was it serious?"

"No." *It could have been.*

Knock it off. It couldn't have been, because he didn't want it to be.

Hmm.

Hmm? Don't hmm me.

"—ago?"

Crap, Trey was talking. "I'm sorry, I missed that."

"I was asking if it was a while ago, or fairly recent."

Yesterday counted as recent, didn't it? "Recent. But like I said, it wasn't serious."

"So you're not hung up on this guy or anything? Like, it wouldn't keep you from dating someone else?" He seemed hopeful.

She wanted to smack herself. Trey was visually stunning. He was warm and funny and good natured. He was nice to the waiter. He was nice to Millie. He took the gawking Ladies' Society in stride. He was *interested*. And she couldn't muster up anything resembling attraction. On the other hand, there was no sense in burning a bridge. Maybe she was freaking out because she'd seen Rowan yesterday. Maybe once he was water under the bridge – *what's with the bridge metaphors?* – she'd feel something for Trey. "No, it wouldn't keep me from dating someone else."

"Good." He finished his glass of wine.

Finishing her own wine, she slid the glass away. "Does that mean tonight wasn't a disappointment?"

"On the contrary. I'd like to see you again." Trey reached across the table and lightly touched her hand.

Sarah waited for the flutter of excitement, but it just wasn't happening. She *willed* it to happen. He was exactly her type. More than her type, really. What more could she possibly want?

Rowan.

Shut up.

"That'd be great." It wasn't stringing him along to go on one more date and see if the chemistry was just being a jerk this time, right? Right.

"Let me know when's good for you."

"Depends on what you had in mind." Well *that* sounded much different than she intended. "Like dinner versus bowling or something."

"Ah, the effort quotient. Is it worth doing on a weeknight or not."

She laughed. "Yes. That's exactly what I meant."

"I'm usually home by six thirty on the weeknights. We rotate Saturdays, so I work this upcoming one."

"Me, too."

He offered, "There's a new exhibit at the Whitaker Center."

"What is it? I was there when they had the Titanic exhibit, which was amazing."

"I don't remember exactly. I just remember seeing the ad. I'll check. Or we could go to the Flower and Garden show at the Farm Show building."

She considered. "That could be fun. I always need ideas for landscaping. Not that I ever use them."

"Saturday evening then? Or Sunday?"

"Saturday evening is fine."

He took a firmer hold of her hand. "Actually, I'd kind of like to see you before then. How about dinner Wednesday?"

"Oh. Sure." He wasn't wasting any time, was he?

His face lit up. "Perfect. Can I pick you up?"

She was still mentally poking herself in the brain. *Come on, this guy is perfect. Feel something!* "Why don't we figure out where we're going, and then we can decide what makes the most sense."

"Okay. We'll text."

"Great."

Trey held her gaze. "Those ladies are still staring at me."

Sarah stifled a giggle. "Maybe we should get going. Let them speculate without us distracting them."

The thought sobered her. What was Millie going to run off and tell Rowan? What was there to tell? She was having dinner with Trey. Would he even care? *Wait. Why should I care whether he cares or not?*

Trey paid the bill and held her coat up for her to slip her arms into. Walking toward the exit, he put his hand on her back and nodded to the table of nosey ladies. Outside, he walked her to her car.

"I'll see you Wednesday?"

"Sure." Growing doubt about the wisdom of seeing Trey again consumed her.

"I can't wait."

She forced a smile. "Great."

"Would it be presumptuous if I gave you a kiss?" He leaned forward a little.

She stepped back and hit the button on her key to unlock the car. "It would." She softened her words with a smile.

"I hope I didn't offend."

"Not at all." She turned and opened the door. "We'll talk soon."

"Okay." He took a step back, gave a little wave, then went to his own car.

Suddenly tired, Sarah just wanted to be home. Wrapped up in her jammies.

Once she got home, she fumbled with her house key in one hand and her phone in the other. "Corinne. You're never going to believe this."

Chapter Thirty

Rowan pinched the bridge of his nose, glad she couldn't see his expression over the phone. "No, Auntie, I have no idea what you saw this evening."

Millie's voice was breathy and urgent, like she was about to impart some great secret. "Well. The Ladies' Society had a planning meeting for the Fourth of July event tonight at DiMaggio's. They have a delicious turkey dinner special on Sundays, but I got the roast beef because I wasn't particularly hungry for turkey. It was a dollar more, but I decided to get it anyway."

"Okay?" As much as he loved Millie, he didn't need to know what she had for dinner.

"Agnes had made us a reservation, so when they took us in, we happened to run into Sarah."

"Okay." He didn't like where this was going.

Millie's voice dropped to a conspiratorial whisper. "She was on a *date*."

What could he say? Nothing, since his jaw clenched and his throat tightened.

"With a *man*."

He swallowed hard. "I, uh, would assume as much."

"I thought the two of you were really getting along."

"We were. As friends. We weren't anything more than friends." So then why did he feel like this? He didn't like this mixture of jealousy and… and what? Regret?

"Friends." The tone was incredulous. He clearly wasn't convincing Millie any more than he was convincing himself.

"Yes, Auntie. Friends. A man and a woman can be just friends, you know."

"Not you and Sarah." She was so matter of fact it was annoying.

"Even me and Sarah."

"I'm not trying to interfere."

He laughed at that. "You're totally interfering. I appreciate the sentiment behind it, but Sarah and I aren't going to happen."

"Not if you insist on being an ass."

He nearly dropped the phone. Did Millie just call him an ass?

"I know you don't like to hear it, or admit it, but sometimes you're wrong. This is one of those times."

"Okay."

"Now you're annoyed. Sorry, but you need to hear it."

Rowan squeezed his eyes shut and shook his head. He pulled in a breath and tempered his tone as he said, "I've heard it. More than once. More than a dozen times. So please consider me duly informed."

"Rowan."

"Millie."

"He was very handsome. And nice."

"Good. She deserves someone nice."

"She wasn't interested in him."

His curiosity was piqued. Which annoyed him. "Oh?" He

could feel her satisfaction through the phone. He hurried to add, "Sarah's dating life is none of my business."

"You're her *friend*. You should give her a call."

He let out a long sigh. "I'll talk to you later. Love you."

"Love you, too."

He disconnected the call. Sarah was out on a date. Less than twenty-four hours after she'd been out with him. So what. So frigging what. It wasn't like he cared. *Bullshit*. Fine. It stung. But only a little.

Blue whined and pawed at his leg.

"Sorry, buddy." He went through the kitchen and opened the door, but Blue stayed beside him and dropped his butt to the ground.

"What's up?"

Blue ran off and brought his tire toy back and dropped it at Rowan's feet.

"You, too? Go pee." He pointed to the yard.

Blue huffed a not-quite bark and trotted outside to do his business.

Rowan heard a voice and took a step outside to investigate.

Derek stood on the other side of the fence, talking to Blue, who wagged his tail. "I'll have to get you some treats, buddy." He looked over. "Hey, what's up?"

Rowan walked to the fence. "Not a lot. You?"

"Corinne was on the phone, so I came outside to pick up some of these branches all over the yard."

"In the freezing cold."

"Yeah, there's only so much shrieking and dissecting a date I can listen to."

"Date? Must be Sarah."

Derek gave him a side eye. "You, uh, you know about that?"

"Millie ran into them and called me to report back as soon as she got home."

Derek picked at the bark on a small twig. "It doesn't bother you?"

"We're just friends."

"That's not what I asked."

Rowan didn't like being put on the spot. "Why would it?"

Derek gave a little snort-laugh. "Okay, man."

"Whatever. Everyone's on this 'get Rowan and Sarah together' campaign and it's kind of tiresome." He crossed his arms.

"Relax, I don't think you and Sarah should get together."

Rowan toppled off his high horse. "You don't?"

"She's like a sister to me. Why would I want her to get together with a guy who needs to be convinced she's worth it? I think you're kidding yourself and you're more invested than you think, but no, I don't think she should be with you."

"Thanks." He bit the word out.

Derek shrugged. "You don't want people thinking you should be with her, and you don't want anyone telling you that you shouldn't. Got it."

"I don't want anybody in my business at all," Rowan snapped.

Derek didn't miss a beat. "Sarah *is* my business."

Rowan stared at Derek, hard, but the other man wasn't budging. "Whatever, man, I'm done with this conversation."

"See you later," Derek answered mildly.

Rowan stalked back to the porch and snapped his fingers for Blue to come. Inside, he tossed a treat to the dog. "Can you believe that?"

Blue couldn't believe it, either. He swallowed his treat and stared longingly at the treat box.

Rowan absently tossed him another one. As it was in mid-air, he said, "Hey. I already gave you one."

Blue wagged his tail and looked at the box again.

"Nice try, I'm not falling for it twice."

Blue gave up and went to his water dish, where he loudly slurped.

Rowan filled a glass with water and sat at the table, doodling in his sketchbook. He wanted to sketch some furniture designs, but all he could think about was making a porch swing for Sarah. With turtles carved in a wide headrest. Damn it, he didn't want to think about Sarah. Frustrated, he shoved the sketchbook in a drawer and went to park himself in front of the television.

A couple of mindless hours later, he crawled into bed, glad for the day to be over.

Work on Monday was a good distraction. Until he walked to his vehicle and happened to see one of the guys being picked up by his wife. Grump. Rowan didn't even know his actual name. The guy was surly and always kept to himself. Rowan hardly recognized him with a huge smile on his face as he hopped into the car and leaned over to give the woman a quick kiss.

Well, wasn't that special. Even Grump had a woman who made him smile.

He kicked a small stone, which ricocheted off a larger stone and bounced up to put a small ding in the door of his Jeep. He sighed as he rubbed the spot. Thankfully, the layers of dirt were the only thing injured.

Figuring he'd only burn the house down if he tried to cook something, he stopped at the diner. Which was probably his brain's attempt at driving him deeper into misery, since odds were good that he'd run into Sarah, or at least Corinne.

Or both.

Rowan pushed the door open and immediately saw Sarah sitting on a stool at the counter, an empty bowl in front of her. Why did she have to be so beautiful? She sipped on a soda while Corinne plated slices of pie and put them on a tray.

He slunk past them both and settled into the far corner booth, where he could look up and see her.

Corinne took his order, and he knew her wordless nod let Sarah know he was here. She didn't look. It was just as well.

Twenty minutes later, she got up, put her coat on and left, without ever looking in his direction. Ouch.

His phone vibrated for the third time in a row. He pulled it out. It was a local number, but not one he recognized. Something told him to answer it rather than let it go to voicemail.

"Hello?"

"Rowan Graham?"

"Yes, who's this?"

"Rebecca at Mercy General. Millie Van Houten asked us to call you."

He dropped his quarter-full cup and a stream of coffee bled toward the far side of the table. "What's wrong? Is she okay?"

"She's being taken into surgery. I'm sorry, I don't have a lot of details."

"I'm on my way."

He felt, rather than saw, Corinne materialize at the table. She tossed a cloth onto the pool of coffee.

"Millie's in the hospital. I gotta go." He stumbled out of the booth and yanked his coat on, then patted the pockets for his wallet.

"Go. Don't worry about it." Corinne waved him away.

He only hesitated for a second. He'd settle up with her

later. "Thanks." He ran out of the diner and jumped into the Jeep.

At the hospital, he got no new information. Millie was in surgery. For what, no one seemed to know. He sat with his head in his shaking hands. He couldn't lose her.

He'd been in the waiting room for an hour when he thought of Blue. Poor dog had probably had an accident in the house. He texted Derek.

> At the hospital for Millie, can you let Blue out?

He knew he wasn't Derek's favorite person at the moment, but surely he could still count on him to let the dog out. He sent a second text immediately after the first.

> Please?

A minute later, his phone vibrated with an incoming text.

> Already did, C called me. Millie ok?

> In surgery. Nobody's telling me anything.

> Keep us posted. Don't worry about Blue.

> Thanks.

He slipped the phone back into his pocket.

The chair grew more and more uncomfortable by the minute. He got up and walked around the waiting room. A television played in the corner, with no volume, and no remote control in sight. He stared at it for a few minutes, then went to stand in front of the windows. The view was little more than blackness, the reflection of the room behind him, and the occasional twin bright dots of headlights.

It was after ten when a doctor finally came out. "Van Houten?"

Rowan jumped to his feet. "Yes. How is she? What happened?"

The doctor held out his hand and shook Rowan's. "Dr. Weston. You're her son?"

"Nephew. I'm her only family. Blood, I mean."

"Sure. Ms. Van Houten came in via ambulance with acute abdominal pain. We determined it was appendicitis and had to do an emergency appendectomy. While we were in there, Ms. Van Houten went into cardiac arrest."

"What?" Rowan's own heart seized in his chest.

"We were able to get her stabilized and complete the surgery. She's resting and we're monitoring her closely, but the worst seems to have passed."

He squeezed his eyes against the relieved tears that threatened to spill. "Can I see her?"

"Yes, but only for a minute."

"Okay." Rowan felt like he was sleepwalking as he followed the doctor through a maze of machines and people and randomly arranged cots.

Millie lay on crisp white sheets, tubes snaking out of needles in her arm. Machines beeped and chirped and spit printouts into overflowing trays. She looked so tiny and frail.

The doctor patted his shoulder. "Five minutes."

"Okay." Rowan inched closer to Millie's side as the doctor walked away. "Hey," he whispered as he wrapped his fingers around her small hand. It was still and freezing cold. If he didn't see the rise and fall of her chest, he could have easily imagined she was dead.

His chest tightened and tears stung the backs of his eyes

like pricks from a thousand needles. "I'm here." He gave her hand a gentle squeeze.

Five minutes passed, and another five. He couldn't bring himself to leave her side. A loud series of new beeps startled him and a nurse came over, studied the machine, turned off the noise and smiled at him. "She's doing good."

He nodded, unable to speak, grateful for the little bit of encouragement, no matter how generic.

Sometime after midnight, Millie's eyelids fluttered and blinked open. The faintest smile touched her pale lips.

Rowan's legs ached from standing in one spot for so long, but he was glad he hadn't moved.

Millie squeezed his hand and drifted back into her drug-induced sleep.

The same nurse came by again and touched his arm. "I'm going to have to kick you out now." She softened her words with a smile. "Go home and get some rest."

"Okay." He leaned down and kissed Millie's forehead. "I'll be back soon," he whispered near her ear.

Back in the waiting room, he sat and put his head in his hands. A couple sat in the waiting room now, clutching each other's hands and staring vacantly at the awful carpet. He wondered what their story was, then figured he probably didn't want to know. Hospital waiting rooms had too many stories without happy endings.

It was nearly one when he got up and decided to go home. He probably wouldn't sleep, but he could shower and change clothes and check on Blue.

Chapter Thirty-One

Tuesday morning, Sarah checked her phone after she got out of the shower. A late text from Corinne let her know Millie was in the hospital. "Oh, no."

> Just saw your text, is Millie ok??

She dressed quickly. If she left soon enough, she'd be able to run in and check on Millie before work.

> D says she's ok. Sounds like rough going last night tho.

Her fingers flew over the screen.

> Thx. I'll stop in before work.

She yanked her coat on and grabbed her purse. "See you tonight, sweetie."

Harvey watched her leave.

Sarah pushed the speed limit, just a bit, and pulled into her parking space. Instead of turning left inside the door, she made a right and wound through a couple of corridors until she got to the ER. "Hey, Karen, where's Millie Van Houten?"

The receptionist tapped a few keys. "Up in 318."

"Thanks." She hurried to the bank of elevators and jumped into a car just as the doors began sliding shut after its passengers got out. She pushed the button for the third floor.

She went down the hallway and smiled at the nurse at the station. In the doorway of 318, she hesitated. A peal of laughter urged her forward.

Agnes, Ruth, and Gertrude sat in plastic chairs beside the bed, where Millie sat upright. She held her arms out. "Sarah!"

"Hey." She gave Millie a gentle hug. "What happened?"

Millie pointed to her abdomen. "Silly appendix. I thought it had been taken out years ago, but that was my gall bladder. They tell me I went into cardiac arrest during surgery, but I don't remember a thing."

Sarah nodded. "That's for the best, I'm sure."

"You didn't have to go out of your way to stop by and see me, not that I don't appreciate it. It's always nice to see you."

Sarah patted her hand. "I work over in the MRI center, it's not out of my way at all."

"Oh, that's right. You're so sweet to visit."

"Let me know if you need anything." She turned to Agnes. "Let me know if she needs anything."

Agnes winked. "I will."

"Have they said how long you'll be in here?"

"You know how it is, they'll kick me out as soon as I can hobble to the bathroom on my own."

Sarah nodded. "Don't you let them send you home before you're ready."

Millie scoffed. "I'm ready now. It's so loud in here it's impossible to get any rest."

"I have to get to work, but I'll stop back after I'm done, okay? Do you want anything? Magazines? Puzzle books?"

"Rowan's bringing me a few things, so I'll have plenty to read. Thank you, though."

"Of course. Take care and I'll see you later."

As she was leaving the room, she overheard Millie saying, "Nice girl."

Agnes chimed in. "Too bad Rowan didn't snap her up."

She had to smile. In spite of whatever was going on with her and Rowan, it was nice to know Millie liked her well enough to want her around.

Down the hallway, she pressed the elevator button. The doors slid open and she came face to face with Rowan. Stepping back to let him exit, she smiled. "Hey."

"Hey."

"I was just in to see Millie. She looks great. Heads up, Agnes and Gertie and Ruth are with her."

"Thanks." He held up a canvas tote bag with cats all over it. "I feel like a weirdo carrying this thing around."

"Pffft. Own it. Be all 'Heck yeah I'm carrying a cat bag, you only wish you were, too.'"

He laughed.

"Are you okay? You look exhausted." Dark circles underscored his heavy eyes. She wanted to reach out and touch him, but she kept her hands to herself.

"I am."

"Are you working today?"

"No, I called off."

"Good. You probably shouldn't be operating heavy machinery." She could only imagine how scared he'd been. He'd lost so many people. Losing Millie would gut him.

"Probably not."

"I have to get to work." She pushed the elevator button again. The doors slid open immediately.

"Okay. Thanks for stopping by to see Millie."

"If you need to talk, let me know." She got in the elevator car and pushed the button for her floor, wanting to kick herself for putting herself out there again.

"Thanks, Sarah."

The doors closed and the car dropped down.

The work day passed in bland genericness, with nothing to stand out or distract her from incessant thoughts of Rowan. Which pissed her off to no end. Just because he was down and vulnerable because of Millie didn't mean she had to think about swooping in to save him.

"Earth to Sarah."

Becky held a clipboard.

"Sorry, what?"

"I said the doors are locked, do you have anything else to log?"

"No, everything's done on my end."

"Good. Go home." Becky shooed her away from the desk.

"I'm going up to see Millie first."

"Then home. That's an order."

Sarah saluted. "Yes, ma'am. Millie, then a drive-through. *Then* home."

"Close enough. See you tomorrow."

Sarah retraced her earlier steps down the hallway to the elevators, then rode up and went to Millie's room. It was quiet. Poking her head in, she saw Millie was asleep. Rowan slumped in a chair beside her bed, his head propped on his fist. Sarah watched him for a moment, letting herself wish things could be different, before turning away and tiptoeing from the room.

Chapter Thirty-Two

Rowan woke up just in time to see Sarah's back as she snuck from the room. He glanced over to Millie, who was fast asleep, then got up and hurried after Sarah. The corridors were empty. He went to the elevators and heard the clunk of the doors closing, no doubt behind her.

The hallway was home to the elevators, a set of restrooms, and a wall of windows. In the restroom, he washed his hands, then splashed cold water onto his face. Hopefully he could convince himself to sleep tonight, now that Millie was strong and stable and feisty.

Back in her room, she stirred as they brought her supper in.

"Rowan, honey, go home."

"Are you sure?"

She gave him a look. "Of course. I'm going to do a crossword, then watch Wheel of Fortune and Jeopardy." She paused. "Did you see Sarah this morning?"

"Yeah, she was just here again, but we were both asleep. I saw her as she was leaving."

"Oh. Too bad."

"I went out, but she was already in the elevator."

He waited for the unveiled hints, and was almost disappointed when her only comment was, "I wonder if she'll stop tomorrow morning. You're going to work tomorrow, I assume?"

"I'm planning to. Unless they're going to release you and you need a ride home?"

"If they do, I'm sure Agnes can give me a lift."

"No, you call me. I'll take you home. I don't want you falling or something when Agnes is the only person there to help."

Millie laughed and patted his arm. "My, how the tables have turned. Now you're fussing at me. Isn't that supposed to be my job?"

"Turnabout's fair play." He held her hand.

"I suppose it is. Now go so I can eat and finish my crossword before my shows come on."

"Okay. I'll see you tomorrow. If you need anything, or if they're discharging you, call me right away. I'll keep my cell on."

"Yes, sir." She gave him a broad smile he could tell was a little forced. She must be exhausted.

"Love you," he said as he kissed her forehead.

"Love you, too."

He got in his car and headed home.

No one greeted him as he came through the door. "Blue? I'm home."

Nothing.

The skin on the back of his neck prickled. "Blue?"

He walked from the living room to the kitchen, circling the island, then went back the hallway. He poked his head in the bathroom, then went into the bedroom. Nothing seemed out of place until he heard a whine. Rounding the bed, he dropped to his knees beside where the dog lay. "Oh, Blue. Hey, buddy, it's okay."

Blue's tail flicked slightly and he tried to lift his head.

"Shh, shh, stay still. It's okay." Rowan fumbled to get his phone out of his pocket with one hand, while petting Blue with the other. "It's okay buddy, I'm here."

Blue whined and his tail lifted and dropped again.

"I got you, Blue. It's okay."

He could barely see the screen on his phone as he searched for the vet's phone number. The office was closed, and when he tried to push the button to connect to the emergency line, the phone disconnected. With a desperate curse, he dialed again, not waiting for an answer before he scooped Blue into his arms, growing even more concerned by Blue's compliance. Somewhere in his mind, he registered piles of vomit on the floor.

The dog panted, not resisting Rowan's movements.

Rowan rushed back out the front door into the freezing cold. He realized he'd forgotten his coat, but he wasn't going back for it. He gently put Blue on the back seat. "Hang on, buddy, we're going to get you to the doctor, okay?"

Racing around the Jeep, he jumped into the driver's seat and… no keys.

Cursing, he ran back into the house and grabbed his keys from the pocket of his coat.

He sprinted back and jammed the keys into the ignition, his shaking hands nearly dropping them.

Blue's whine forced him to calm himself. It wouldn't do Blue any good if he got them into an accident. He had to pull himself together.

He finally connected to the emergency vet, who listened for a moment and then told him to come in. Rowan didn't mention that he was already on the way.

He pulled out of the driveway, carefully checking for oncoming traffic. "Okay, buddy, we're on our way. We'll be there soon." He stifled more curses as all three traffic lights he had to go through turned red as he approached. He reached back and touched Blue's foot. "Hang on."

As he drove to the clinic, he found himself praying, something he hadn't done for years. Having Millie *and* Blue in danger was more than he could handle on his own. He struck every bargain with God he could think of.

A few minutes into the trip, the panic subsided enough for him to think clearly. He turned down the back road that led to the Hickory Hollow Veterinary Clinic, and slowed to make the sharp turn into the driveway. Lights came on inside the office just as he parked.

Jumping out, he opened the back door. Blue tried getting up, but Rowan commanded, "Halt," and he stilled. Rowan picked him off the back seat, shoved the door closed with his foot, then carried the dog to the door, which was held open by a woman in animal print scrubs.

"Is this Blue?"

Rowan could only nod.

"It's chilly out here tonight."

He had zero interest in small talk.

"You'll be going through that door, it'll just be a minute."

She'd only finished speaking when another woman in scrubs opened the door. "Blue? Come on back."

Rowan followed her through the door into a hallway with three doors on either side. She took him to the middle door on the left and stood aside to let him in.

Relief coursed through his veins. "Margo."

Margo Lewis, his regular veterinarian, patted the stainless steel table in front of her and gave him a kind smile. "Hey, Rowan. I'm glad I'm on call tonight." She turned her attention to Blue. "Let's see what we have here." She whipped her stethoscope over her head and popped the earpieces in, then listened to Blue's heart while scratching his head. "What's the matter, buddy?" He lay on his side, still, but watching her every move.

She ran her hands over the dog, lifted his lips to see his teeth, then quickly shined a penlight into his eyes and away.

The technician assisting her frowned a little. "There's something wrong with his leg."

Rowan said, "He's a veteran. Lost part of his back leg in combat."

Margo finished her brief exam. "What's going on with him?"

Rowan told her the relatively short tale of coming home and finding Blue lying beside the bed. "Oh, and there was vomit everywhere. Probably six or seven spots."

"All on the carpet, of course," she said with a smile designed to put him at ease.

"Yeah."

"How was he this morning?"

"Fine. I let him out to do his business, he came back in and I gave him his treat. Then I left for work."

"Nothing unusual you've noticed over the past few days, weeks?"

He wracked his brain. "Nothing."

Blue's ears perked, watching everything.

"My guess right now would be vestibular disease." She scratched Blue's head again. "It's very common, especially in dogs of his age. It happens suddenly, usually due to infection in the middle ear, but sometimes there's no real cause we can pinpoint."

"What does all that mean? Is he..." He couldn't finish the question.

"In laymen's terms, it's basically an infection that got out of control. It's very common, especially in Shepherds that are Blue's age."

"How did I miss—"

Margo held up a hand. "No, Rowan, you didn't miss any signs. It's just one of those things, and it goes from zero to sixty in a snap. The good news is that it usually clears up on its own, could be within minutes or hours, could be days."

"What do I do?"

"It's up to you. If we can do a few tests, I'll be able to give you more accurate information." She consulted a sheet of paper taped to the wall beside the sink. "We're looking at about $300."

He nodded. "Yes. That's fine."

"We'll draw some blood and get an x-ray." She nodded to the technician, who drew a couple of vials of blood from Blue's back leg, then took them out a back door.

"If you want to wait here, we'll take Blue back for an x-ray. It'll just be a few minutes."

"Okay."

Blue didn't look impressed when she scooped him up and carried him from the room. Rowan paced, looking at the posters and artwork on the walls, but not really seeing any of it. The only thing that caught his attention was a poster of dogs, and one of the dogs in the front looked like Blue.

A little while later, the door opened and Margo walked in, Blue walking slowly beside her. His head tilted to the side, and he wasn't walking in a particularly straight line, but he seemed alert. When he saw Rowan, his tail went into overdrive and he nearly tipped over.

"Easy, buddy," Margo said as he stumbled into her leg. "He wasn't interested in being carried again."

Rowan dropped to his knees and scratched both sides of

Blue's face, planting a kiss on his snout. "That sounds like him. Stubborn."

"I'm prescribing some antibiotics for Blue. You'll need to give them to him twice a day, morning and evening starting tomorrow. We gave him the first dose already. Try to space them as close to twelve hours apart as possible."

"Okay." He got to his feet.

She put an x-ray film onto a lightbox on the wall and clicked the light on. "There's some inflammation here," she pointed, "in his inner ear. It could indicate an infection, so we'll do the antibiotics mostly as a precaution. Bloodwork looks fine, so I'm pretty sure that's what we're looking at."

"What's it called again?"

"Vestibular disease. It'll be on the papers they give you when you check out."

"Okay, thanks."

"I want you to keep an eye on him, and call me in a couple of days to let me know how he's doing."

"Is there anything I should do?"

"Just the antibiotics. Most likely he'll improve significantly over the next forty-eight hours. The head tilt may end up being permanent, but it's not problematic in and of itself. Make sure he's eating, drinking, relieving himself, and acting like himself. If he's not improving, or if you have any questions, give the office a call anytime."

"Thank you so much."

"My pleasure. Take care."

Blue's gait was crooked and slow as they left the exam room and went to the front desk where Rowan's credit card was put through a workout.

Rowan walked slowly, trying once to bend down and pick Blue up, but Blue wasn't having it. If there was one thing Rowan understood, it was pride.

The empty parking lot was slick and dark, except for small pools of light from the streetlamps. "Take it easy." He let Blue set the pace, even though he was freezing without his coat. A little voice chided him for all the crap he'd given Sarah for being coatless in the cold. At the Jeep, Blue didn't object when he picked him up and set him inside.

As he pulled out of the parking lot, little drops of freezing rain bounced off the windshield. "Great." The wipers only smeared the drops and made them freeze on the glass. They inched home, the fifteen minute drive taking nearly forty-five. He was grateful to pull into the garage, after nearly sliding into the garage door while it slowly opened.

He let Blue out the back door to do his business, watching closely while the poor dog made an awkward circle into the icy grass and finally found an acceptable spot to relieve himself. He came back inside, ignored his treat, went straight to the living room and flopped down with a huff.

Rowan went to the bedroom to change and stifled a curse. No magical cleaning fairy had come to take care of the piles of vomit.

He was grateful for the carpet spot mini-shampooer Millie had given him last Christmas. She'd been talking about it for months, and he'd insisted he didn't need such a thing to sit in the closet and collect dust. Score one more point for Millie. Couldn't she be wrong about anything? Just one small thing?

Maybe Sarah? Couldn't she be wrong about that?

Chapter Thirty-Three

Sarah stopped by Millie's room Wednesday on her way to work. She looked around the room and said, "You better hope I don't get caught. It's from the diner."

Millie's eyes lit up as Sarah handed over a Styrofoam cup.

"Oh, you're wonderful. I'm rewriting my will and leaving everything to you," she joked. "It smells so good. The food's not terrible, but I haven't had a decent cup of coffee since I've been here." She made it sound like it had been months, then scrunched up her nose. "They only give me *decaf*."

"That's horrible. Corinne made this just for you."

"I'll put her in the will, too." She took a little sip. "Hot."

"Very, so let it cool."

"Have you talked to Rowan?" There was something different in her voice. It wasn't quite the playful conniving she usually employed.

"Not for a few days, why?"

Millie set the coffee on the stand beside her bed. "Poor thing. He had a rough night. That sweet dog of his had some problem and he had to take him to the emergency vet."

"Oh, no, is he okay?"

"I think so. The vet said it was some big long name I can't remember."

"I'll give him a call." Sarah's heart squeezed. If something happened to Blue, Rowan would be devastated. Her phone dinged with an incoming message. For a second, she thought it might be Rowan, but it wasn't. "Becky's son is sick, she's going to be late. I have to run and get the office open."

"Thanks for stopping by. And thanks for the coffee."

"No problem. I'll see you later."

On her way down in the elevators, Sarah typed out a quick message to Rowan. Despite their last meeting, she wanted him to know she cared.

She was just hanging her coat in the closet when her phone dinged with a response. Smiling she pulled it out and found herself a little disappointed that it was from Trey. Okay, a *lot* disappointed it was from Trey.

Trey, who was taking her to dinner in ten hours.

Trey, who'd barely occupied a single thought since she'd seen him on Sunday.

Trey, who checked off all the boxes on paper.

Trey, who wasn't Rowan.

Dropping her phone back into her pocket, she hurried to get the office ready for the day. It was nearly nine when Becky let her know she wasn't going to make it in at all.

Sarah groaned. It was supposed to be her half-day, so that probably wasn't happening. A little voice suggested it was the perfect reason to cancel dinner with Trey.

Another little voice called to mind the book cover featuring Trey's abs and asked how she couldn't be full of anticipation.

Yet another voice – how many were there?? – suggested it might be wise to see him again just to be sure there was no possible way she could see potential with him. That's the voice that won.

The day was uneventful, slow, even, so although she didn't get to leave at lunchtime, Julie kicked her out at three.

Back home, Harvey offered no advice about dinner with Trey, although he did seem to share her chagrin that Rowan hadn't texted her back.

"What do you think?" She twirled so the skirt of her dress flared out.

Harvey was noncommittal.

"You're right. It looks like I'm trying too hard." She changed into dark jeans and a sweater. "How about this?"

Harvey definitely approved of this outfit.

"Casual but nice. Appropriate for pretty much anywhere." She pulled on black boots, refreshed her mascara, scrunched her curls, and called it done.

She checked her phone again. This time, she had three messages she'd gotten while in the bathroom. Holding her phone up so Harvey could see, she rolled her eyes. "Do you see this? When I've got it glued to my hip, nothing. When I walk away, I get all kinds of messages. I swear it knows."

The first message was from Trey, acknowledging the time to pick her up. The second was from Corinne, demanding every detail, as usual.

The third was from Rowan.

Thanks, he's doing okay.

Just as she was contemplating the depth of the message and any underlying meaning, he texted her again.

Can I call you?

She checked the time. Trey was going to be there any minute. She hit the button to dial Rowan's number.

"How's Blue?"

"He's good. I had to pay a jacked up emergency fee since it was so late. Not that I'm complaining." He sounded tired.

"I always have to pay a jacked up fee for Harvey since he sees an exotic animal vet."

"He needs a special vet?"

Sarah twisted one of her curls around her finger. "Most vets are experienced with mammals. I'm sure they have to do a semester or something with reptiles, but I'm more comfortable with a vet who specializes so they're more likely to recognize a problem right away."

"Makes sense."

It felt like they were dancing around something important, deliberately ignoring an elephant in the room. "I only have a minute. I'm going out for dinner."

There was a long pause. "Same guy from Sunday? Millie told me."

"Yes."

"Oh. Well. Okay."

She squeezed her eyes shut. "What am I supposed to do, Rowan? You've told me over and over you're not interested in a relationship."

"I know."

"Are you saying something different now? Or are you wanting me to sit at home and wait while you decide?" She hated knowing that if he said the word, she'd cancel dinner with Trey in a heartbeat.

"Can we talk later? Tomorrow?"

Sarah felt a sudden tightness in her throat. Like their next conversation was going to be the end for real. Closure. She swallowed hard. "Sure. I'll call you tomorrow evening. After I get home from work," she added unnecessarily.

"Okay. Good. So, um, have a nice dinner."

"You, too. I mean, thanks. Have a good evening. Give Blue a scratch for me." She disconnected the call before it could get any more awkward.

The headlights from Trey's car flashed into the window as he pulled in. She gave herself a pep talk. "Get it together, Winchester. It's just dinner. Maybe this time will be different. Maybe there'll be a spark."

He came to the door and handed her a single red rose.

"Aw, thanks. I'll put it in some water." She tapped the glass as she walked past. "This is my turtle."

Trey looked mildly interested. "Oh."

The fact that he didn't even ask what his name was annoyed her. "Yep. Red eared slider. Do you have any pets?"

"No."

She put the flower in a glass with water. "Did you ever?"

Trey leaned in the doorway and shrugged. "Not really. Do you like soccer?"

"It's okay. My brother played in high school and college, but I haven't been to a game since then."

"Ah."

"I'm ready if you are."

Trey took her coat and held it so she could slip her arms in, a swoon-worthy gesture for sure. Or it should have been. On the way to the restaurant, Sarah kept trying to talk herself into being interested in him. He checked off every column on her must-have list for a man, and then checked off all the columns on the nice-to-have-bonus list. She was clearly missing something.

Even the hostess practically fluttered in Trey's presence, which objectively *was* rather magnificent, but Sarah couldn't stir the butterflies in her own belly.

"I haven't been here in ages," Sarah said, just to say something.

"Me, either."

They studied their menus and when the waitress came, she barely acknowledged Sarah's presence. "What can I get you?"

Trey raised an eyebrow. "Ladies first."

Madyson, according to her name tag, blinked rapidly. "Of course." Her tone shifted comically. "What would you like?"

"The lobster ravioli with shrimp, please."

Madyson looked back to Trey. "And for you?"

Sarah cleared her throat. "House dressing for the salad, and iced tea, please."

"Oh. Yes. Of course."

Trey gave his order. When Madyson left, he shook his head. "Sorry."

"You have nothing to apologize for. You didn't make our waitress obnoxious."

"Well, I wouldn't say 'obnoxious'…"

Sarah smiled, done with the train of conversation. "What do you do for fun? Hobbies?"

"I don't have a lot of time for hobbies. I mostly work and work out. What gym do you belong to?"

She nearly choked on her tea. "I don't belong to a gym."

"Too bad. I was hoping you could give me a recommendation."

"I think there's only one gym in town, so there you go."

He asked, "What about you? What do you do for fun?"

Sarah waited while Madyson set their meals in front of them and looked at Trey. "If you need anything else, let me know."

"I'd like some more tea, please," Sarah said to Madyson's back.

"Sure," she said to Trey.

When she left, Trey apologized again. "This doesn't happen all the time, I promise."

"It's fine." She waved her hand, dismissing the unnecessary apology. "As for my free time, I like to spend time with Harvey, my parents, my friends, that sort of thing. Hanging out, watching movies or whatever. I make quilts."

"Quilts? Wouldn't it be easier to buy one?"

"Easier *and* faster. And probably cheaper. But I enjoy it. This ravioli is incredible."

"I wish I could eat pasta. Too many carbs."

With that, even the voice who thought Trey was almost perfect stopped arguing. Yep, this was going nowhere.

The rest of the dinner passed with little more than generic small talk. Sarah passed on dessert, but definitely not because of the carbs. Then, she insisted on paying the check, mostly to ease her conscience about going out with him a second time. It seemed to confuse Trey, even though he didn't raise more than a cursory objection.

On the way home, the conversation was forced, and she couldn't wait for the drive to be over. After forever, Trey pulled into her driveway, put the car in park and popped his seatbelt off.

"You don't have to walk me to my door."

His hand hovered over the key. "Oh."

"Thanks for tonight. It was nice."

"Sarah, I have to ask. Did I do something? I feel like you weren't really into this tonight."

"Sorry. No. I wasn't. It's nothing you did or said or anything. It's not you at all. I just don't think we have much in common."

"And that's not something you want to work on? I might be willing to make a quilt if you're willing to do some kickbox-ing." He smiled, a perfect, straight-white-toothed smile that should have sent tingles all through her body.

Nope. Not even a tiny zap of anything, anywhere. "You're great. But no."

"Okay."

Sarah couldn't quite read his expression. "I'm sorry, Trey."

"No, don't apologize. If it's not there, it's not there. No big deal."

"Okay. Good luck finding a gym." She gave him a smile and got out of the car.

Trey waited until she was inside, then pulled away.

She tossed her purse on the side table. "Why couldn't I like him?"

Harvey was smug – he knew the answer but he wasn't talking.

Chapter Thirty-Four

The next evening, Rowan tried to keep from checking his phone, but failed miserably. He'd swear half an hour had passed, but when he pulled out his phone to make sure he hadn't missed a call, only five minutes had gone by.

He decided she wasn't going to call. Then he decided to call her himself. Then he decided not to.

When the phone finally vibrated in his hand, he jumped, caught completely off guard. Sarah's name on the screen gave him a spike of anxiety.

"Hey! Um, hi. Hello."

"Hi, did I catch you at a bad time?"

"No, I was just... um, I was busy." He mentally kicked himself for not having anything better to say.

"I can let you go if you're busy."

"No, it wasn't anything important." A long silence stretched out. "How was dinner last night?" Well, that was a stupid question.

"Fine. I had a lobster and shrimp ravioli that was to die for."

"Nice. So, the reason I wanted to talk to you." This would

be so much easier in person, where he could see her face and gauge her reaction. Talking on the phone always felt awkward to him, and he hated the feeling. "I guess I didn't understand why you were getting so mad at me. But I knew I was doing something. And then you told me to get myself together."

"I wasn't saying it to be mean."

"I know. But I took it to heart, because I've let a lot of the bad stuff that's happened to me in the past keep me from moving into the future. So I talked to an old friend and got a recommendation for, um, someone to talk to."

He heard her suck in a breath, then hold it. "Like a professional?"

"Yeah. I can't keep using my old lousy therapist as a reason to not see a different one. So, um, I have an appointment on Friday. This guy specializes in grief and trauma and has experience with military issues. The therapy trifecta." He gave a little laugh. "I have a lot of work to do, I know that. But I'm optimistic about this, and might even be looking forward to it."

"That's great, Rowan."

"I just wanted you to know." What he really wanted to tell her was how badly he wished they'd met when he was in a better place. With his stuff together.

"I'm glad you told me." There was another long pause, but this one didn't feel as strained. "How's Blue?"

"He seems a lot better today. Walking straight. He even chased a bird when he went out to pee earlier so he must be feeling better, too."

"Good."

"How's Harvey?"

"Great. Right now, he's walking around on the table. I think the bumpers offend him. He keeps walking over to them and putting his foot up like he's going to climb over, but he can't."

"I'm sure he's annoyed."

"No doubt. He's also upset because we're out of crickets."

"Poor guy's having a heck of a day."

She laughed. "I'll make it up to him."

He knew this was the time to end the call, but he hated to. He knew he wasn't just ending the call, he was ending his connection to Sarah, and it sucked. "I guess I should let you go."

"Sure. I'm glad we talked."

"Me, too."

"How's Millie?"

He knew she'd seen Millie earlier, so maybe she wanted to keep talking to him, too. "She's good. They're sending her home tomorrow, so I took the day off to take her home. They said she'd be discharged around ten."

"Which means closer to noon, if you're lucky. You might have to take her for lunch, too."

"I can probably handle that."

"You won't have much choice."

"What? You think frail little Millie would strongarm me?"

Her laugh was music to his ears. "I think Millie would body slam you if she had to."

"I think you're right."

"Um, I don't know if you'd want to know or not, but I had my lawyer send Thomas a nastygram reminding him about the penalties for violating the restraining order. I guess he got whatever paperwork he needed somewhere else, because he's back in California."

"Good riddance." He nodded even though she couldn't see. "I'm glad he's gone."

"Me, too. Okay, I'll let you go now." She sounded reluctant, but that might be wishful thinking.

"Okay. Take care."

"You, too."

He disconnected the call and sat, staring at the phone. Blue yawned and lay down on his feet. "Guess I can't get up now, can I?" He sat back and scrolled through the pictures on his phone.

Pictures he'd thought were silly and pointless at the time, but he'd been wrong. Again. He stopped on a picture of Sarah grinning, her cheeks red and windburned, one hand up against her head to keep her flyaway curls in check. He'd taken it right after their first time tubing down the slope.

With a sigh, he clicked his phone off and set it on the arm of the chair. "Whatcha think, Blue?" He wiggled his toes, but Blue ignored him.

"You know my feet are falling asleep, right?"

He waited a minute, then said, "You wanna pee before bed?"

Two magic words in one sentence. Blue stood, stretched, yawned, then looked back the hallway and into the kitchen like he was trying to decide if he had to pee bad enough to go outside instead of going straight to bed.

"Nope, you're not getting me up in the middle of the night. Go pee."

With a huff, Blue trotted through the kitchen and waited for Rowan to open the door.

The next morning, Rowan got dressed and went to pick Millie up. Much to his surprise, she sat on the side of the bed, dressed and ready to go.

She said, "I'd like to stop and see Sarah on the way out."

"Auntie, she's working. We probably shouldn't bother her." She must be feeling better if she was back to her not-so-subtle matchmaking.

"Psht, I just want to pop in and thank her for visiting."

"If you're trying to force us into the same room, you can save your breath. We talked last evening."

"Oh." Her eyebrows rose.

Score one for Rowan. He'd actually surprised her. He took advantage of it and changed the subject. "Are you hungry?"

"I suppose."

Rowan tilted his head. "Auntie."

"Fine. Yes. I'm hungry. They were supposed to have me out of here before eight, so I didn't order breakfast."

"Yesterday they said ten."

"And later yesterday they told me eight. I didn't bother calling you because I assumed it would still end up being closer to ten."

In fact, it was almost eleven when a nurse gave Millie the green light to leave.

Rowan picked up her tote bag. "Is this everything?"

"Except my water bottle. They said I could keep it."

He took the big plastic cup and balanced it on top of the mishmash of periodicals and a sweater in her bag, then held out his free hand. "Alrighty, let's go."

In the elevator, he said, "I assume we don't have to stop by to visit Sarah while she's at work?"

She shot him an annoyed look, like she was not at all pleased he'd seen through her flimsy reasoning. "Fine. But only because she's probably very busy."

He stifled a grin. Small victory knowing Millie didn't win *every* time. "Where would you like to eat?"

"Oh, I suppose anywhere's fine."

"How about the diner? They serve breakfast all day."

They crossed the lobby and exited through the sliding doors. "Maybe I'll get pancakes. I haven't had pancakes in a while."

At the diner, Millie did indeed get pancakes, three massive

beasts that were bigger than the plate they were served on. "Goodness, there's no way I'll be able to eat all this."

"Get a box. Take one or two home so you can have them for breakfast tomorrow."

Millie eyed the pancakes. "I don't know…"

As if by magic, Corinne appeared with a Styrofoam box. "How about we put a couple of those in the box for later?"

Millie gave her a sheepish smile as she put two pancakes in the box and closed it up. With a wink, Corinne said, "I'll get you some butter packets and a cup of syrup, too."

Rowan had no trouble polishing off every bite of his own huge breakfast, one specifically designed to provide a month's worth of saturated fats and carbs in one sitting.

"When are you seeing Sarah again?" Right to the point.

"I don't know."

"Oh, Rowan." Her voice dropped with disappointment. "But she's perfect for you."

"I know."

Her eyebrows shot up in surprise. "Then why—"

"Because *I'm* not perfect for *her*." He lifted a hand to stop her before she could argue or interject. "Just because she'd be able to put up with my crap doesn't mean she should have to. She's had enough with her crazy ex-husband, don't you think? She deserves a man who's got a lot less baggage."

"Hmm." She finished her pancake.

"What?"

Pulling her napkin off her lap and setting it neatly on the table, she sat back and stared at him intensely. "I don't like this."

"What?"

"Being wrong."

It was Rowan's turn to sit back while his eyebrows climbed up his forehead. "Wrong?" This felt like a trap.

"Yes. I was only thinking about what was best for you, which Sarah clearly is. I wasn't wrong about that. But I didn't stop to think that it might not be the healthiest thing for her." She reached over and patted his hand. "I think you're wonderful, no, I *know* you are. But maybe you have to work some things out before you'd make a good partner for her."

"Exactly." It was a little disconcerting how relieved he was at Millie's words. It meant the world to him that she understood. Or maybe it meant the world that she approved.

"Don't take this the wrong way."

He steeled himself for another suggestion on how to make it work with Sarah.

"Maybe you should talk to someone like Dr. Phil. He has some good advice sometimes. I suppose there's a long waiting list to get on his program, but maybe there's someone around here?"

He wasn't quite ready to admit to her that he was going to see a counselor, so he simply nodded. "Maybe you're right."

"I'm not trying to insult you. It's not that you need your head shrunk or anything."

Chuckling, he pulled out money for the bill. "Maybe if it shrunk I wouldn't have any room for all the crap floating around in there."

Her eyes narrowed. "I worry about you."

"I appreciate it. Mostly." He wasn't sure why he didn't just come out and tell her he was going to talk to someone. It would probably give her some peace of mind, but it just felt too private. "How are you feeling?"

"Oh, I'm fine. A little tired."

"Let's get you home." He waved Corinne over to hand her the check and money. "No change, thanks."

She thanked him, said goodbye to Millie, and walked away.

Rowan stood beside Millie's seat and held out his hand to help her to her feet. He grabbed her box of leftovers and let her hold onto his arm until she was situated comfortably in the Jeep. Her skin felt thin under his hand, a reminder of her age that belied her fiery spirit. It was easy – and preferable – to think of Millie as immortal, so any weakness on her part was rather alarming.

The thought of having to live without her... he shoved the notion aside. It was just as possible he'd be hit by a bus while Millie lived to be a hundred and twenty.

"Don't you think?" she asked.

"Huh? Sorry, I didn't hear."

"I said it looks like it might rain later."

"It does. Hopefully it doesn't snow."

She made an unladylike noise. "I certainly hope not. I've had my fill of snow and ice."

"It's already March, spring will be here soon."

"Not soon enough."

He took Millie home, where Agnes and Gertie were already sitting in the kitchen with a fresh pot of coffee waiting for Millie's return.

"Ruth will be here in a bit. She's stopping for bagels."

Millie groaned. "Rowan just took me for breakfast. There's no way I'll be able to eat a bagel."

Agnes said, "Cinnamon crumble bagels."

Rowan laughed as he put Millie's leftovers in the fridge. "It won't be easy, but I bet you can eat a bagel too. Wouldn't want to make Ruth's trip a waste."

"Well, no, I wouldn't want to do that..."

"I'm heading home." He kissed Millie's cheek then pointed to the other ladies. "No shenanigans. She just got out of the hospital."

"Oh, you," Gertie laughed.

"Shame about you and Sarah," Agnes said. "You made such a nice couple."

Rowan made a noncommittal grunt. "Yeah, well, sometimes it works out, sometimes it doesn't."

Agnes sighed dramatically. "We tried."

He cocked an eyebrow. "Really? I thought it was all by chance."

"Hmpf."

"You're incriminating yourself, Agnes."

"I'm doing no such thing," she answered with a twinkle in her eye.

He backed toward the doorway, gave them all a final wave, then hurried out the door. That group was just too much.

Chapter Thirty-Five

Two months later, the office had a slow Saturday, so Sarah spent most of it texting back and forth with Corinne about her upcoming date with one of Derek's friends.

Aaron was recently divorced and had two kids. Corinne promised he was cute and had a great sense of humor. Even so, Sarah wasn't overly excited about the date. Her stubborn heart was still stuck on Rowan.

The clock crawled to noon. Finally, Sarah locked the door, put on her jacket, and turned off the lights.

Stopping at the grocery store on the way home, she picked up a bundle of carrots for Harvey and a selection from the salad bar for lunch for herself. By the time she left the store, the sun had finally decided to make an appearance.

She drove home and carried her bags to the kitchen. "Ugh, today was brutal," she complained to Harvey. "We had one patient. One. And it was a wrist. I mean, I'm sure the patient was glad it wasn't more complicated, but gee whiz. I had everything – and I mean everything – done before nine. Then I just sat around and texted Corinne."

She sat down and ate her salad. "I did get you some fresh carrots. I'll get you one as soon as I change."

Cleaning up her trash, she took a drink of water and capped the bottle. She walked into the living room and paused by Harvey's tank. "And how was your – Harvey?"

She tossed the bottle of water onto the chair and lifted the tank lid. Harvey's legs and head were stretched out of his shell and seemed limp. "Harvey? Whatcha doing, sweetheart?" She reached in and touched his leg but there was no reaction.

Swallowing back the rising panic, she lightly pinched his foot and he moved his leg. "Okay, honey, we need to go to the doctor, okay?"

She shoved her feet back into her sneakers and yanked her jacket on, then ran to the bathroom and got a towel. She gently wrapped him and settled him into his carrier, grabbed her purse, fumbled for her keys and phone and hurried back out to the car. "At least the car's still warm, right?" The May afternoon felt warm to her, but it was still cold for him.

Turning the heat on high, she backed out of her parking space and headed to the animal hospital in Capers, half an hour away. Pressing a button on her steering wheel, she instructed her phone to dial the vet so they knew she was coming.

Sarah forced herself to keep both hands on the steering wheel and both eyes on the road, even though she wanted to keep checking on Harvey.

The parking lot was full when they arrived. She carefully took the carrier in, checked in at the reception desk, and sat down to wait. She barely held back tears while they waited to be called back. Finally, they were led down a long hallway and into an exam room, where she gently unwrapped Harvey from the towel and handed him to the technician, who weighed him as the doctor came in, a young man she hadn't seen before.

"What seems to be the trouble?" he asked as he began examining Harvey.

Sarah took a deep breath, got herself under control, and explained the symptoms, and calmly answered all his questions about Harvey's diet and habitat.

"We usually see Dr. Kim, he was just here a few months ago for his checkup."

The doctor put his stethoscope against Harvey's chest and nodded. "I took a quick look at his file. I'd like to do some x-rays."

"Of course."

"It can be a little pricey."

Sarah shook her head. "Whatever you need to do. Tests, medication, whatever will make him better." This is what credit cards were made for, right?

"Okay. We'll be right back. C'mon, Harvey, we're going to take a little walk."

Twenty minutes later, after Sarah had paced the length of the room dozens of times, the doctor and vet tech came back in with Harvey. "Looks like we have a respiratory infection. I'd like to keep him overnight, get some fluids in him and take another look in the morning."

"Overnight? I have to leave him here?"

His brow creased. "You don't *have* to, but I'd *highly* recommend he stay here so we can get him better."

"Yes, yes, of course. I just wasn't expecting him to need to stay overnight. What would have caused a respiratory infection?"

"Bacteria, fungus, germs. There are a number of causes. You'll need to make sure his habitat is the correct temperature, that it's clean, has good lighting. If the room it's in is carpeted, vacuum frequently since germs can get tracked onto the carpet and then get in the air, that sort of thing."

Sarah nodded. "I must be doing something wrong." A wave of guilt sucker-punched her in the gut.

The vet shrugged. "People get sick, animals get sick. There's not always fault." He lifted the pages of Harvey's chart and glanced through. "Since he's always been healthy, I'd imagine it's a one-off, and he just caught a cold. Of course I'd recommend you go home and give the tank a thorough cleaning, change the filter, all that fun stuff."

"I will, thank you."

"Leave your number with reception and if you'd like, we'll text you updates periodically."

"I'd really appreciate that. Thank you." She stroked Harvey's shell and said, "I'll be back tomorrow, okay? They're going to give you some medicine and help you feel better."

He didn't answer, but Sarah knew he appreciated her assurances.

The tech smiled at her. "We'll take good care of him."

"I know." She left before she could burst into tears. Stopping by the front desk, she left her number and the kind woman at the counter reiterated that they'd send her updates via text. She went to the parking lot and sat in the car for a few minutes to calm down. She hated leaving Harvey overnight, even if it was the best thing for him.

She stopped at the pet store and bought new filters for the tank, and a new deep-sea diver with a treasure chest. And a new plastic plant. And a new rock for Harvey to stand on. And some new pH test strips.

"Setting up a whole new tank?" Midge asked when she piled her selections on the counter near the register.

Sarah managed a smile, but she really felt like crying. "No. Harvey's sick." The tears did come then.

Midge came out from behind the counter with a speed that

belied her age and wrapped her arms around Sarah. "Oh, honey. What's going on?"

"He has a respiratory infection." She sniffled against Midge's comforting shoulder. "He has to stay at the vet's overnight."

"Well, that's the best place for him right now. You go to the place in Capers?"

Sarah nodded and wiped her face as Midge drew back. "Yeah."

"That's where we take Ginger. They'll take excellent care of him."

"I know. It just stinks. I don't know how he got sick."

Midge echoed the vet. "People get sick, animals get sick."

"I just feel guilty. Like I should be able to keep him healthy."

"You are. You take wonderful care of him, and you took him to the doctor right away." Midge patted her arm and went back behind the counter. "Were you done shopping?"

"Yeah. Oh, no, I wanted to get some of that tank disinfectant."

Shaking her head, Midge said, "I'll sell it to you if you want, but bleach works better and it's cheaper. Just cut it, one part bleach, two parts water."

"Are you sure?"

"It's what I use. Here *and* at home. Don't tell the sales rep."

That made her smile a little. "Your secret is safe with me."

Midge rang up her purchases. "Do you have your coupon?"

"No, it's at home."

Against her clearly posted and oft-stated policy of no-coupon-no-discount, Midge rang in the coupon discount code anyway.

"You didn't have to do that, but I really appreciate it."

"You're a good customer. I don't mind at all."

Sarah swiped her credit card while Midge bagged the purchases. The machine beeped and spit out a receipt.

"Let me know how Harvey makes out." She reached across the counter and patted Sarah's hand.

"I will, thanks."

Sarah took her bags out to the car and started it. Her phone vibrated with an incoming text from Corinne, asking about the upcoming date. "Crap." She tapped out a message to Aaron, then deleted it and called instead. After five rings, it kicked into his voicemail.

"Hey, this is Sarah. I'm so sorry for the short notice, but I have to cancel tonight. I had to take Harvey to the emergency vet and they admitted him and now I have to disinfect everything and it's going to take all night and I'm so sorry this sounds like a terrible made up excuse, but it's really not. I'm sorry, please let me know when you get this message. Sorry."

She drove home, kicking herself for the ridiculous rambling message. When she was parking, her phone dinged. Aaron.

Who's Harvey?

She texted back,

My turtle.

Turtle?

Yes.

She carried her bags into the house and checked her phone. No response. She changed into old sweatpants and a flannel shirt and tied her unruly hair back, then cranked up some music and started unloading the tank and carrying everything to the kitchen sink.

A few minutes later, a beeping interrupted her one-woman concert. She paused the music and answered the phone.

"Hey, it's Aaron."

"Hi. I'm really sorry about tonight."

There was a long pause. "Look, if you didn't want to meet, it's not a big deal."

"I did want to meet."

"Come on, you had to rush a *turtle* to the vet?"

She bristled at his tone. "What's your point?"

"I thought it was an actual pet, like a cat or a dog. Nobody wastes that much time or money on a turtle."

She blinked rapidly, marveling at the heartless stupidity of his words.

"For future reference, make better excuses."

Sarah wasn't sure how to respond, so she simply hung up. No point in continuing to be insulted or end up saying something she might feel bad about later. Well. At least she hadn't wasted an entire evening on this jerk.

Twenty minutes later, her phone buzzed with an incoming call. Corinne.

"What's going on with Harvey?"

With a sigh, she told her everything.

"Is he going to be okay?"

"They seemed to think so." It occurred to her that she hadn't updated Corinne. "Should I ask how you know?"

After a long pause, Corinne said, "Aaron called Derek and was griping about you standing him up with a lame fake excuse. After he told Derek what the excuse was, Derek gave him an earful. He said he was going to call and apologize to you."

"He hasn't and quite frankly, he can shove his apology. He

told me he thought I had an emergency with a *real* pet like a cat or dog."

"Ouch."

"Yeah. I thought you said he was smart."

Corinne chuckled. "Clearly I was mistaken."

"It was bound to happen sooner or later," Sarah joked. "I do have to get off the phone and get this stuff scrubbed."

"Call me if you need me. Love you."

"Love you, too."

They hung up and Sarah filled the sink with hot water and poured in some bleach. It was going to be a long evening.

Chapter Thirty-Six

Rowan clipped Blue's leash to his collar and went out the front door. The May afternoon air was finally warm. He turned down the sidewalk and headed toward Derek and Corinne's house. Blue sniffed and peed against the mailbox post.

"Really? You couldn't wait until we got to that mean old lady's house and pee on her mailbox instead?"

Blue finished his business, ignoring Rowan's suggestion.

Derek and Corinne came out their front door and walked off the porch toward their car in the driveway.

"Hey, neighbor," Derek said. "Nice day for a walk."

"Finally. We might actually stroll today instead of speed walking to get back home."

Corinne shoved her hands into her jacket pockets. "I don't know if you'd want to know or not, but Harvey's really sick."

Rowan jerked his head up. "What happened?"

"I don't know the details. Just that Sarah took him to the vet and he has to stay overnight. Some kind of infection."

"I hope he's okay."

Rowan heard Derek mumble something that sounded like, "What are you doing?"

"I guess Sarah has to disinfect everything he touches. I was going to go over and help, but," she gestured to the car, "we had plans."

Derek gave her a confused look. "We—"

"We should get going. You and Blue have a nice walk." Corinne hurried around the car and got inside.

Derek shrugged.

"See you guys later." Rowan hurried Blue past their driveway and took Blue for his walk. When they returned home, he didn't bother taking his shoes off.

"I'm going for a little drive. I'll be back." He gave Blue a treat and walked out the door. He stopped at a convenience store for gas, then went inside and got two large coffees, plenty of cream and sugar.

Arguing with himself the entire way, he had to talk himself into pulling into her driveway. They hadn't spoken for two months, and he was probably the last person she'd want to see. Still, he took a deep breath, turned off the ignition, pocketed the keys, and grabbed the coffees. "Here goes nothing."

He hesitated again at her front door, then poked the doorbell button. As he was debating whether or not to ring again or leave, she opened the door. "Rowan. Hi."

He held up the coffee. "Heard you might be in need of this."

She smiled and his heart skipped a beat. He was more nervous than he had been picking up his date for his senior prom. Maybe because it mattered more than he wanted to admit that she was happy to see him. Two months hadn't even put a dent in how much he wanted to see her, and he could only hope she might not slam the door in his face.

"Come on in." She stood back to let him pass, then closed the door. "I'm cleaning Harvey's tank. I assume you talked to Corinne or Derek?"

"Yeah. Blue and I were out for a walk and they were out. How is Harvey? What happened?"

Sarah blinked a few times in rapid succession, then shook her head. "They say he'll be fine. I just got a text, actually. It's definitely a respiratory infection. They're giving him antibiotics and are watching him overnight. They suggested I disinfect everything, so I'm on track for a wild Saturday night."

Rowan handed her a coffee. "I'd love to help. I mean, if you want."

It was a long, uncertain minute before she said, "Sure. If that's how you want to spend your Saturday."

Yes. This was exactly how he wanted to spend his Saturday. "I'm at your disposal. Just tell me what to do."

She led him into the kitchen. "I'll wash, you dry."

The radio played classical music in the background while they scrubbed and disinfected everything from Harvey's tank.

"Do you have to change the water? How do you dump it out?" Even empty, those buggers were heavy.

"Siphon."

"No kidding."

"Yeah, so if you ever need to steal gas, I'm your girl."

Oh, how he wished that were true. "Good to know."

She laughed and handed him Harvey's sunning rock she'd just scrubbed. "I try to have a well-rounded set of skills that will make me valuable in the inevitable post-apocalyptic world."

It was Rowan's turn to laugh. "I think you've seen too much Walking Dead."

"Too much? Impossible."

They finished washing the items for Harvey's tank and spread them out on the counter so they could air dry.

"Do you need help emptying the water?"

"It's already done. Now I need to scrub the glass and change the filter."

"How about I scrub while you change the filter?"

"Deal." She handed him a pair of hot pink rubber scrubbing gloves.

He snapped them on and held his hands up, admiring them. "Sweet, they're just my color."

They spent the next hour and a half getting Harvey's entire house back in order. Conversation was easy and light.

Sarah set the deep-sea diver in the tank. "And now we're done." She held her hand up for a high five.

"Harvey'll like the new diver. Give him somebody to talk to when you're at work."

She giggled a little.

His throat clenched with words he desperately tried to put in order. "Sarah, I know I'm not good at this, and maybe this is a bad time to say anything because I know you're worried about Harvey and the last thing I want to do is stress you out even more. We both know I have a lot to work through. I've got a long way to go, but I'm making a lot of progress, too. The therapist I'm seeing is amazing, and things are finally clicking. You mean a lot to me, and I'd like to try giving us a chance, if you're willing to." He held his breath, afraid to look at her.

"Try?" The single word held a lot of doubt.

"Is try a bad word?"

"I'm not some thirty-day free trial option."

"Well, yeah, when you put it like that." Rowan ran his hand through his hair. "I'm trying to say I'm not ready for some big commitment or marriage or moving in or anything."

Her eyes went wide. "Wow, that's a big leap."

Rowan cleared his throat. "Like I said, I suck at this."

She looked him in the eye. "Okay, let me lay it out for you, and you can take it or leave it. You mean a lot to me, too, and we could have something amazing. I'm so proud of you for working through everything. But if you're in, you're in. No calling me tomorrow and waffling how you aren't sure you want to be with me. We're either together or we're not. Period. If it's not working out and we break up, that's one thing and it would suck but it's totally fine. But I'm not something you try out to see if you can handle being in a relationship. There's no on again, off again."

"Okay." He agreed with every word. He'd never intended to jerk her around or lead her on, but now he had the tools to recognize that's exactly what he'd done. It wouldn't happen again, that was for sure.

"I know what I deserve, and I can't settle for less because you've got some issues. I'm not trying to be cold, heaven knows I have plenty of my own baggage. We treat each other with respect, call out each other's bullshit, fight fair, be honest, and committed to being together. I need to be able to count on you. Trust you. That's the bottom line. In or out."

"Okay."

"I'm not in any hurry, Rowan. Taking it slow is fine, as long as I know where we stand. We don't have to talk about moving in or marriage or anything more until we get there."

His heart skipped a beat. Did this mean she was giving him a chance? He shoved his hands in his jeans pockets. He was afraid to ask the direct question, so instead, he said, "Can I take you to pick up Harvey tomorrow? Maybe we can grab takeout on the way home and just hang out with him while he checks out his new digs?" He knew she'd want to keep an eye on Harvey once he was home.

Sarah nodded. "Okay."

He reached out, feeling awkward while his hand hung in midair, until Sarah launched herself at him, wrapping her arms around his waist and burying her face in his chest. Her fingers dug into his back. "I missed you," she said into his shirt.

His chest squeezed with a hundred emotions. She was in his arms again, and nothing had ever felt so right. "I built you a porch swing," he blurted out. It was the best proof he had to give her that showed he hadn't stopped thinking about her.

She looked up at him, her eyes wide. "You did?" she whispered.

"After we get Harvey home and settled, maybe your dad could help me put it up." He touched her face, overwhelmed by sheer gratitude. He'd made a lot of bad decisions in his life, but he knew beyond a shadow of a doubt that this one was very, very right. He swallowed the lump in his throat. "I'm in, Sarah. I promise I'm all in."

Epilogue

Two months later
July 4

"Gather round, everyone." Mayor Clifton Riggle shouted into the microphone. "The Hickory Hollow Ladies' Society would like to make an announcement."

Agnes, Millie, Ruth, and Gertie crowded onto the little platform in the middle of the fairgrounds. Unsurprisingly, Agnes grabbed the microphone from the mayor. "Happy Independence Day!"

The crowd, made up of pretty much the whole town, cheered and whistled.

"As we've done every year, we'd like to recognize the couples who were paired up at our Valentine's Ball and are still a couple. This year, we have three wonderful couples that have come from the Ladies' Society's meddling, as my family likes to call it. *We* like to call it what it is. Simply the luck of the draw."

A ripple of laughter ran through the crowd.

Sarah and Rowan exchanged a knowing look. She muttered, "Luck, my ass."

"Mike and Juanita, wave your hands."

Sarah turned and clapped as they waved.

"Greg and Erin."

More applause.

"Rowan and Sarah."

Sarah lifted her hand and waved. Beside her, Rowan did the same, albeit with less vigor.

"Congratulations to our couples. As promised, we have a prize to give out. One of our couples will win a one-night weekend stay at the local Hickory Hollow Bed and Breakfast." She didn't quite pull the microphone away in time, so everyone heard her grumble, "Best use it after they're married," under her breath.

Everyone laughed. Agnes realized she'd been heard, and her cheeks pinked a little. "Mayor? Would you do the honors?"

Mayor Riggle reached into the box and pulled out a folded sheet of paper. "And the winner is..." He paused for greater effect. "Mike and Juanita! Congratulations!"

Sarah clapped hard until her hands hurt. Rowan whistled, then put his hand on her back.

"Before everyone runs off, we have one more prize. The brand new Hickory Hollow Pub would like to host all three couples for dinner next Saturday evening. The Ladies' Society was there for their grand opening, and I must say, the food is excellent. Enjoy the fireworks!"

Another raucous round of applause erupted, then morphed into crowd chatter as everyone moved away from the podium and back to their blankets and lawn chairs to watch the spectacular fireworks show, also sponsored by whomever the Ladies' Society "asked."

Rowan put his arm around her shoulders as they went

back to the blanket they were sharing with Derek and Corinne. Derek sat on a lawn chair facing Corinne, massaging her feet, while she contentedly rubbed her growing belly.

Sarah kissed the top of her head as she went past her. "How you feeling, mama?"

"Perfect, now that the sun went down. That breeze is straight from heaven."

Rowan pushed their lawn chairs closer together and sat down. Sarah snuggled in next to him.

"Is that what brought us together? The luck of the draw?"

Sarah chuckled. "Nah. It was Millie and Agnes's questionable ethics."

"So it was luck that got us *back* together?"

"Nope."

"What, then? My charm? Good looks? Sparkling personality? Outstanding people skills?"

"No, no, and no." She put her hand on his knee and leaned up to kiss his cheek. "You know why I decided to give you another chance?"

"Why?"

"You talk to Harvey."

"Well, he *is* an excellent conversationalist."

Sarah laughed just as the first bursts of light bloomed high up in the sky.

"As a matter of fact," he slid to the edge of his lawn chair.

Sarah wondered what he was up to. She glanced at Corinne and Derek, who were watching them and not the fireworks.

"I consulted Harvey and Blue, and they both helped me pick this out." He slid to one knee and pulled a velvet box from his pocket.

Her heart thumped in her throat. So much for Rowan needing to take things slow.

"I don't know a lot, Sarah, but I know that I love you, and I want to spend the rest of my life with you." He popped the box open. "Will you marry me?"

Colorful reflections from the fireworks bounced off the diamond.

Sarah slid to her knees and put her arms around his neck. "Yes."

Derek and Corinne, and several people in their immediate vicinity, cheered loudly and crowded around to congratulate them.

Rowan slipped the ring on her finger, then kissed her.

As Sarah snuggled against him to watch the rest of the fireworks display, she wished she could tell Millie and Agnes how thankful she was that they'd rigged the Love Drawing.

They still refused to admit it, though, insisting it was simply the luck of the draw.

Enjoyed this trip to Hickory Hollow? Keep those warm fuzzy feelings going and dive straight into Book 5 in the Hickory Hollow series, Cat Burglar.

When Avery moves back home to save her family's business, she's not prepared for the neighbor's cat to steal her undies... or for her neighbor to steal her heart.

Hickory Hollow. Get comfy, stay a while!

You don't want to miss news of upcoming books, events, and behind-the-scenes sneak peeks! Sign up for my newsletter today at carriejacobs.com!

Acknowledgments

I'd first like to thank my eagle-eyed mom for proofreading this book so you all didn't have to be subjected to my poor math skills or egregious misuse of lay/lie/laying/laid.

Thanks to Geri Krotow, fellow author, friend, and US Navy veteran who helped me with some details of Rowan's military past, but let's be clear - if I got anything wrong, it's on me. You can check out her books here: https://gerikrotow.com/

Jen and Laura – There aren't words to tell you how much I love you guys and our writing sessions. All the words, none of the filters.

Michelle – You're the best. Thank you for letting us crash your store with our laptops and snacks! Cupboard Maker Books is a *must* if you're in central Pennsylvania. Books and cats, y'all! https://cupboardmaker.com

As always, my biggest thanks go to my husband Scott.

And thanks to YOU, dear reader, for picking up this book and reading this far. Every review or newsletter signup is like a little Christmas present.

In Chapter 16, I mention a fictional food bank. I'd love to encourage you to support your local real food bank. Despite the stereotype to the contrary, most food bank clients are hard-working, employed folks who use the services on a temporary basis. Check with them first to find out what they need/can accept, but some of the best donation items are feminine products, toilet paper, and cleaning supplies.

About the Author

Carrie's love of storytelling began in early childhood and never wavered as time marched onward. She reads in pretty much every genre imaginable, but found her writing happy place in small town contemporary romance and romantic comedy.

From that love came Hickory Hollow, a mashup of her hometown and places she's either visited or would like to. Her favorite part of Hickory Hollow? The residents don't have to drive an hour to get to Target, like she does in real life.

Carrie lives in beautiful central Pennsylvania with her family and very spoiled furry editorial assistants.

Connect with Carrie through her newsletter or social media!

Website: carriejacobs.com

facebook.com/writercarriejacobs

instagram.com/carriejacobsauthor

goodreads.com/carriejacobs